# moderate
# violence

# moderate violence

## Veronica Bennett

RICKSHAW PUBLISHING

Rickshaw paperback

First published in Great Britain in 2013 by Rickshaw Publishing Ltd,
102 Fulham Palace Road, London W6 9PL

www.rickshawpublishing.co.uk

A CIP catalogue record for this book is available from the British
Library.

ISBN 978-0-9565368-5-3

Cover designed by Richard Smith.

Printed and bound in Great Britain for Rickshaw Publishing Ltd by
CPI Group (UK) Ltd, Croydon, CR0 4YY

RICKSHAW
PUBLISHING

# Acknowledgements

In March 2011, I was lucky enough to be elected a Hawthornden Fellow, and spent a very productive month at Hawthornden Castle in Scotland, working on Moderate Violence. The Hawthornden Foundation runs a writers' retreat at the castle, where writers can concentrate on their project surrounded by the tranquility of the Esk Valley. This is made possible by the continued generosity of Mrs Drue Heinz.

I am very grateful for the opportunity granted me by Mrs Heinz and the Hawthornden Committee, and would also like to thank Hamish, Jonty, Colin, Sarah and James for a stimulating and enjoyable four weeks. Without their comments, suggestions and expertise, the book would be greatly diminished. Meanwhile, if it hadn't been for Sarah Molloy of A. M. Heath and Jo Doyle and Paul Michaelides of Rickshaw, the book would never even have been finished. Many thanks to them.

Veronica Bennett 2013

# Chapter One

Jo was leaning on the wall beside the door that said 'Mr B. Treasure, Headteacher'. The corridor wall felt cold through her school blouse. She pressed her shoulder blades harder against the bare bricks.

"Joanna Probert?"

Mr Treasure's secretary's face came round the door and regarded Jo with the sort of look cops give serial rapists in American TV shows. "Wait there."

The face disappeared. Something deep beneath Jo's skin - maybe her spleen or her gall bladder - rolled over. Here she stood against a wall, imprisoned. Why couldn't a school just treat you like a human being? In the real world, if a secretary was as rude as that to someone waiting to see her boss, she'd get fired. But if you were wearing a white polyester-cotton blouse and a navy blue polyester skirt, everyone wearing ordinary clothes could be as unpleasant as they liked.

The face reappeared, still with its you're-going-down-for-life-buddy stare. "All right, go in."

Jo smiled pleasantly. "Thank you".

The secretary stood back. Jo walked through the outer office and opened Mr Treasure's door.

"Ah. Jo," he said, in the same voice he'd used when Jo was in Year Seven, and had come to get a Good Work Certificate (the kind that no one bothered to try to get *after* Year Seven).

He stood up and motioned her to the visitors' chair. "Sit down. I won't keep you long."

Jo sat down. "Is it about my dad?"

Mr Treasure, who was just sitting down again, stopped half way, as if she'd warned him that the paint on his chair was wet. His normally benign expression sharpened. "Well, yes, partly."

"What's the other part?"

He settled into his chair, put his elbows on the desk and made a tent with his fingers. Jo thought he looked very tired. There were dark patches under his eyes. Being a headteacher was surely a terrible job. "Let's take one thing at a time," he suggested. "Your dad first?"

Jo shrugged.

"Don't shrug, Jo," said Mr Treasure steadily. "This does concern you, you know."

Jo was annoyed at herself. She could feel herself going pink. Mr Treasure was just so good at being *right*. When he was telling you off you always felt like an idiot.

"Your father had an appointment to see me today..." – he glanced at the open diary on the desk – "...at twelve thirty. But he didn't appear. I think you probably have a good idea why, don't you?"

Jo went pinker. "Yes, sir," she whispered.

Mr Treasure sat back and looked at her calmly. "I don't like being messed around."

Jo tried to look at him, but her nerve failed and she looked instead at her hands. They felt sticky and school-stained. She spread them on the blue skirt that soon, with luck, she'd never have to wear again.

"No, sir," she said. "I'm sorry he let you down."

Mr Treasure didn't go all martyred and teacherish. He said, "Look, we both know that he's either got to sort this out himself or someone else has. And meanwhile, some sorting out has to be done in *your* life too, doesn't it?"

Jo still couldn't look up. "Is this the other part of why you wanted to see me?"

Mr Treasure didn't give her an answer. He gave her another question. "How do you feel, Jo?"

She didn't know what to say. "Now, do you mean?" she ventured, finally looking up at him, searching his face for clues. "Or in general?"

"Either."

Jo still couldn't work out what he was fishing for. "I feel...OK, I suppose," she said warily.

He didn't speak. He waited, alert for her next words. That thing inside her, whatever it was, rolled over again. "Er...lots of people manage without their mothers," she said. "I mean, she's not dead or anything."

He still didn't speak.

"And it's not as if I'm a young kid," she added.

She felt weary. Today hadn't worked out well. Pascale had told her that she and Ed Samuels were having a trial separation so, since Jo sat next to Ed in History, she'd broached the subject. "Your limit of endurance is three months, then, is it?" she'd said casually as he'd slid into his chair. But he'd given her a God-you're-stupid look and slammed down his history book, swearing at her under his breath.

Holly had explained. "Pascale's trying to make Ed jealous by pretending she wants to go out with Tom Clarke. "You know what she's like."

"Why, though?" Jo had asked. "Ed's her slave."

Holly had gazed at Jo, her eyes full of sympathy. "You just don't get it, do you? Pascale has to have at least two boys

9

drooling over her or she won't even get up in the morning. And she's got this extra thrill with Ed, because *you* like him too." She'd paused, still watching Jo. "Well, you do, don't you?"

Jo sighed, doing her best to look straight at Mr Treasure so that he didn't think it was a shifty, or insolent, or teenage-moody sigh. It was just weariness. "Look," she said, "I'm not going to jump out of the window like Serena Wilkinson did when *her* mum and dad split up. Honestly, I'm OK."

His eyes left her face. Jo watched while he altered the position of his blotter, very slightly, and moved the fountain pen lying beside it a few millimetres. "Sixteen isn't a young kid, I agree," he said. "But it's not quite an adult either, is it?"

Jo frowned. *Now* what did he want her to say?

He took a cardboard folder from a drawer and placed it on the desk in front of her. "These are copies of your reports for this year," he said. "Do you want to look at them?"

"I know what they say, sir."

"So do I." He leaned forward. "But I also know that despite what they say, you're apparently about to leave us."

"Sounds like I've got a terminal illness" said Jo, wondering if she was smiling or grimacing. Maybe she *did* have a terminal illness. Terminal inability to work out what was going on.

"You know what I mean, Jo, so leave out the acting tough, will you? You'll do very well in the Sixth Form, and afterwards at university, so why give up now?"

Into Jo's mind came a picture of Ed Samuels sitting in his usual place by the window in the science lab, one elbow on the windowsill and the other hand doodling on his notepad. Jo's seat was in the corner behind him. She could watch him without anyone seeing. "Um..." She tried to concentrate on what Mr Treasure had asked. "Well, it's not because of my parents splitting up, sir. I mean, I'd want to leave school even if they hadn't."

His face didn't change. "Why?"

"I just don't see the point of it any more. I...I think I want a rest from it. Or I want a rest from *something*." She looked into his face. "I don't know what it is."

"Had enough of exams?" he suggested.

"Maybe. Or maybe just...the whole thing."

"School?"

Jo didn't know how to answer. She thought about how weird it is that by the time you've been in a school for five years it might as well be five hundred. The place is wired into your consciousness as indelibly as your name. For the rest of your life you'll remember the smell of the gym, the wads of chewing gum stuck on the undersides of the desks, and every single annoying thing about every single teacher. School would be with her whether she left now or in two years' time. So it wasn't school as a *place*. It was school as *life*, and Jo's life was what she wanted to have a rest from. Or maybe escape from. She just wanted to be somewhere she wasn't right now. But she couldn't say all that to Mr Treasure.

He waited a long time for her to speak. When she remained silent he said, "Right."

Jo looked at the unopened folder on the desk, waiting for what was coming next. Mr Treasure never shouted, so he wouldn't do that. But once he'd opened that folder, she knew that whatever he said would make her feel bad.

He didn't open the folder. "Will you do me a favour?" he asked quietly, with no undercurrent of frustration. "In fact, two favours?"

She nodded, watching him. His face didn't have that bunched look teachers' faces usually had when they were

11

disappointed with you. He spoke calmly and gravely, like an actor in an appeal for a cancer charity.

"First, pass my message to your father and ask him to make another appointment." When he saw that Jo was about to protest, he raised his palm. "No, don't say there's no point because you're leaving school anyway. I want to speak to him, as arranged. And second, whatever you decide, I want to speak to you too. Come and see me..." – he consulted the diary – "...at two o'clock on the twenty-eighth of August."

"That's in the holidays," said Jo stupidly.

"I'll be here."

Jo felt small. She seemed to have lost some sort of argument. "Why do you want to see me?"

"You'll find out then." He pushed back his chair. "Two favours, then. Don't forget."

Jo stood up. "I'll put a reminder in my phone."

"Good idea," he said, standing up too. The interview was over.

\* \* \* \* \* \*

"Come on, Trev, one more step. That's it. You can do it, now."

Jo's dad was even drunker than he'd been on the day Wales beat England 33-5, when he'd vomited into an empty dustbin then fallen asleep in it, upside down. He was too unsteady to find the front door without his friend Ken's help. And Ken had had a few, too.

"I know where my own bloody house is, man," said Trevor grumpily.

Watching from her bedroom window, Jo saw him push Ken away, stumble, sit down hard in the hydrangea bush and burst into laughter. Jo ran downstairs and opened the front door. "For

12

Christ's sake, Trevor!"

"For Christ's sake, Trevor!" said Trevor and Ken together in high voices, and then collapsed into laughter again. Trevor was too weak to get out of the bush. He half sat, half lay among the broken branches, clutching his chest, his mouth open, his eyes blissfully closed.

"Will you help me get him out of there?" Jo asked Ken. "If you're sober enough?"

"Don't you be so bloody cheeky!" bellowed Trevor. "You're not too old for a punishment, Jo-girl."

He allowed Ken to take one arm, and Jo the other, so that they could pull him on to his feet and guide him, lurching, into the house.

"Jo-girl, Jo-girl, give it a go-girl," said Trevor in a sing-song voice. "Jeez, I should be a bloody songwriter."

"You might *have* to be a songwriter now, mate," said Ken. "Come on, Jo, let's put him on the sofa."

"What?" asked Jo.

"I said let's put him – "

"No, about him having to be a songwriter now."

Ken, who was younger and chubbier than her lanky father, looked at her with watery, just-stopped-laughing eyes. "Oh..." They lowered Trevor to the sofa, where he lay with his head on a cushion, snorting. "I think I'd better leave your dad to tell you."

"He's asleep," said Jo.

"No he's not, he's just arsing around." He jabbed Trevor's shoulder. Trevor didn't move. "All right, he's asleep. But it's for him to tell you."

"Is it the reason he's been in the pub all afternoon?" she asked.

"Well..." Ken sat down in an armchair and put his elbows on his knees.

"He's lost his job, hasn't he?"

Ken looked at the carpet. Poor Ken, thought Jo. Trevor had dropped him in it, as he had countless times before. He shouldn't have to be doing this. "Yep," he said. "But they've given him a redundancy payment."

"How much?"

"Er..."

"How *much*, Ken?"

Ken interlaced his stubby fingers. He was still looking at the carpet. "Not enough, he thinks."

"So he's pissed off as well as pissed, is he?" asked Jo coldly. "Guinness pissed off, or whisky-and-chaser pissed off?"

He lifted his head and they looked at each other.

"*Neat gin* pissed off?" she suggested. "In the middle of the afternoon?"

Ken didn't say anything. They went on looking at each other. Then a sudden deluge of not-giving-a-toss flooded over Jo, and she opened the door.

Ken took the hint and got up. He nodded towards her sleeping father. "Maybe stay out of the way when he wakes up," he said apologetically, and shut the door behind him.

\* \* \* \* \* \*

The truth was that Trevor was a drunk. Jo didn't blame him. If your wife walked out, leaving you to look after your only child, but was always criticizing how you did it, and you hated being an accountant as fiercely as it's possible to hate a job (and only did it in order to support the wife), you'd probably be a drunk too.

But it was inconvenient, for sure. Sometimes it made Jo so angry that she would flip impatiently through *Key Pathways in*

*Triple Science*, a textbook unparalleled in its tedium, looking for ways to poison him, electrocute him or blow him up without anyone noticing it wasn't an accident. At other times it made her sorry, in the way you'd feel sorry for a saucer-eyed African child, helpless in the face of disaster. But she had given up trying to talk to him about it, because he would go all daddy's-girl and hug her, saying that she was the Sparkliest Diamond in the Princess of Perfection's Crown. She would unwind his arms and tell him he stank of beer and fags, and start to do her homework with hot eyes and a jerky heartbeat. Then, when she came downstairs, he'd be snoring on the sofa and she'd have to get herself spaghetti on toast for dinner.

Recently, the whole thing had begun to make her feel numb with boredom. Not resigned, not intolerant, not even resentful. Just utterly, indescribably uninterested. Life with Trevor was like the soap operas on TV, which Jo had stopped watching because they were all about divorce and drunkenness. She resented acting in a soap opera without even getting paid, so ignoring the problem seemed the best way to go. She was, as Mr Treasure had reminded her, only sixteen.

This time, it took a long time for Trevor to wake up. Jo had eaten beans on toast and washed up and watched two episodes of *The Big Bang Theory* and revised for an hour by the time he stirred. She was working at the dining table, so she could keep an eye on him. She'd read somewhere that drunks can choke if they vomit. It wasn't that she minded Trevor choking, but that she might be held responsible, and probably sent to prison for murdering him.

Suddenly he sat up, coughing. Jo resisted the impulse to impale him with spiky questions, the kind of questions that her mum, Tess, had always made sound so ugly. And she had no desire to look torn-up and jagged-edged like Tess had looked when she'd asked them.

"It's all right," she said, "you've just been asleep. Cup of tea?"

Trevor had his head in his hands. "No, no," he groaned.

"Water, then. And a headache pill?"

He didn't say anything, so Jo got the water and the pills anyway, and held them out to him.

He looked awful. His eyes, which old videos told her had been bright and attractive when he was young, hadn't looked like that for ages. They were bloodshot, and he needed to clean his teeth, and maybe shave and comb his hair, too. She looked at his hair. It was the best thing about his appearance. It still looked like it did in the old videos, since he hadn't lost much of it. It was made of a hundred different colours, from almost blond to dark red, and changed in every light. It was what had made Tess first notice him. Now it was flattened where he had been sleeping, and it wasn't very clean.

"Who was in the pub?" she asked, watching him jerk his head back as he swallowed the pills. That can't help a headache, she thought. "All the regulars? You must have had a jolly old time."

Trevor's head lolled against the back of the sofa. His eyes were closed. "Shut up and leave me alone."

"Aren't you hungry?"

"I'll get something later."

"In the pub?"

"Shut *up*."

Jo began to gather her books from the table. "I had to go and see Mr Treasure after school, because you forgot to go and see him at twelve thirty."

Trevor's eyes opened. "Oh bloody hell," he said, and closed them again.

"He wants you to make another appointment."

"I'll phone him."

"And he says to tell you that he doesn't like being messed around."

"All *right*." Trevor's eyes opened again and looked at Jo. "He'll be OK when I tell him I was doing something important."

"You were in the pub, Trev."

"I was being made redundant! Isn't that more important than going to see some stupid headmaster?"

"He's not stupid," said Jo, struggling to stay calm, "and if you knew anything at all you'd know that headmasters are called headteachers these days."

She went upstairs. She wanted to cry but not cry, shout but not shout, lie down on the bed and run around the garden, all at the same time. She sat down at her computer. Maybe she'd email her mother and tell her that Trevor had lost his job. But Tess would only start to bleat about Jo coming to live with her now Trevor didn't have any money. It was Trevor's inability to be as rich as Tess wanted that had sent her back to Prattland, as Trevor called Tess's parents' house, in the first place.

Ah, life at Prattland! Comfortable, well-appointed, sherry before dinner and gin and tonic after, the *Daily Telegraph* crossword and Sunday lunch at the golf club, forever and ever amen. And Granny Pratt's remarks about Welsh people, with "nothing personal, Joanna darling," attached to the end of them.

There was no getting round it. Tess's Home Counties family had a lot of money and Trevor's South Wales family didn't. Tess had met Trevor in a pub after an international rugby match at Twickenham straight after she left university. She'd got pregnant with Jo, married Trevor, who was already working in London as an accountant, and had never bothered to get a job. Her parents thought, correctly as it turned out, that Trevor would never earn enough to keep their daughter in the style she liked. So for the whole of Jo's life Trevor had gone to work every day while Tess had stayed at home, all the time taking handouts from Grandad Pratt and complaining about not having enough money. She said that looking after Jo and keeping the house that Grandad had practically paid for, was a big enough job, thank you. And now she'd gone.

Since she'd moved out, three months ago, Trevor had begun to sleep in the spare room. Jo's narrow room above the hall had become a junk room and Jo had taken over the main bedroom. The fitted wardrobes, which had been too small to hold Tess's clothes, were too big for Jo's. And the dressing table that used to be covered with Tess's expensive bottles made a good desk. The bed was too huge to fit into any of the other bedrooms, so Jo had had to keep it.

She'd pushed the bed against the wall and filled up the empty half with soft toys. Sylvia the Chinese Cleaner who came on Thursdays, always complained about having to move the toys when she changed the duvet cover. But Jo took no notice. Sylvia lived with her parents, grandmother, brother and sister-in-law in a maisonette, so the idea that you can have more space than you want must have seemed like madness to her.

Jo looked at her reflection in the large, side-lit mirror behind the dressing-table desk. She hadn't inherited Trevor's red-gold-auburn-copper genes. Tess had given her darkish, straightish hair that stayed close to her head whatever she did to it. It would never spring up healthily like Holly's, or tumble about harlot-style like Pascale's. Jo thought her face looked odd too. Fat at the top and thin at the bottom. Was it possible to have a fat forehead and a thin chin? But at least her skin wasn't as bad as this time last year, when Tom Clarke had said that revolting thing about her.

She switched on the computer, shut her eyes, selected a random DVD, opened the tray and slotted it in. It was *The Fellowship of the Ring*, the first film of the *Lord of the Rings* trilogy. Jo had seen it recently when she should have been revising. Watching DVDs on the computer was easy to hide from Trevor. If he came in she could shrink the screen and pretend she was working.

She didn't want to watch the film again, even the creepy bit with the Black Riders going *sniff, sniff*. She slid down in her chair and put her chin on her chest. Her right handed rested on the mouse. With her other hand she turned the DVD case over and over, slapping it lightly on the desk.

The PG symbol on the back of the case made her think about Trevor's puny attempt to tell her off. Parental Guidance, indeed. Why did parents imagine their sons and daughters might want to be guided by them, or anyone? And Parental Guidance was even more useless if the parent was drunk. Trevor might as well have a white stick, for all he could see of what Jo's life was like. She smiled, imagining him and his self-pity tap-tapping around like an idiot in a sightless world.

When she read the guidelines on the DVD case, she stopped smiling. 'Some scenes may be unsuitable for young children'. How would the censors describe that scene downstairs just now, with Trevor moaning and Jo giving him pills? 'Moderate drug use'? Jo felt tears behind her eyes, but she wasn't upset. She didn't care if he wanted to kill himself with alcohol. But she was angry. In fact she was furious. Trevor might even be worse, Jo decided, than Tess, whose crimes against being a parent were numerous and spectacular.

The top shelf of her bookcase was littered with piles of DVDs, some in their cases, some not. Jo grabbed some cases, put them on the desk and began to flip each one over, reading the guidelines on the back. She had never realized before that they were so...what was that word Mr Gerrard said in English that made all the babies in the class honk with laughter? *Pithy*. Right, DVD guidelines were pithy. They said things in a short, no nonsense way. No one would think 'mild peril' could mean anything other than mild peril. A perfectly pithy phrase.

She looked at some more. 'Coarse' language was obviously different from 'bad' language, which was different again from 'strong' language. It was all clear and simple, like movies themselves. In movies people weren't people, they were characters. The actors spoke words written for their character by the screenplay writer, and the director told them what to do. Jo wished real life had a script and a director. But no-one wrote the words for you to tell your headteacher why you couldn't carry on any more, and no one told you how to change things.

She frowned at the computer screen. If DVDs could have little labels that went to the heart of what they were like, maybe people could as well. She pulled the keyboard towards her, opened a new Word file and typed 'Trevor'. She paused a moment, and then wrote: 'Unsuitable for young children'. He could be *gross*, especially on whisky-and-chaser days, when he would belch or fart fruitily, and swear at newsreaders.

Under Trevor's name Jo typed 'Tess'. But then she left a space. Tess was difficult. Jo was tempted to put 'mild nudity', since Tess thought she was still nineteen and didn't wear enough clothes. But that was only a small part of the wide-ranging problem of Tess. She scanned the backs of more DVDs. Labelling people as if they were movies might seem a horrible thing to do, but the point of labels was that they told you what to expect. Maybe, thought Jo, if you could learn not to expect more of people than their label showed, you wouldn't be disappointed.

She typed Pascale's name under Tess's. As she did so, a thought she didn't want to think forced its way into her mind.

In the back of Trevor's car last Saturday night, Pascale had huddled close to Ed. "Your place or mine?" she'd said in his ear.

"Ready for it anywhere, darlin'," Ed had replied in an exaggerated I'm-a-geezer voice.

Jo had been in the front passenger seat, watching Trevor as he drove, hoping he wasn't very far over the limit. He had obviously heard this crass exchange between Pascale and Ed, but had had to pretend not to have heard it, and Jo had had to pretend she didn't know he was pretending not to have heard it.

Without hesitation she labelled Pascale 'Explicit sexual content'. Then she typed 'Strong sex references' next to Ed's name. Immediately her heart found its way to her throat and stayed there, pushing her blood around so hard she could feel her temples throbbing.

"Grow up, you *child*," she murmured, sitting up. She typed Holly's name below Ed's.

What was Holly like? Teachers were always saying things like, "That's very sensible, Holly." She *was* sensible, in a way, but the face she displayed to teachers was a conscious one, learnt by heart. The unrehearsed version of Holly was much harder to define. Jo's fingers hovered over the keyboard for a moment, and then she typed 'Fairly adult' alongside Holly's name. 'Fairly' was a suitably vague word for Holly's level of maturity. And of course, Holly did have 'fair' hair, which made the sort of satisfying pun Mr Gerrard would enjoy.

God, this was stupid. Jo took hold of the mouse, ready to delete the incriminating list before Trevor came in and read it over her shoulder. But she didn't do it. She looked at the names, and the scattered DVD cases, and her reflection in the mirror behind the computer, and remembered how Ed's shirt had come out of his trousers when he'd been kicking a football around at lunchtime, and she'd stood and watched him tuck it in again as if she were a no-brain fourteen-year-old. But it was just that he'd had to loosen his belt...

She pushed the keyboard away. Her head sank forward of its own accord and landed among the DVDs. There were still tears inside her somewhere, but they wouldn't come. All she felt was embarrassed – at her own behaviour, at Pascale's, at Trevor's. She wanted to disappear somewhere impossible to reach. Heaven, maybe. Or space, or history. No one would miss her, or try to bring her back. Not even Mr Treasure.

She stayed there for a long time, her breath dampening her cheek as it condensed on the cover of *Knocked Up*, her hair covering her nose and mouth. Her hair smelt of school, and her breath was giving it a damp smell too. The smell of hairdressers' salons. It made her feel enclosed in her own, physical self, as if her body had been wound in a shroud and placed in a coffin.

She had to press her top teeth as hard as she could against the bottom ones, to try to stop that thought. It always led to one about worms eating her eyeballs.

She felt the edge of one of the plastic cases dig into the bony part of her cheek. Without thinking she shifted and pressed harder. A sudden stab of pain shot through her body.

It really hurt, but instead of releasing she just pushed harder and harder until the pain enveloped her entirely, like a black hole swallowing the Universe.

She sat up breathlessly. Her whole body was tingling. She shut her eyes tightly and lived the electric moment. It didn't last long and when she opened her eyes, she saw the consequences. The mirror displayed an L-shaped weal on her right cheekbone. She felt suddenly disorientated, and gripped the edge of the dressing-table desk. Leaning closer to the mirror, she saw that the DVD cover hadn't merely imprinted its corner into her flesh, it had torn it. In the crook of the L, a drop of blood was gathering.

She looked down at the pile of DVDs. The cover she'd pressed her cheek onto lay open and empty. Jo picked it up and inspected it. It wasn't the corner of the case that had drawn blood, but the plastic prongs that slotted into each other when the case was closed. The edge of one of them had been broken, leaving a sharp point.

She dabbed the wound on her cheek with a tissue. It wasn't a big deal, but people would notice it, so she'd have to think of a lie to tell them. Futile behaviour like sticking a DVD case into your face would elicit bafflement from Pascale and a telling-off from Holly, and Jo didn't want to experience either.

The case was still in her hand. She fingered it, feeling a lingering sense of shock. Such an innocuous object; such an electrifying result of...what? Drawing blood? She studied her reflection, looking for the reassurance in the sight of her own familiar features. But there was an expression in her eyes that *wasn't* familiar. She looked like someone in a TV news film who had just been rescued from a capsized boat, or an earthquake, or a flood. Adrift, only half in the world, and possessed of a sudden, unwelcome wisdom.

## Chapter Two

"*Wales*?"

"Yep," said Trevor. He was sitting in the kitchen with his feet on the table. "It's a principality of some three million souls, situated in the west of the British mainland. It enjoys a constant supply of mountains, castles, rugby and rain, and is God's own country. As every Welshman knows, and so should you, Jo-girl."

Jo put the teapot down quickly and sat at the table, keeping her eyes on Trevor's face. "Stop being such an arse. What will you do there? Get a job?"

"I doubt it. I got some money from the firm. Fifteen thousand."

"Is that all?" Jo was surprised. No wonder Trevor had felt the need to get off his face on gin. "So when that's gone, what will you do?"

It was Saturday morning, so Trevor wasn't at work. But he only had three more days to work anyway, because they owed him holiday time.

"Well, my little love," he said, biting off a mouthful of toast, "you remember Mord Davies?"

"No."

"Yes you do. He's my mother's cousin, or nephew, or something. Mordecai, his name is. Anyway, he's been asking me for years, on and off, if I want to go into business with him. Bed and breakfast, in this farmhouse he wants to do up, see."

"Good grief," said Jo faintly. The thought of Trevor and someone called Mordecai running a bed and breakfast establishment wasn't even funny. It was just ludicrous.

"So I think the time's come to take him up on his offer, don't you?" said Trevor.

Jo tried to understand. "So if you go into business with him, you'll take half the profits, will you?"

"Mm," nodded Trevor with his mouth full.

"So you're going to put your fifteen thousand into setting it up, then?"

As she said this, Jo could feel her heart doing something weird inside her. She was sure, before he spoke, that Trevor wasn't going to do that at all.

"Nope," he said. "Needs much more than that. I'll put in what I get from the divorce. Half this house, for a start."

Jo poured the tea and they sipped it. She knew that if she asked Trevor to take his feet off the table he wouldn't, so she didn't bother. "So you sell a nice house in London and you use half the money to help Mordi-whatever-his-name-is to do up a crappy old house in Wales," she said after a while. "What will Tess use her half for?"

"That's up to her, Jo-girl. But if she's got any sense, which I doubt, she'll invest it."

"You mean buy another property?"

Trevor nodded, trying to look wise. He'd had a shower and his hair was still wet on the top. He was wearing trainers and jeans and a faded Guns 'n' Roses T-shirt. "Well, she can't live with her parents for ever, can she?" He reached for the teapot. "Top up?"

Jo shook her head. "Trevor, half the money will only buy half a house. A flat."

"That's right." He looked at her with sympathy, or almost-sympathy. "It's that or Prattland, babe."

Jo could see her face in the glass of the kitchen door. She looked pale, the mark on her cheekbone showing dark. Her hair was separating into strands and her shoulders were hunched. "Sit up *straight*," Tess was forever saying, with that funny 'r' sound that came from speaking French when she was a child, "or you'll grow up to be uglier than the Hunchback of Notre Dame, and he was *ugly*."

"Actually," she said, cradling her mug, "it's that or begging on Victoria Station."

Trevor had stopped listening. He'd taken his feet off the table and picked up Blod, the tortoiseshell cat Tess had rescued then neglected. "Come on, let's get you fed, shall we?" He opened a can and put some food in Blod's bowl. Then he picked up his keys and jingled them on his palm. "You know, love, I was bloody angry yesterday. I thought the world had come to a freakin' end, losing my job. They think I've got a drink problem, see. But then I was on the phone to Granny Probert last night and she said Mord was still open to offers, and it would be great if I could come back to Wales and be near her and Dad, and I thought, why not? So things aren't so bad after all." He gave Jo the lopsided look he thought was charming, and jingled the keys again. "Think I'll have a walk and buy the newspaper. What are you going to do with your Saturday?"

Jo began to clear the table. Granny Probert, she thought, should keep her mouth shut. "My interview's today," she said.

They looked at each other. Trevor's face was blank.

"I told you," said Jo. "It's in a shop. They want someone for the summer, then maybe permanently."

"What sort of shop?"

"I *told* you. A clothes shop."

"What about your exams?"

"It'll only be on Saturdays until after the exams. Then all week during the summer. But the interviews are today."

He opened the kitchen door.

"What time's your interview?"

"Eleven thirty." Jo looked at the clock on the cooker. It was already five past ten.

Trevor took his jacket off the rack in the hall. "Well, good luck, then." Unexpectedly, he squinted at her. "What have you done to your face?"

"Walked into a rose bush."

"A *rose bush*?"

Jo was ready for this. Trevor hadn't consciously seen her yesterday. "It was sticking out from someone's stupid garden, and scratched me as I walked past on the way back from the bus stop. It bloody hurt, I can tell you."

Trevor grinned. "Try not to get tetanus."

"Thanks for the sympathy."

"See you later, then."

The front door crashed behind him. Jo topped up her mug of tea and took it upstairs. After her shower she dried her hair, trying to push it up a bit so that it looked like there was some air between it and her scalp. But it just wrapped itself round her head and neck as flatly as a scarf. Whoever interviewed her would wonder whether that branch of Rose and Reed could risk giving a job to a girl with a scab on her cheek and such disappointingly dull hair. Dull hair, dull brain, dull personality.

At least her jeans were clean, and she had one unworn top left in the drawer. Once it was on and she'd done her eyeliner and put concealer on her cheek she felt better. She even dug out a pair of earrings and a belt that roughly matched the top, and put on her jacket with the stand-up collar that kind of pushed the bottom of her hair up. The top of her hair just sat there as usual, though.

On the bus she re-read the letter. It wasn't very businesslike, even though it had the shop's familiar Rose and Reed logo at the top, with the two capital Rs entwined. It was printed in bright blue ink except for 'Dear Miss Probert', which was in untidy round handwriting. It was obviously a standard letter sent to all the candidates, of which there would be hundreds. Five pounds an hour. For a Saturday, forty pounds. For six weeks in the summer, over two hundred pounds a week. It was more money than Jo could envisage.

She thought about how long an hour was. An hour of Computer Studies felt like five minutes, but an hour of Biology, or History, or especially French – oh Jesus, French! – seemed much, much longer. The hours at the job she'd had last year, in the pet shop, had gone at a sort of jogging speed, rather than serious running. So what would an hour selling expensive clothes feel like? Waterskiing? Or doing a marathon with blisters on her feet?

There weren't hundreds of other interviewees. There were only two. One was a girl who was older and had much better hair than Jo, and the other was a good-looking boy.

"Now," said the man whose identity tag said Gordon Ritchie, Manager, "I've asked you all to come at eleven thirty so I can show you round the shop together before interviewing you separately. That OK? Oh, and there are two vacancies today."

Jo considered making an excuse and leaving. She could have handled being one of a hundred rejects. But the humiliation of spending time with these two nice-looking people, even chatting to one while the other was interviewed, then being the only candidate left unemployed at the end of the morning was just too great.

"Welcome to Rose and Reed! Do you wear our clothes?" the

manager said as he led them up the stairs. "My name's Gordon. I'm the branch manager. I thought we'd start with Menswear."

Gordon had a Scottish accent, tight trousers and expensive pointy shoes. He talked a lot during their tour of Menswear, then Womenswear, then Lingerie, without leaving them a space to answer any of his questions. Jo was relieved. Older-Better-Hair Girl could obviously afford to shop at Rose and Reed, and Good-Looking Boy was too good-looking for it to matter. She wished she was at home with Blod on her stomach, watching Saturday morning TV.

"Joanna Probert!" Gordon consulted his list and fixed Jo with his rather bulbous eyes. "You don't mind going first, do you, darling?" His fingers closed around the arm of a passing sales assistant. "Oh, Eloise. Get some coffee for our intrepid interviewees, please."

"Black for me," said OBH Girl. "I mean, black coffee." Eloise was black. OBH Girl went red. Eloise smiled.

"Can I have a Coke?" asked GL Boy.

"'Fraid not," said Eloise. "Coffee or tea?"

"Nothing, thanks."

Eloise turned patiently to Jo, still smiling. Jo wanted to smile back, but found that her smiling muscles wouldn't work. "White, please," she mumbled. "One sugar."

"Now..." Gordon took Jo into the office, guided her to a chair and sat on the desk. "Have you worked in a shop before?"

"Yes, a pet shop. It says it on my CV."

"Have I got your CV?" He moved some papers around on the desk. "Doesn't look like it." He smiled brightly. "Sorry! So what goes on in a pet shop that might be relevant to working with fashion?"

Jo still wanted to run away. But she persevered, telling him that she had learnt about stock control and knew how to work the till, and understood what customer relations were. "People don't know how to treat pets, you see," she pointed out. "So they're always bringing them back and complaining that they're not doing what they're supposed to."

"Like the Monty Python sketch!" exclaimed Gordon in delight. He put on a face. "This. Parrot. Is. No. More!" Jo smiled patiently.

Eloise came in and put Jo's coffee on the desk beside Gordon's thigh. As she left the room she gave him a look that Jo wasn't supposed to see. It said, "Get on with it, Gordon, it's Saturday out here."

"Well, yes," continued Jo. "You hear quite a lot about that Monty Python sketch when you work in a pet shop. And the other thing about animals is that people often buy them for other people, and the people they've been bought for don't like them, and want the shop to take them back, and of course they haven't got any proof of purchase, and one gerbil's very like another, so – "

"When could you start, if you get this job?"

"Next Saturday?"

"The pay's five pounds an hour. All right?"

Jo tried to remember the questions she'd lined up. Always ask the interviewer at least one question, people said. It makes you look interested. "Yes, thank you. Would I get a discount on the clothes?"

"Certainly. Twenty percent."

"Oh...well, good."

There wasn't anything more to say. He hadn't read her CV or her reference from Mr Piper at Piper's Pets. He was trying to get rid of her. Jo picked up her coffee. But it was too hot, so she put it down again.

"I'll phone you by Wednesday," said Gordon. "What's your

number?"

"It's on my CV."

The frog gaze landed on her face again. "I'll just write it down again, shall I?"

She dictated the number and took two sips of scalding coffee. Then she picked up her bag. "Goodbye, then."

"Goodbye, er..." – he checked his notes – "Joanna." They shook hands. "Thanks for coming."

As she opened the door she almost flattened GL Boy. "Sorry!" she said without looking at him.

"In a hurry?" he asked.

"Things to do," she said over her shoulder, hauling open the swing door to the shop floor.

"See you next week, maybe."

"I doubt it," said Jo, and set off for the bus stop.

\* \* \* \* \* \*

"But you like Ed, don't you?" asked Pascale. "Holly told me you do. Didn't you, Hol?"

Holly, Pascale and Jo were in the school library, whispering. "I *do* like Ed, but not in the going-out-with sense, obviously," explained Jo.

Pascale frowned. "Are you telling me my boyfriend's not fanciable?"

"No, of course not. But isn't Tom Clarke your boyfriend now?"

"Jo, how can you be so *stupid*?" Pascale looked at Jo critically. "And by the way, did you know you've got a spot coming on your cheek?"

"It's not a spot, I walked into a rose bush."

"A *rose bush*?" said Holly and Pascale together.

31

Mrs Alder, the librarian, passed by their table, her lips pursed in a silent "Sh!"

"I can't stand this," said Holly, closing her folder. "Let's go."

"But we're revising," said Jo.

"No we're not, we're talking about boys. And study leave starts next week, thank God."

It was a perfect May day. The windows were open to the kind of sunshine that made Jo suddenly remember what summer felt like. It was the first period after lunch, and the bench under the blossom tree at the edge of the field was empty. Holly sat down at one end of it. "Tell us about this job, then, Jo," she said.

Gordon had called the afternoon before and, to Jo's great surprise, had offered her the job. She assumed one of the others must have been hit by a bus or been offered something better somewhere else.

"Do you get money off the clothes?" asked Pascale. She was standing with her back to the sun, which lit the edges of her plentiful hair and threw the face that launched a thousand crushes into shadow. Even as Jo said the words she could feel herself regretting it.

"Twenty percent."

"Ooh! Can you buy things for other people?"

"I expect so, if I pretend they're for me."

"Shotgun first go, then!" Pascale settled herself and her pile of books next to Holly, barely leaving room on the bench for Jo. "I'll come and try some things on this Saturday."

"No you won't," said Jo. She sat down on the grass. "I've got to buy some things to wear while I'm working, and there's a limit on what I can spend. They're not completely stupid, you know."

"So who else works there? Anyone nice?" asked Holly. Her

whole face was smiling. She looked ridiculously pretty, as she always did. She was more beautiful than Pascale in every way except possibly her one crooked front tooth. But the boys still went for Pascale. Since when had boys been put off a beautiful girl by a wonky tooth? Jo had abandoned the search for an explanation years ago.

She knew she shouldn't tell them, but she couldn't help it. "I don't start until Saturday, so I don't know which of the two other people who were interviewed got the job. But they both looked OK."

"Anyone from Kingsgrove?" asked Pascale.

"No, they're more like college students," Jo told her. She paused, trying to picture OBH Girl and GL Boy. She couldn't, after such a brief acquaintance. "Or maybe they're just people who want a part time job that might turn into a full time one."

Like me, she thought.

Pascale had her boy-detecting antennae flashing. "So when you say they look OK..."

"All right, Cal," said Jo. "One of them's male. And yes, he's quite good-looking. But that's all I know about him."

"And he might not have got the job, so you'll never see him again anyway," observed Holly sensibly.

"But there's a chance you *will*," insisted Pascale. "How sweet! Our little Jo in a shop all day with a good-looking boy!"

Holly leaned towards Jo, the sun full in her face, brightening her hair to an even more blazing gold than usual. "Don't listen to her," she said. "Jealousy's rotting her brain cells. Personally I hope the *girl* got the job if it'll shut Pascale up."

"So do I," said Jo, though this was untrue. Making Pascale jealous was a novel experience. "And by the way, look who's turned up."

Mrs Cadwallader, the Deputy Head, crossed the field and

gave them a look of loathing. "Have you permission to be out here, girls?"

"Yes, miss," said Holly, who was always the boldest in these situations. *Fairly adult* indeed. Holly was always doing thoughtful things like defending Jo against Pascale's shamelessness. Yet here she was, lying with demure proficiency to Mrs Cadwallader like every actress's portrayal of a schoolgirl.

"Well, I just hope you *have*," said Mrs Cadwallader uneasily.

The bell rang. Sandwiched between Holly and Pascale as they walked across the field, Jo longed to be left to herself. When they reached the crowded corridor, she quickened her step.

Holly immediately caught up. "So what are we doing on Friday?" she asked. Someone's bag clouted her in the chest. "Excuse *me!* Are you trying to kill me? God, this school's full of hooligans. Can't wait till Sixth Form. I could have given that clown a punishment if this was next year. I mean, we should go somewhere to celebrate the start of study leave."

"Um..." Jo didn't consider several weeks of being in the house all day with newly-unemployed Trevor a cause for celebration. "Press Gang?"

Press Gang was a café-bar. Until a couple of years ago it had been an ordinary riverside pub, but new management had restyled it. The dark wood interior had been replaced with polished floors and metal tables, and the bar now served coffee, cakes and cocktails. It now seemed to be more of a café really, and it was generally accepted in the neighbourhood as a gathering-place for anyone who was too young to get into a real pub. Jo didn't like it much. The garden tables and benches were sticky, the ashtrays seldom emptied, and you had to check your change.

"We *always* go to Press Gang," complained Holly. "What

about a Chinese instead?"

"Since when have I eaten that muck?" asked Pascale, who had caught up too. "*And* it'll only be the three of us," she added gloomily. "Ed works at Burgerblitz till eleven thirty on Friday nights."

"Tom Clarke?" suggested Jo.

Pascale stopped, ignoring the two people behind her who walked into her. She gave Jo's shoulder a small push. "Will you just *shut up* about Tom Clarke?"

Mr Phipps was already in the Maths room, writing on the board.

"What's up with Cal?" whispered Jo as she and Holly sat down at the front with the no-hopers. Pascale was good at Maths, so she sat in the back row. But even if she hadn't been, Mr Phipps would have put her there. He knew that if he wanted the boys to do any work he mustn't let them see her. Even her back view.

"Tom didn't bite, I think," said Holly, searching her pencil case busily.

Jo suddenly felt, very strongly, that she didn't want to go to Press Gang with Holly and Pascale, or Tom, or Ed, or anyone, on Friday or any day. From nowhere the memory of pressing her cheek into the DVD flooded her head. Unconsciously she raised her hand to the wound. The mark had scabbed over, and Jo had picked the scab off and blobbed make-up on the crater, which was why Pascale had assumed it was an incipient spot. But it wasn't a spot, it was a cut she'd inflicted on herself. The DVD case resting against her cheek. The feeling of pressing down on it. The sudden jolt of pain. More pressure, more pain, growing and growing, blotting everything else out...She took a deep breath, suddenly feeling dizzy and nauseous. "Look, Hol, you two do what you like, but I think I should get an early night on

35

Friday as I'm starting work in the shop the next day."

Holly started to say something, but at that moment Mr Phipps roared for the class to shut up, so Jo didn't have to answer her, or even look at the astonishment on her face.

\* \* \* \* \* \*

His name was Toby.

On that first morning, Jo hardly saw him as he worked upstairs in Menswear, supervised by Gordon. Downstairs in Womenswear Jo tried to take in what Eloise was explaining. Eloise was patient, but training Jo had to be fitted between serving customers. It was slow work.

"Look, Jo," Eloise said at half past eleven, glancing round the crowded shop. "There's new summer stock in the stockroom to be sorted. T-shirts. Will you unpack them and put them on hangers? When you've done that you can go to lunch. Just tell me when you're going."

Eloise needed a break from having to look out for Jo, and Jo couldn't blame her. "OK," she said, watching Eloise wrap up a raspberry mini-skirt for a woman who looked at least thirty years too old to wear it. Of course, it could have been for her daughter. Or granddaughter.

"Just make sure the size on the T-shirt is the same as the size on the hanger," said Eloise. "They're already priced. Here's the card for the stockroom door."

Even someone as new as me can do a simple job like this, thought Jo. She smiled with what she hoped Eloise would think was confidence. "Right. I'm on it."

Rose and Reed's classy decor ended when you pushed the door marked *Staff Only*. The office where Gordon had interviewed Jo was the only room with a window. Everywhere else was below street level. There was the stockroom, a tiny toilet and the optimistically-named Staff Room, which was an oblong space with a lockable cupboard for employees' belongings, two hard chairs and a kettle. These rooms were artificially lit, with no air conditioning and nothing on the walls except staff rotas and a notice about fire regulations. Jo slid the card Eloise had given her down the slot on the stockroom lock, feeling as if she were descending into a bunker to await the end of the world.

It looked to Jo as if there were more T-shirts than every branch of Rose and Reed could sell in the entire summer. They filled three huge boxes, one of which had been damaged, so that its polythene-bagged contents had slid out like lava across the floor. Jo looked around. "So where are these hangers, then?" she muttered.

Toby's head came round the door. "You talkin' to me?" he said, like Robert De Niro in *Taxi Driver*.

Jo went pink. "No, I didn't know you were there. I was just wondering where the hangers are. I've got to put these T-shirts on them."

He came in and looked around. "Nice place you've got here."

Jo couldn't think of a reply, so she shrugged.

"I'm on my lunch hour," he announced. "I've got to go now because Gordon wants his lunch later, and there's only the two of us up there. But I could run out for a sandwich and come back and help you. This looks like a big job."

Jo tried to refuse, but he ignored her. "Look, why don't I get you a sandwich too? You hungry?"

"Yes, but you don't need to do this."

"What do you like? Meat or veggy? Cheese?"

"BLT's my favourite." Jo tried to listen to herself. She'd only exchanged a few sentences with him in her life, and now he knew her favourite sandwich. If he asked her what size her bra was, would she tell him?

"BLT it is, then. And a Coke? Or juice, or water?"

"Diet Coke would be good. Thanks."

"No problem." He started to close the door, then opened it again. "The hangers are in a box behind those rails," he told her. "The sizes are all mixed up, though."

"Thanks," said Jo again.

When he'd gone she stood in the middle of the stockroom floor and sighed. She felt like the miller's daughter in *Rumpelstiltzkin*, a story Tess had eventually refused to read any more because four-year-old Jo always started crying when Rumpelstiltzkin demanded the newborn baby. The miller's daughter couldn't spin straw into gold, and Jo wasn't confident she'd be able to unfold and hang up all these T-shirts on the right hangers. But the miller's daughter still got her prince.

When Toby came back with the food she'd made a start on sorting out the hangers into sizes. "Eloise is trying to bury me down here for the rest of the day," she told him sheepishly. "I must be totally useless."

"No you're not," said Toby, handing her a paper bag. "You're just new. I started on Thursday, and in two days I've learnt where they keep the hangers. Big deal."

"Thanks for this," said Jo, opening her sandwich. "How much do I owe you?"

Toby looked at the ceiling. "Um..." Then he looked at Jo. "Can't remember. Pay me some other time."

He opened his own sandwich. "Come on, we can eat and work at the same time. We'll clear this in a couple of hours."

"Eloise'll think I'm Superwoman," said Jo.

"Maybe you are, but you just don't know it."

Jo watched him while he pulled hangers out of the box, his

sandwich in his other hand. He was definitely the Good-Looking Boy she'd labelled him as at the interview. Separately, his features may have been relatively ordinary – thin lips that didn't show his teeth much when he talked, a high-bridged nose, far apart eyes of an indeterminate colour – but together, in Jo's eyes, they made something amazing.

He had the kind of hair that curls on the top and is straight at the sides. He was tall, but not so tall that he had to stoop to speak to her, and when he stood with his feet together there was a space between his thighs. Pascale wouldn't even go to a movie unless the actor in it had that all-important space.

"I like these T-shirts," he said. "I'm going to buy two."

"Less twenty percent, of course."

"Of course. And I've got my eye on a pair of jeans a customer returned, but Gordon doesn't think he'll put back on the rail. Might get them *really* cheap."

Jo had finished her sandwich. She began to take T-shirts out of bags. "You like clothes, don't you?"

"And you don't?" His eyes looked amused, but interested. Closer up, she saw that they were greyish blue, with flecks of darker grey.

"Yes, I suppose I do. But usually, you know, boys..."

"Everyone *I* know likes clothes," he said decisively. "Here, I've sorted all the men's hangers. You get the XLs out of the bags, and I'll hang them up."

They worked in silence for a few minutes. Jo knew Toby was looking at her every now and then, as he turned between the boxes and the rails. She was glad she'd washed her hair, because he was looking down on the top of her head as she sat on the floor among the polythene bags. She wanted him to approve of her appearance, since he was a boy and she was a girl and there was no way round that situation. But she wasn't sure if she wanted him actually to think beyond that, and consider *her*. If he did, he might be disappointed.

"How old are you, Jo?" he asked her conversationally. "Seventeen?"

"Sixteen," she said, undoing another bag. "I'm just doing my GCSEs."

"Oh. You seem...I mean, I'm eighteen."

Jo handed him the T-shirt, considering him in the light of the Upper Sixth Form boys at school, who would be his age. "I would put you at older," she said, "if that's not an insult."

"It's a compliment!" he said, smiling a small, no-teeth-showing smile. He hung up the T-shirt and pondered, fiddling with his hair. "I can't remember what it felt like to be sixteen. It's been a long two years, one way and another."

Jo took in breath to ask him what he meant, but was stopped by a noise from the doorway. Gordon stood there, one hand on his hip, the other holding the stockroom key card. "So this is where you're hiding! Tobe, it's like Harrods sale up there, and I've got a lunch appointment." His gaze landed on Jo. "Are you all right, darling?" Then he looked at Toby again. "Come on, you. I haven't got all day."

Toby gave the finger to Gordon's retreating back view. Jo smiled. "Thanks for your help."

"That's OK." Suddenly, he bent down and, producing a pen from the pocket of his jeans, took her hand and wrote a number on the back of it. "See you later. Happy hanging."

When he'd gone Jo stared at the number. She couldn't stop herself grinning. Toby was eighteen, and worked for his living, and had given her his phone number. How sad did Pascale's little drama over Ed and Tom look now?

# Chapter Three

"Jo, darling..."

"Don't call me darling."

"Why not?" Tess removed her sunglasses and looked at Jo accusingly. "You're my precious only daughter, aren't you?"

"I just hate it, that's why not." Jo, who was sitting in the swing seat, braced her feet against the table, pushed off and swung as violently as she could. "Gay Gordon at work calls everyone darling. It's meaningless."

"I agree," said Trevor. "I never use it myself."

"We'd noticed." Tess waved away the smoke from his cigarette. "You call your only child 'Jo-girl'. And must you blow smoke all over her?"

"She's used to it," returned Trevor, glancing at Jo out of the corners of his eyes. Jo knew he was about to say that it was Tess who had left him, and he could do what he bloody well liked now she'd gone. She had to stop him. They were here to discuss Mord Davies's business venture, and that was all.

"Anyway," she said quickly to her mother, "what were you going to say, when you called me darling?"

Tess frowned. Her hair, darker than Jo's but just as flat, was parted in the centre and drawn into a chignon. She called it her Charlotte Brontë look, though Jo could never fathom why anyone would want to look like a woman who had lived when hairstyles were at their most unflattering in the whole of history.

The sunshine, which had brought out the garden furniture, also shone on Tess's fake tan, strappy dress and pink sandals. Not very Charlotte Brontë.

"Can't remember," Tess said at last. She put her sunglasses back on and sipped her drink, but then she took them off again. "Oh, I know! I was going to ask you about school."

Jo took the paper umbrella Tess always put in soft drinks out of her Coke and dropped it on the table. "What about school? I thought we were going to talk about Trevor's new business."

"Trevor and Mordecai!" said Tess, smiling. "You know what everyone'll think, don't you? Two men running a bed and breakfast?"

"You know what a bigoted craphead you sound, don't you?" said Trevor. He picked up the paper umbrella. "I'll use this for an ashtray, since your parents haven't thought to provide me with one."

Oh God, thought Jo.

Tess had gone a bit pink, and her nostrils twitched. She turned exaggeratedly to Jo. "What I wanted to ask," she said testily, "is about your plans for next year. A Levels?"

"Give me a break, will you?" sighed Jo. "I haven't even finished my GCSEs."

"I know that, but shouldn't you have decided by now what subjects you want to continue? Have you spoken to the teachers about it?"

"No." Jo swung the seat again. "In fact..." She paused, and swung it again. "I'm not sure that I want to stay on at school at all."

Tess slammed her fist down on the table, so unexpectedly that Jo spilt some Coke on her T-shirt. "I *knew* this would happen!"

"Oh, calm down, will you?" said Trevor wearily. "Get off the stage, for Christ's sake."

Tess looked at him with her eyes narrowed. "Thank you, Mr Responsible Parent. I turn my back for five minutes and you've messed everything up!" She sat back and pressed her fingers to her forehead. "And now you've given me a headache."

"Well, you've given me a bum-ache," said Trevor. He flicked some ash into the makeshift ashtray, not looking at Tess or Jo.

Tess had her hand over her face. There was petulance, but no real anger in her voice. "It's up to me to do what's best for Jo," she said, "because *you're* clearly incapable of it."

"Why did you walk out on her, then?" retorted Trevor.

"I didn't walk out on *her*. I walked out on *you*. And I wish I'd done it years ago!"

Jo leaned forward. "I'm here, remember? I'm listening to this!"

Tess took her hand away from her face. Her mouth had collapsed into a tight line, so that her lipstick was almost invisible. "We know that, darling," she said to Jo, though she was still looking at Trevor. "But there's no need for you to feel bad. This isn't about you. It's between me and your father."

"It *is* about me!" The back of Jo's neck felt sweaty. Impatiently, she swept her pony-tail up onto the top of her head and held it there with one hand. "It's *my* decision whether I want to do A Levels, isn't it?"

Trevor tried to say something, but Jo wouldn't let him. "Look," she said to Tess, "you can't make me into the person you want, whatever that is, by trying to control me and then taking it out on Trevor because I don't do what you want!"

Tess didn't like this at all. Her face hardened, the muscles in her jaw puckering. "I do *not* do that, so stop fantasising, you...*little girl*! What do you know?"

"I know that I can't stand you telling me what to do as if I *were* a little girl! Which I'm not!" This was so obvious Jo almost felt silly saying the words. Frustration was turning to anger. Everything – the stupid paper umbrellas, the way Trevor slumped in his chair brushing cigarette ash off his dirty jeans, Tess's bra straps cutting into her shoulders, the mean, strained expression on her face – was making her angry. "I'm just *me*! For God's sake, is that so hard to understand?"

Trevor poured himself another glass of wine and drank it in two gulps. Tess let out one of the "Sshk!" noises that she used to show disgust. Jo knew that they were doing these things because neither of them knew how to answer her.

Jo let go of her hair. Tonight, she decided, she would type 'Moderate horror' in the space next to Tess's name. Why hadn't she thought of this before? Everything about Tess was scary enough to be in a horror film. Her talon nails and salon hair, the light that came into her eyes whenever any object of consumer desire was mentioned, the depth of her snobbishness and the shallowness of her taste. It was all unrelenting, tedious and clichéd, like the very worst straight-to-DVD slasher movie.

"OK, then," said Trevor at last, holding the wine bottle upside down over his glass. A dribble came out. "Any more wine?" he asked, looking around the garden as if he expected a waiter to cross the lawn with a bottle wrapped in a white napkin.

Tess's lipstick was visible again, but her expression was still hard-edged. She shrugged, put on her sunglasses and offered Trevor and Jo her profile.

"Anyway, Jo," went on Trevor in a tolerant voice, "I think *you've* got to understand something too. Tess and I are very concerned about this idea of leaving school. Why exactly don't you want to stay on? Perhaps if you give us a good enough reason, we'd – "

"Trevor!" hissed Tess. "leave it for now!"

This was so predictable that Jo almost laughed. "Yeah, Trevor. Only speak when given permission, remember."

Trevor sat forward suddenly, so that his face was about fifteen centimeters from Jo's. His eyes looked pink round the edges. She could smell alcohol when he breathed out. "That's *enough*!" he told her in a clipped whisper. "Don't you be so bloody rude."

Jo stood up. A picture of Toby silently writing his mobile number on her hand came into her head. She wished he could be there, in Granny and Grandad Pratt's garden, right now. She wanted – she had quite possibly never wanted anything so much – to be with him. Just to be with him, wherever he was.

"I'm going now," she announced, clenching her fists so hard her nails dug into her palms.

She found herself imagining the little crescent-shaped indentations they would leave. "I was about to talk to you about leaving school, but you can't be bothered to listen because you're too busy playing some insane game."

Trevor pushed back his chair, but Jo held up her hand. "And if you say, 'I'll drive you, Jo girl', I'll say 'five glasses of wine, Trevor!' I've got my front door key. I'll go on the train."

\* \* \* \* \* \*

On the train Jo thought of crying, so that she could have a little drama-queen moment in public like Pascale would. But she decided against it. She didn't want to behave like Pascale. Boy magnet Pascale might be, which was useful sometimes, but she had her drawbacks. Ever since Saturday, everything she had said implied that the only reason Toby had been so nice to Jo was that he hadn't met Pascale...yet. It was inevitable that he would, since anyone could come into the shop. But it was up to Jo to sort out what *didn't* happen next.

She took her phone out of her pocket. Two messages waiting. They would be from Holly and Pascale, asking her what was going on tonight. It was a warm evening, and Ed was working at Burgerblitz again. He'd taken on more hours since study leave had started. Jo didn't look at either of the messages.

Her insides jumped about a little as she scrolled down to Toby's number. A thousand times this week she'd looked at it, and a thousand times she hadn't dialled it. Supposing, for a laugh, he'd put someone else's number on her hand? His girlfriend's? Never assume a boy hasn't already got a girlfriend, Pascale was always reminding her. They never throw out dirty water until they've got clean. But this time, the thousand-and-first time, Jo had to risk it.

"Hello?" Well, it wasn't a girl. She couldn't tell if it was him, though.

"Is that Toby? It's Jo."

He paused before he spoke. He definitely paused, as if he was thinking, "What the...?" Or maybe he knew more than one girl called Jo. Then he said, "Jo!"

"That's right." Her voice was actually shaking. She couldn't breathe properly. "You gave me your number."

"How're you doing?"

"You sound like Joey from *Friends*."

"What?"

*Shut up, Jo. Not everyone's as sad as you.* "I'm OK. I just wondered..."

"Are you free tonight?" he asked. "Where are you?"

Jo's breath disappeared completely. But she managed to tell him that she was on the train.

"What station are you getting off at?"

"Kingsgrove."

"What time will you be there?"

"In about twenty minutes."

"I'll meet you there. See ya."

When he'd hung up Jo sat limply, resting her head against the window, allowing her heartbeat to calm. Never phone a boy, Pascale said. But it had worked, hadn't it? He'd obviously just been sitting there, wondering what to do with his Wednesday evening, when suddenly the phone rang, and there was the Saturday girl he'd given his number to. What did Pascale know?

She tried to conjure Toby's face in her memory. She tried to picture the scene in the stockroom. She'd stood there, eating her BLT, with him saying he liked the T-shirts and was going to buy two. She'd tried to watch him without looking as if she was watching him, so she could report accurately to Holly and Pascale.

She could see it all perfectly clearly in her mind's eye. But oddly, since it was only a few days ago, she couldn't see Toby's face. All she could think of was the way he'd filled up the place that would have been empty if he hadn't been there. Was that what people meant when they talked about someone's 'presence'? Or was that just a load of nonsense? But it wasn't so much what he looked like, it was what he *was*.

Three minutes from Kingsgrove she remembered that she had a Coke stain on her T-shirt and no make up on, and that her hair was in a pony tail. She shook it out and consulted her reflection in the window. Disaster. She combed it. Worse.

"Would you not do that in public, please? It's most unhygienic," said the woman opposite. She was about forty, with diamond rings on her fingers. "I mean, what are you going to do with the hair in the comb? Drop it on the floor, I suppose?"

Jo went pink. "Sorry." She put the comb, hair and all, in her pocket. Then the train stopped and she had to get out. She made sure she hit the woman's shoulder with the corner of her bag, though. "Sorry!" she said again.

She ran along the platform and over the bridge, dodging briefcases and backpacks. Her heart felt as if something were compressing it into the size and consistency of a blob of chewing gum. She put her ticket in the machine, scanning the station entrance. And there he was.

"Hey," he said cheerfully. "Where do you want to go? Cinema?"

"I haven't got enough money. I've just come from my mum's, and I had to spend what I had on the train fare."

"I'll pay. Or we could just get something to eat. Have you eaten?"

"No. That would be good. But I haven't got – "

"I'll pay, I told you. Do you like curry?"

Throughout this exchange Jo had felt hot and self-conscious. Toby was clean. He was dressed in the Rose and Reed clothes he'd got on discount. He was neatly shaven, and smelled of aftershave or shower gel or something. Her own appearance was gross in comparison. But when she'd called him, she'd just thought she was going to talk to him on the phone.

"Look, I'll go home first and change, and get some money," she told him as they came out of the station. "I mean, you paid for my lunch on Saturday. I just live along the road. I won't be long, I promise."

Toby leaned on the railing outside the station. "I'll wait here, shall I? I don't particularly want to meet your parents right now."

"Oh, you wouldn't!" Jo assured him. "I live with my dad, and he's not in."

He gave her the kind of look that Jo recognized from a thousand screen close-ups. His mouth and eyes competed with each other for which could look the more amused/sexy/pleased. She could almost hear the director: "Gimme more funny! Gimme more sexy! That's it, and look pleased at the same time!" Boys were just conceited, everyone knew that. But Toby did look nice, even with The Look all over his face.

"Home alone, then?" he said. He was smirking, but Jo forgave him. He had every reason to laugh at her.

"Um...yes, I suppose so. My dad won't be long, but if we're quick we'll miss him."

For the first time since she'd met him, he smiled with his teeth showing. It was a good smile, not too cheesy, even though his teeth looked as if they'd been chemically whitened. "Lead the way, then."

When Jo opened the front door, evening sunshine slanted through the hall, showing the dust on the picture frames that Sylvia the Chinese Cleaner wasn't tall enough to notice. Blod came out of the kitchen, mewing, and nudged Jo's legs as she showed Toby into the sitting-room.

"Shall I put the telly on?" she asked him. "Here's the remote. I won't be long." She looked down at Blod. "Oh, come on, you stupid creature, what do you want?"

"Maybe he wants some company," said Toby. "I like cats. I bet he'll climb on me if I just sit here."

"She," said Jo. "She's called Blodwyn. We call her Blod, usually."

"*Blodwyn*?"

"My dad's Welsh."

"Ah." He looked at her for a moment. "You're a Celt, then."

"Well, half."

"My mum and dad are Scottish," said Toby. He sat down in the corner of the sofa and sure enough, Blod jumped up onto the seat next to him and began to sniff him warily.

"Oh, of course!" Jo suddenly remembered that when Gordon had introduced them, he'd said that Toby's other name was Ferguson.

"Aye," he said in an exaggerated Scottish accent. Then, in his normal voice, "But I've always lived in London. And my parents don't talk like Gordon. They come from a different part of Scotland."

Blod had her forelegs on his thigh. "She likes you," said Jo.

"Irresistible to all females, you see."

"I'd better go and get ready."

He began to flick through TV stations. "OK, I'll just stay here with my new pal."

Jo washed quickly, changed her underwear and put on her own Rose and Reed clothes. She sprayed herself with a lot of the contents of a half used-bottle of perfume Tess had left in the bathroom. It was so strong it made Jo cough, and when she got back to the bedroom she had to dab her eyes with tissues. Looking as if she'd been crying when she hadn't was stupid. And eating curry always made her eyes water too. She stuffed some tissues in her bag. Without looking at her hair, which she knew would disappoint her, and wishing she had time to paint her toenails, she dug her feet into her sandals and went downstairs.

Toby looked comfortable, with his head on a cushion and Blod on his lap. He looked as if he belonged in Jo's house. Her stomach tightened when she saw him. He had no right – no boy had any right at all, in fact – to be so nice, and to affect her insides like this. Usually it was unavailable boys who did that – rock stars on videos, who were deliberately filmed to look sexy, and were probably horrible people. But Toby was sexy *and* nice. And, apparently, available.

He turned his head without taking it off the cushion. Then he raised it and looked at her properly. "You look really good."

"It's only what I wore to work on Saturday."

"It's still nice. And you smell terrific. That's *expensive*."

"It's my mum's," said Jo, watching Toby lift Blod carefully off his lap and stand up. Most guys wouldn't have bothered, she told herself. They would just have stood up and let the cat cope. But Toby bothered. Maybe he wouldn't have if his mates had been there, though. Boys' mates always had an adverse effect on their behaviour.

"I thought your mum didn't live here," said Toby, brushing cat hairs off his trousers.

"She doesn't. She just...oh, never mind. I'll tell you another time. Look, I've just got to text Trevor, or he'll wonder why I'm not here." If he's sober enough, she thought.

"You call your dad Trevor?" asked Toby admiringly as they left the house.

"Always have. And I call my mum Tess."

"Must be nice to have such liberal parents!"

Jo pulled the door behind her. One day, when she knew Toby much better, she'd explain to him why her parents were about as far from liberal as it was possible to be, outside of the Middle Ages.

"Mm," she said, pressing the Send button on her phone. "They thought of it as a bit of a joke. Their initials were both TP – she's called Tess Pratt – so they just wanted to be good ol' Trev an' Tess, even to me."

It was still warm, but while they'd been in the house there must have been a shower of rain. The pavements looked patchy as some bits dried quicker than others. The air smelled of earth.

"Nearly summer," said Jo, sniffing.

"Your exams soon?"

Jo nodded. "Study leave started last Friday."

"Are you working in the shop full time, then?"

"No, I'm studying." Then, realizing how geeky that sounded, she added, "I mean, I have to go into school so often to take an exam, it wouldn't be worth it. I'll be at the shop every day after the exams have finished, though."

Walking beside her, Toby had taken her hand so automatically she'd hardly noticed. She was conscious of how his hand felt. Soft in places, bony in others, like anyone's hand. No rings. "Gordon's offered me a permanent, full time position," he said. "Do you think I should I take it?"

Jo didn't know why he was asking her, but she was flattered. "Um...why not, if you like the work?"

"It's OK, but the thing is, I really want to work in fashion buying, not selling. I mean, I want to go to the shows in Paris and Milan, you know, and negotiate with designers and manufacturers and all that."

"How do you do that?" asked Jo, interested. It was normally girls who went on about working in fashion.

He swung her hand a little. "You get a job in a company as a trainee, and work hard and do well, and get noticed. Then maybe you can branch out on your own and make proper money. But all that takes, like, forever. I just want to do it *now*."

"Wouldn't it help to go to art college?" suggested Jo warily. "To study fashion, I mean?"

"Tried that last year. Didn't get in."

"Are you going to try again this year?"

"Jo, you sound like my mum!" He sounded impatient. His hand gripped hers harder.

"For art college you have to do a foundation year, then

three more years. It's too long. I want to be earning, so I can get a car. I'm eighteen and I haven't got a car, which is ridiculous."

Toby was right. Earning money did sound like a good idea, and education did go on far too long. Jo didn't care about having a car, but she longed for some independence. She didn't like living with Trevor, and if he was serious about going back to Wales she certainly didn't want to be Tess's flatmate. If Gordon were to offer *Jo* a permanent job, she'd say yes before he'd finished the sentence.

"Maybe working at Rose and Reed will lead somewhere," she observed. "It's a big company, with lots of branches, so it must employ several buyers. If you work hard and do well, like you said, and keep a look-out for openings, maybe Gay Gordon would give you a recommendation."

He smiled, more to himself than at her. "I doubt it. Since I left school I've been a trainee hair stylist, which was bloody terrible, then a waiter, which was nearly as terrible, and now I'm a shop assistant. It's not a great track record."

Jo didn't know what to say. Surely he had contradicted himself? He seemed to know exactly what was required to fulfil his ambition, but had dismissed her suggestion that he had already taken the first step towards it. Confused, she fell back on a first-date question. "What school did you go to?"

"St Bede's."

St Bede's was an independent boys' school with an academic reputation and a gaudy purple blazer. "And you just *left*?" she said with admiration.

He nodded. "I was totally freaked by the whole exam thing."

Jo pondered. She was freaked by the whole exam thing too. "Your parents must be normal," she told him. "Mine never shut up about A Levels."

"They want you to go to university?"

"Oh, yes. My dad because he *didn't* go, and my mum because she *did*. It's all crap."

"Sounds it!" said Toby cheerfully. "Me, now, I've got my folks house trained. My mum nags me, I ignore her. She's used to talking to the back of my head. And my dad, he's never there. He works abroad mostly, in the Gulf. He does the electrics on new buildings. He goes there to get away from my mum."

Jo wondered whether there weren't easier ways to escape from your wife. "And you haven't got any brothers or sisters?" she asked, still in first-date-land.

"No. I'm an only, just like you." Toby sat down on a low garden wall and took hold of her other hand too. "You're lovely, you know."

Jo found herself giggling. She must be nervous. She moved forward so that she was standing between Toby's legs. He let go of her hands and put his palms on her bottom. His head was level with her stomach. He pulled her further towards him, dipped his head and kissed the little strip of flesh where her top met her jeans. She held his head for a few seconds, wondering what to do next. But then he stood up, and the most intimate moment she'd ever had with a boy was over.

"So...what subjects did you like at school?" she asked as they walked on.

"None of them," he said crisply.

Jo didn't want to sound geeky, but she had to say something now she'd asked the question. "I don't like most things, but Computer Studies is OK. And French would be, too, if we had a decent teacher."

He pondered for a moment, not looking at her. "Sounds like you should take your mum and dad's advice. You like studying."

"I don't want to go to university, though."

He grinned. "Don't go, then!"

It sounded simple. Suddenly Jo was filled with more enthusiasm than ever for not doing what her parents wanted. "Actually, Toby, I'd really like to make films."

He stopped walking, and looked at her with puzzled eyebrows. "Like, movies, you mean?"

She nodded. "Making films is no more ambitious than going to the Paris fashion shows, is it?"

He ignored this. "How do you start?"

"Um...I'm not sure. Maybe by failing to get into art college?"

They both smiled. It was silly, really. Dreams. But did sitting in a boiling Assembly Hall, scribbling until your hand ached, over and over again, paper by paper, necessarily make dreams come true? She let go of his hand and fingered the sleeve of his sweatshirt. "Toby...I mean..."

They hadn't started walking again. He was giving her The Look.

"You haven't got a girlfriend, have you?" she asked, feeling foolish.

He smiled without showing his teeth. "I have now."

Drawing her towards him, he put his hand on the side of her face and kissed her lips lightly. His mouth tasted minty and felt squashy. Then he started to put his hands on her body. He stroked her midriff and her bare arms. His knee slid between her thighs.

Jo put her arms up and caressed his neck, and put her fingers in his hair like people did on TV when they were kissing a boy. He kissed her a bit harder, putting his palms on her bottom again, holding her firmly against him.

Jo's muscles were tense. She tried to slump against his body more, to feel herself cradled, or whatever he was trying to make her feel. She even slid her fingers under the back of his shirt, to show she knew she was supposed to touch him too. They stood there on the pavement in the darkening evening for a few more minutes.

As they broke apart, a jolt of dismay shook Jo. She didn't quite feel what she'd hoped to feel. Was there something wrong with her? Somehow looking at Toby had affected her more than touching him, and being touched by him.

"Are you OK?" he asked. "You've gone all tense."

"Oh...sorry." She rubbed her upper arms. "I'm a bit cold," she told him, though she wasn't. At least, not in a way that had anything to do with the air temperature. "And hungry. How much further to this restaurant?"

# Chapter Four

Tess's name was Thérèse. Her mother, Granny Pratt, was Belgian, and the family had lived in Belgium until Tess was about fifteen. She was perfectly bilingual except for French 'r's in some English words. When Jo had begun learning French herself, she had realized where that throaty 'r' sound came from. But it had taken her ages, much to Mr Peacock's frustration, to allow herself to imitate it. Trevor was fond of telling people how Tess's 'r's had struck him as extremely sexy when he'd first met her. Tess would supply the punchline, "French 'r's or French arse?", and their friends would roar with laughter and sip their wine, and Jo would wonder how long it would be before she would have to hear the story again.

Jo was good at French. But she hated the lessons, because the teacher they'd had this year, Miss Balcombe, was what Grandad Pratt would call a ninny. She was one of those teachers who should never have been a teacher, at least not of comprehensive school kids. Little girls in straw hats, maybe, like the ones whose mothers double-parked their Range Rovers in Jo's road every morning and made Trevor curse. Or boys at Eton, or something. Miss Balcombe's rosy-cheeked, large-bosomed, cardigan-clad body, which Jo always thought should be wearing an apron and have flour on its hands, enclosed a mind of astounding naivety. How could someone of that age – twenty five or six at least – not know *anything*? She didn't even seem to know much about French, and was always saying, apologetically, "Er...you'll have to look that one up, I think!"

The boys were merciless. And when the girls weren't encouraging their cruelty, they were feeling sorry for poor Miss Balcombe. Jo wished she could do something to help her. But how could she say, "Miss, you're in the wrong job. Go and work in a library, or a charity shop," without pulverising poor Miss Balcombe's already crumbling self-esteem?

Now that Jo was on study leave, Tess was going on and on at her about schoolwork. And Miss Balcombe, to Jo's surprise, suddenly took on an important role in the War On A Levels.

"I can't possibly do French, Tess," Jo explained. "The teacher's hopeless. And A Level's hard, so you've got to have a good teacher."

"Would this teacher be taking the A Level class, though?"

"Oh, yes! She's the senior person." This was a lie. Mr Peacock was Head of Modern Languages. But what did Tess know?

"I thought Mr What's-his-name, begins with a P, was the senior person."

Jo thought fast. "Well, maybe, but his subject's German, not French. That's why Miss Balcombe was taken on, to do Sixth Form French."

"I see." Tess was still suspicious.

"It would be *awful*, Tess," said Jo earnestly. "And you wouldn't want me to be unhappy, would you?"

It was five past eleven the next morning. Her mother had called in on her way to her club, which was how she always referred to the gym, with a gift of twenty-five pounds, "for doing your exams, darling," and a box of cakes from the French baker's near the station. Jo knew they were peace offerings after yesterday's row.

The weather was even hotter today, and the kitchen got the full sun in the morning. The chocolatey cakes were wilting on a plate in the middle of the table. "Can't we go outside?" pleaded Jo.

"I told you, I'm not sitting out there until the pollen count comes down," said Tess. "You might not mind being *seen* with a person whose nose is as red as Rudolph the Reindeer's, but I mind *being* that person. The grass in this garden is terrible because Trevor will *not* cut it often enough. Has he decided what he's doing yet?"

This question was so unexpected Jo was bewildered for a moment. Then she remembered. "I don't know," seemed the safest thing to say.

"Oh, come on. Where is he this morning?"

A sudden jolt of pain seared through her body, drowning out Tess' words. Jo looked down into her lap and saw she had been digging her nails in to her arm just below her elbow, where the sleeve of her blouse finished. "In the pub, probably" Tess continued, obliviously.

Press. Release. Press. Release... There would be crescent-shaped marks on her arm.

"Or he's gone off to put the house on the market, hasn't he?"

Red at first, fading to skin-coloured again. Press. Release. Press. Press... She moved her hand away from her arm and sighed.

"No, of course not." Jo said. She didn't remind her mother that the house was, in fact, Trevor's as well as hers. Grandad Pratt had given them the deposit as a wedding present, but Trevor had made the mortgage payments. "Give it a rest, Tess. My head hurts."

"Hangover? Have a cake."

"No, it's not a hangover. I didn't drink anything last night."

Tess had her poor-diddums face on. "Oh, were you all on your ownsome? Serves you right for going off in a huff like that." She took one of the cakes and cut it in half. "Share?"

Jo shook her head. "Actually, I went out for a curry with a boy I know from work." The words came out in such a rush she wondered if they'd made sense, but a glance at Tess told her they had. Her mother was staring at her, the cake half way to her mouth.

"*Really?*"

"Yes. His name's Toby and he's eighteen."

Tess bit into the cake. "So he's off to university next term, then," she said contentedly.

"No, he's got a job on the permanent staff at the shop. He really wants to get into fashion buying," she went on before Tess could finish her mouthful, "so it's a sort of step on the ladder."

"I see." Tess put the cake down. "Has your father met him?"

"No."

"Have you met his people?"

Jo tried to remain patient, though she winced inwardly at the way Tess always referred to anyone's family as their 'people', as if no Ferguson could ever be good enough for a Probert. "Tess, I've only been out with him once. I hardly know him."

"But you like him, don't you?" Tess's expression had softened. Something near to maternal indulgence came into her eyes. "Is my darling girl in *lurve*?"

"No, of course not," said Jo. She couldn't help her face reddening, though. She caressed the moon-marks one final time, wishing she could look at them. Then she took the other half of the cake. "But when she is, you'll be the first to know, since you're so interested."

The front door slammed. Jo and Tess listened to the familiar sounds of Trevor dropping his keys onto the hall stand and calling, "Hi guys, I'm home!" which he considered very modern. "Anyone in?" His head came round the kitchen door. "Oh...hello." His gaze took in them both, and the cakes. He put down the supermarket bag he was carrying and slung *The Guardian* onto the table. "Want to see something I got in the post this morning?"

"Is it a pizza flyer?" asked Tess. "Or a tax demand?"

"Very funny. Any tea going?"

Jo took a bite of cake, got up and lifted the kettle. "So what is it, then?"

Trevor searched his pockets for a folded piece of paper. He spread it on the table. "This is the place Mord's got his eye on," he announced.

Jo put the kettle down again. She and Tess looked at the paper. It was an estate agents' property details. There was a picture of the exterior of the house and several of the interior, and a lot of extravagant description of what a great location it was in. But Jo didn't read the words. Astonished, she gazed at the main picture, which was of an old – perhaps hundreds of years old – house, surrounded by grass, against a backdrop of sunlit mountains.

"It's a farmhouse," said Trevor proudly. "The nearest town is Aberystwyth."

"Aberystwyth! Fancy that!" Tess picked up the piece of paper and thrust it at Trevor's chest. "And you'll sink every last penny into it, won't you? I can't believe even *you* can be so selfish."

"Tess..."

"You're insane, do you hear me? In...*sane!*"

"No I'm not." Jo could hear her father trying to keep calm.

"And I don't think I'm being selfish either. I like it in Wales. I mean, you're always saying you'd like to have a house in Belgium, so – "

"What are you wittering about *Belgium* for?" Tess's voice had got a bit squeaky. "Can't you see how *mad* this is? What do you know about running a business? You're like those imbeciles on TV who buy a house in Provence and find there's no water supply or something. You're going lose all the money from the house, money we could – "

"Who's 'we'?" interrupted Trevor. "This is *my* money, Tess."

"Is it?" Tess stopped squeaking. "I seem to remember something about a wedding present from *my* father."

"And who's paid the mortgage every month for the last seventeen years, and is still paying it?" Trevor's voice was steady, but Jo could hear the frustration in it. "Face it, Tess, the proceeds of the sale of the house are going to be split between us, and so are the contents. It's called divorce."

Tess couldn't refute this. Half-rising, she prodded Trevor's shoulder. "And supposing I refuse to give you a divorce?"

Trevor gave a weary sigh. Jo filled the kettle, feeling almost sorry for him. Why couldn't Tess just let him buy his Welsh farmhouse and leave him in peace? "Look, Tess," he said steadily, "stop fantasising. What's going to happen is this. We'll sell this house, I'll go back to Wales and you and Jo will move somewhere smaller, maybe a flat, or maybe not, if your dad can be persuaded to stump up again. But I'll support Jo, like I always have done."

There was a silence while Tess, still trembling theatrically, pondered this scenario. Jo leaned against the worktop beside the murmuring kettle and folded her arms. "I know, Tess!" she said, pretending enthusiasm, "you could get a job!"

More silence, though Jo was pretty certain Tess wasn't

pondering *this* scenario.

"I mean," Jo went on cheerfully, "if I leave school, I can get a job too and move into my own place, and you won't have to live with Trevor *or* me. Wouldn't you like that?"

Tess stopped pondering. "You're *not* leaving school," she said sharply. "You're going back in September and you're going to do your A Levels and go to university. I *insist*, do you hear? And so does Trevor." She turned on him. "Don't you?"

Trevor, looking exceedingly tired, nodded soulfully at Jo. "Yes, I suppose I do," he said bleakly. He put the farmhouse details back in his pocket. "Hasn't that kettle boiled yet?" Fumbling for his cigarettes, he opened the back door and went into the garden.

"And shut that door!" bellowed Tess after him. "How many years did we live together, and you *still* don't know about my hay fever?" She turned to Jo and patted her hand. "Never mind him, darling. Granny and Grandad want to take us for lunch at the golf club on Sunday, to wish you luck in your exams. That'll be nice, won't it?"

Jo tensed her left forearm. The muscle responded with a light stroke – more of a memory, really – of the press-release sensation. "That'll be splendid," she said, and picked up what was left of her cake.

* * * * * *

At work on the following Saturday, every time Toby's legs appeared before his head as he came down the staircase from Menswear, Jo felt a jolt of recognition. Every time, she watched him cross the ground floor with a sense of propriety, fighting the desire to say to the customer she was serving, "That's my boyfriend, you know!"

63

But at half past five she stopped having him to herself. The scene was so predictable, Jo could have written the screenplay and sent it to a film production company, which would have been encouraging at first, but would ultimately reject it. "Sorry, not *quite* clichéd enough," the rejection letter would say.

Jo was behind the cash desk with Eloise and Sandy, a weekday part-timer who'd been persuaded to come in that Saturday to help train Jo and Toby. Sandy was a slight man in his forties with a quick, professional way of handling the customers. He looked to Jo somehow two-dimensional, as if his clothes were held on by tabs, like the dressing-dolls she'd played with when she was little. "Don't look now," Sandy muttered to Eloise and Jo, "but a dodgy gang of three's just come in. Two girls and a boy."

Eloise nodded. "Just before closing's a favourite time," she told Jo sagely. "Could you watch the girls, please, Jo, especially if they go into the changing rooms? Sandy'll watch the boy. And don't let any of them distract you."

Jo wasn't sure whether to feel embarrassed for Sandy, Eloise or herself. "Actually," she said awkwardly, "they're not shoplifters. They're my friends."

"Oh, my Lord!" guffawed Sandy self-consciously. "Well, you'd better go and see to them." Then he added, with a resigned glance at Eloise, "I don't suppose they've actually come in to spend any money, have they?"

*Ha ha. Very hilarious.*

Jo waved to them, but only Holly waved back. Pascale was examining the price-tags on a rack of skirts, and Ed was standing behind her with his hands in the front pockets of her jeans. Explicit content and strong references right enough.

"So where's the famous Toby?" asked Holly in an excited whisper.

"He works upstairs."

"Let's go up there then."

"OK," said Jo. It was a lot less public upstairs in Menswear. Even if Gordon had to be a witness to this vomit-inducing behaviour, at least Sandy, Eloise, the other Saturday girl Tasha and an assortment of female customers wouldn't. "Follow me, troops."

Some angel was smiling on Jo. The only people in the Menswear department were Toby, a young guy trying on jackets and an older one arguing quietly with his wife. "Where's Gordon?" she asked.

"Stockroom, I think," said Toby. When he saw Ed he put on his customer-approaching face. "Can I help you?"

Pascale and Holly burst into giggles. Here comes the predictable bit, thought Jo. "Toby, these are my friends," she said.

"I'm Ed," said Ed.

Toby had flushed slightly, but he smiled his no-teeth smile and nodded to Ed, then looked at the girls. "So which one's which?"

Pascale and Holly stood there, one each side of Ed, like bridesmaids posing with the groom. To Jo's mystification, Holly was still giggling. It wasn't like her to giggle. In fact, she despised people who did, and often said so.

"I'm Pascale," said Pascale confidently. "It's so great to meet you, Toby!"

Jo knew what Pascale was going to do next, and she did it. Before Toby could escape, she grasped his arms just above the elbows and kissed him firmly on one cheek, then the other, then the first one again. "That's the way the French do it!" she said, fixing him with a mocking, we're-the-grown-ups-here look.

"And this is Holly," said Jo unnecessarily. She just didn't

want Holly to pipe up, "And I'm...Holly!" like the last girl in a girl band's intro.

Jo could tell Toby thought Holly was beautiful. She *was* beautiful. She put her arm around Jo and bestowed her wide, crooked-toothed smile on Toby, whose flush deepened. "You take care of my friend Jo now, won't you, Toby?" she said. "I love her!"

"I love her too!" chipped in Pascale.

Jo slid a look at Ed, who was fingering the price tag on a soft leather jacket. She wondered if Pascale and Holly were embarrassing him. If so, he was hiding it well.

"We came in just before closing time so that we can all go out somewhere, if you want," said Pascale. "Didn't we, Ed?"

Ed turned away from the jacket. Six months' wages wouldn't be enough to pay for it. He took his sunglasses from his pocket and put them on. "Yeah," he said. "I've got the night off."

"Ed works at Burgerblitz," Jo explained to Toby.

Toby looked at Ed, who was leaning on the rail at the top of the stairs, kicking the floor idly and looking bored. He was wearing deliberately creased clothes, she thought. But he couldn't let the light of a Saturday afternoon shine on greasy hair or undeodorised armpits. Despite the studied scruffiness of his outfit, he was still supercool Ed Samuels.

"I had a mate who flipped burgers," Toby told him. "Said he could never get the smell out of his hair."

Jo couldn't see Ed's eyes. The dark glasses made his sharp features sharper. His appearance was quite different from Toby's neat face and easy, strolling gait. Jo could suddenly see the two years between them. Ed looked like he was posing, but Toby didn't need to. An arrow of guilty pleasure darted through her.

"Well, if I *do* stink of hamburger, Pascale's never

complained," said Ed frostily.

"Oh, I'm sure you don't, Ed," Holly hurried to say. "Now come on, where shall we go?"

"I can't," said Toby unexpectedly. They all looked at him. "Tonight, I mean. I'm not free."

Pascale put her hand on his arm. "You mean you want to take Jo out on her own. That's OK, we get it."

"No," said Toby. In his eyes Jo saw a lie. But she didn't know what the lie was – that he didn't want to go out with her friends, or he didn't want to go out with *her*. "I mean, I'd come if I could. But I've got to go up to London. I promised someone." His gaze fell on Jo. "Sorry, I forgot to tell you."

It wasn't so much a lie, Jo decided, as an excuse. He didn't want to spend Saturday night with four sixteen-year-olds, or even one. He had his own friends, to whose company Jo's Saturday night would be sacrificed. She minded, but she couldn't let him think she was immature enough to mind. "That's all right," she told him warmly. "I should be revising anyway." She looked round at the others. "We all should!"

"On Saturday night? Even *you* can't be that geeky, Jo," said Pascale. Her dark eyes widened in Toby's direction. "Maybe see you soon, then, Tobe."

No one argued. Holly gave Jo a he's-lying-isn't-he look, but that was all. The three of them said goodbye to Toby, less enthusiastically than they had said hello, and disappeared down the stairs. Trying not to imagine what Ed, Pascale and Holly would be saying once they got outside the shop, Jo smiled at Toby encouragingly. "Are you going to see something in London? A show?"

Gordon appeared at the top of the stairs. "Any customers up here?" he said softly out of the side of his mouth.

The young guy and the middle-aged couple had gone.

"Nope," said Toby.

"Thank God for that. My feet are balls of fire," said Gordon in his usual voice, bustling about behind the cash desk. "Did I hear you say you're going to a show?"

"Nope," said Toby again. "I'm just meeting a couple of friends." Then he added, more quietly, to Jo, "We might go to a club, but we might just have a drink. I haven't seen them for ages."

Jo stopped herself asking if one or both of them were female. "Have you got lots of friends in London?" she said conversationally as they went down the stairs. Jo hardly ever went 'up to town' as Tess called it, even though Waterloo Station was only 30 minutes away on a commuter train. Kingsgrove was part of London really, but to Jo it always felt like it was on a different planet from the dirty, noisy, traffic- jammed London so few miles away. She didn't much like London. She thought she would rather live in New York, or Los Angeles. But then most people probably thought that.

"No, not lots," said Toby. He took her hand and they walked through the shop, which was empty except for Tasha, who was tidying the changing-rooms. Toby leant on the cash desk. "But the ones I have got, I like to see sometimes."

"Oh. OK."

"Sorry," he said. "You'll meet them eventually."

"In the flesh, or only on Facebook?" she asked, as light-heartedly as she could.

Toby dropped her hand. "No, not on Facebook."

"Why not? I'll friend you, or you can friend me, and – "

"I haven't got a Facebook account," said Toby. He gave a small, self-conscious laugh. "Not everyone has, Jo."

Jo was puzzled. "Yes they have. Even my mum. Even my gran in Wales, for God's sake."

"Well, I think the whole thing's bollocks," said Toby, decisively but not aggressively. "I'd rather phone someone any day, or email them. You want my email address?"

"OK," said Jo. She felt uncertain. How did he conduct his social life, or keep up to speed with everyone's else's, or tell hundreds of people about things instantaneously, without Facebook? How could he stand to miss out on all those photos, or someone's hilarious post, or tragic news, or brilliant news? How could he just ignore the *necessity* Facebook was?

"You working tomorrow?" he asked, scribbling on the back of a promotion flyer from the pile on the cash desk and handing it to her.

"No." She looked at the email address: fergieman120@hotmail.com.

*Fergieman*?

"Me neither," he said. "Let's go somewhere, since it's Sunday."

"I've got to go out to lunch with my grandparents. The other ones, who live here. Sorry, um...Fergieman."

He grinned. "What's *your* email, then?"

She wrote the address below his and tore the flyer in half. "jo dot probert hyphen pratt at yahoo dot com," she said as she gave it to him. "Not as snappy as yours."

"Thanks." He put the address in his pocket. "Look," he said, "call me when you're finished with your grandparents. We'll have the rest of the day."

"All right."

He stepped closer and kissed her lightly on the tip of her nose, and then on her lips. She kissed him back, hoping Tasha, whom she suspected of fancying Toby, would see her doing it.

"So...what did you think of Pascale and Holly?" Jo asked as Toby released her.

He took a comb from his pocket and drew it through his hair. "Holly's really nice," he said without hesitation. Then he *did* hesitate, flicking a glance at Jo. "And Pascale's *hot*."

"Nice too? Or just hot?"

"Oh, nice too," he said, laughing with his mouth almost closed.

But she thought afterwards he probably only said this because Pascale was her friend. Usually, hot was hot and nice was nice. And she didn't ask his opinion of Ed. She couldn't bear to hear it.

# Chapter Five

Jo's plan of escape from the golf club straight after lunch worked perfectly. As the car tyres crunched between the posts of the exit gate, she pretended to fiddle with her bag on the floor, surreptitiously texting Toby. A few second later, her phone rang.

"Oh, it's Toby!" She spoke to him for a few moments, then said to Tess, who was driving, "If you drop me at the corner of Whittaker Road, Toby'll meet me there."

"Aren't you coming home with us, Joanna?" Granny Pratt asked from the passenger seat.

"Evidently not," supplied Tess moodily.

"Well, I suppose we don't provide much excitement." Jo thought this was unusually perceptive of Granny. "We'll fall asleep in our armchairs after that big lunch, anyway. You go and enjoy yourself, dear."

Tess couldn't very well protest, though Jo was sure she'd lined up the next round of ammunition in the War On A Levels. While Granny and Grandad slept, she would have released it all over a captive Jo, and Jo would have had to endure it.

When Tess stopped the car in Whittaker Road and Jo got out, Toby pushed himself off the wall he was leaning on, put his arm around Jo and waved to the occupants of the car. Tess looked at him over her sunglasses through the lowered window. "Hello, Tony," she said.

"Hello," said Toby, not correcting her, and nodding politely to Granny and Grandad, who nodded politely back.

Tess gave Jo one of her Angelica Huston looks. "Don't get back too late, will you, darling? You've got work to do. And I hope you've got your key, because you know where your father'll be."

"Don't worry about me," said Jo.

Whittaker Road was on her route home from school. From the top of the bus she'd often noticed a series of cul-de-sacs leading off it, all called after poets. Milton Rise, Wordsworth Place, Keats Close, Tennyson Walk. When Tess had driven off, Toby led the way into Keats Close. "This is it."

He stopped at the gate of a medium-sized brick house with a little roof over the porch like the one on Jo's old dolls' house. In fact, the whole house was a little girl's fantasy, with lacy curtains and window boxes full of petunias. There was even a plant stand in the shape of a small wheelbarrow beside the front door.

"It's lovely," said Jo. She kissed him on his cheek and giggled. The champagne she'd drunk at lunch was making her feel inanely happy.

"Your mum's really fit, if I'm allowed to say that," he said, squeezing her close to him and smiling. It was the smile she'd first seen when he'd met her at Kingsgrove station on Wednesday. A candid smile, that smoothed his face and showed that perhaps, despite being so good-looking, he truly liked her.

They walked up the path, still entwined, and he unlocked the front door. "My mum's not so fit, I warn you. She'll be back soon too. She's only gone shopping."

"This seems to be the day for meeting mothers," said Jo. "Should I be nervous?"

"Oh no, Mum's cool."

Taking her hand, Toby led her from the tiny square hallway into a sitting-room that occupied the whole depth of the house, with windows at the front and sliding patio doors at the back. These were open onto a garden, lovingly kept. A long-legged, drooly dog bounded in, its claws clicking and sliding on the polished floor. "I told you, I've got my mum trained. She's as obedient as Robson here." He released Jo's hand, squatted and rubbed the dog behind its ears. "Hey, Rob, what's going on?"

Jo looked around the room. It couldn't, she realized with a sinking heart, be any more different from the sitting room where she had left Toby with Blod on his lap that first night. All the furniture looked brand new. There were expensive rugs on the floor, and everything sparkled with conscientious cleanliness. No one cleaned Jo's house except Sylvia the Chinese Cleaner, who only came for two hours each Thursday. The carpets and furniture bore the evidence of Trevor's smoking habit, and bits of *The Guardian* that always became separated from each other, junk mail, CDs, beer bottles, half-read books and half-watched DVDs littered every surface. The smell of stale booze, cat litter, un-emptied bins and un-opened windows was noticeable the moment you opened the front door, except on Thursday evenings. But Jo was willing to bet that in Toby's house the kitchen worktops would be strangers to bacteria, and every lampshade, curtain rail and skirting board free of dust. And there was no smell, not even of dog.

"Does your mum do all this herself?" she asked warily.

"Do all what? Come on, let's go in the garden."

Robson was running around them in excited circles, hurling himself against their legs. Jo almost fell over.

"Sorry, he can be pretty crazy," said Toby. He caught the dog's collar and wrestled him to the grass. "Come on, you stupid animal, lie down." He looked up at Jo, squinting against the sun. "How was your lunch?"

"All right," muttered Jo.

"What did you eat?" asked Toby, scratching Robson's ears.

A vision of the golf club restaurant came into Jo's head. The swirly carpet and pink tablecloths, the parties of intoxicated golfers and murmuring middle-aged couples, the young waiter who flushed with embarrassment when Granny Pratt spoke French to him. Overcooked lamb on Jo's plate, Grandad pursing his lips seriously when he tasted the wine, Tess chirruping pointlessly about the importance of A Levels. And university, of course. University was the only thing Tess had ever done in her life. Jo had to go to university; it was what everyone did, except Trevor, of course, but that was another story.

Jo's mood suddenly darkened, almost to misery. Is that what champagne does to everyone, she thought? Make you feel happy, then daft, then plunge you into depression? How much alcohol did you need to drink, and how often, to achieve Trevor's level of tolerance? He drank as if getting drunk was a project he was working on, requiring dedication from which nothing would distract him. But for all his tolerance it never seemed to make him happy, or daft, or even depressed. It just sent him to oblivion, a place where all feelings – good or bad – disappeared.

"Roast lamb," she told Toby. "And sticky toffee pudding. And champagne."

Toby was still crouching beside Robson, looking up at her. "Were you celebrating something?"

Granny and Grandad Pratt often ordered champagne in restaurants, usually after a serious discussion with the man they and Tess called the *sommelier* and Trevor and Jo called the wine waiter. "I think they wanted to wish me good luck," she said.

"In your exams?"

74

She nodded.

"Wow." He fondled Robson's ears more vigorously. "What will they do when your results come out? Take you to Las Vegas for the weekend?"

Jo didn't smile. "No, that would be far too naff. Venice, perhaps, for an art lesson. Or the Pyramids, for a history lesson."

Toby let go of the dog and stood up. "Blimey. Your family's something else."

Something else. What, exactly? Toby could have no possible idea what the Probert-Pratt experience was like. Suddenly, Jo thought about how ugly Tess's mouth got when she said things that exasperated Trevor, and how Trevor narrowed his once-nice eyes when he retorted with things that annoyed Tess.

There was a light all round the edge of the garden. Jo watched it get brighter and brighter, wondering what it was, and why Toby seemed unthreatened by it. She felt panicky.

"It's very bright out here, isn't it?" she said. She couldn't make her lungs draw in enough breath; the words came out very quietly.

"Haven't you got any sunglasses?"

Sunglasses wouldn't help. The sun was on its mid-afternoon trajectory, making defined shadows under a recently-planted row of saplings, but the light crowding Jo's vision wasn't the sun. It was a relentless glare, barging in from all directions, flattening the contours and perspective of the garden into two dimensions, bleaching the lawn, the dog, and Toby himself into an over-exposed Kodak print.

Jo didn't want to be here. She didn't want Toby's mum to come home to find a strange girl, possessed by a rush of elemental loathing, in her spotless house. Bewildered, she clutched the nearest thing, which turned out to be the back of a plastic garden chair. "Toby, I don't feel right. Maybe I'd better go home."

"What's the matter?"

"I don't know. Maybe I drank too much champagne. My head feels funny, and I can't see properly. Maybe it's a migraine or something."

His lips tightened, and he blinked a few times, searching her face. "Come in out of the sun and lie down, then. Take an aspirin or something."

Jo's panic increased. She had to get home. She couldn't stay in this place. "I can't do that, Toby."

"Why not?"

"Because I can't!"

She was almost shouting. Toby gave her a "Whoa there!" look. "All right," he said suspiciously, "I'll take you home. Come on."

As they walked through the house the front door opened and a short woman with a supermarket bag in each hand eased her way in. "This is Jo, Mum," said Toby. He didn't offer to take the bags.

Mrs Ferguson was tawny-haired, with peachy skin and a fleshy face. Her jeans squashed her hips and thighs, and she had on a yellow blouse with very short sleeves, the kind that were at the top of Tess's Unflattering Sleeves list. Her sweet, eager expression didn't make her look like the sort of woman whose husband would go all the way to Saudi Arabia to avoid her. "Hello, Jo," she said in a Scottish accent. "I won't shake your hand, if you don't mind. Supermarkets are full of germs, aren't they?"

Jo couldn't speak. Her head pounded. Images of the DVD case floated through her mind. The sharp pain, the shock of blood. The light around her increased, but when she closed her eyes she saw redness, not darkness. She swayed, and had to put her hand on the wall to steady herself.

"Too much champagne" said Toby to his mum. "I'm just taking her home."

"Sorry," blurted Jo. She hoped Mrs Ferguson didn't think they were leaving because she'd come in.

"She's not usually like this," said Toby, more sarcastically than apologetically. He must think Jo was making all this up, just to get away from him. He must think she considered the house, or the garden, or even his dog, unsuitable in some way. Jo's family were something else, he'd said. Something different from his, he'd meant. Oh bloody hell, he thought they were too refined for him. Of course he did; he hadn't met Trevor.

"Well, I'll maybe see you when you're feeling a wee bit better, Jo," said Mrs Ferguson, smiling thinly.

Toby took Jo's arm firmly and steered her out of the door. "We'll wait for ever for a bus on a Sunday. Let's walk."

"I can't walk."

He stopped and looked at her. "What do you mean, you can't walk?"

"I feel like I might faint." She couldn't muster more than a whisper. She took her phone out of her pocket. "I'll call my dad to come and get me."

"Oh." Toby was still holding her elbow. "So I'm staying here, then, am I?"

She hardly heard him. She had to concentrate on pressing the right keys, getting Trevor's number, listening to the ringing sound, willing him to answer.

"Y...ello!" said her father in his Homer Simpson voice.

"Will you come and pick me up?" she asked, hoping he could hear her properly over the pub noise. "I'm not feeling very well."

"Where are you?"

"Toby's house. Keats Close. Off Whittaker Road. Number six. Trev, are you sober enough?"

"Have to be, won't I? See you in a minute."

She shut the phone. The brightness was still all around her, obliterating Toby.

"Why did you ask if he's sober enough?" he asked, his suspicious tone darkening. "Is he in a pub?"

Jo shrugged. She couldn't embark on an explanation.

"What's wrong?" asked Toby. "Why are you shivering?"

Because I'm dying! She though. She gasped for breath. What the hell was happening? Panic? Is that what it was, a panic attack? She'd heard that's what Juliet Parslow had had at Thorpe Park when they'd gone there on a school trip in Year Nine. Mr Phipps had told her to sit down and put her head between her legs, and the boys had sniggered. "I don't know. Maybe I ate something bad." She clamped her teeth, but the shivering didn't stop. "Sorry, sorry," she muttered through her teeth.

"Look, come back in the house to wait for your dad," suggested Toby. He sounded uncertain, and much more concerned.

"No!" It came out more aggressively than she intended. "I mean, I'm all right here, thanks. Just ignore me."

He didn't ignore her. He put his arms around her and held her stiff, trembly body, murmuring comforting words until Trevor's car drew up with all the windows down and the sun roof open, and 'Hotel California' on the stereo.

"You must be Toby," said Trevor, silencing The Eagles. "I'm Trevor Probert."

Jo registered vaguely that Trevor had got Toby's name right. "Hello," said Toby He opened the passenger door and helped her in. "Jo's not well." He did up her seat belt for her. "I'll call you later and see how you are," he told her, and shut the door.

"Thanks for looking after her," said Trevor.

As the car pulled away from the kerb, Jo turned. Toby was standing on the pavement with a gap between his thighs and his hands in the pockets of his jeans. Panic swirled around her, but she summoned her voice. "Toby!" she called. He was too far away to hear her.

But what would she have said anyway? It's nothing to do with you? I really like you and want you to be my boyfriend? Please don't think this is *anything* to do with *you*?

"What's the matter anyway?" asked Trevor as she turned back, defeated.

She leaned against the headrest and closed her eyes, ambushed by nausea. "Don't know, I just feel crap."

"Better phone the golf club, then." Jo could feel that he was driving slightly too confidently. He broadened his Welsh accent. "Listen, you toffee-nosed bastards, you've poisoned my daughter. Fancy a court case, do you?"

"Very funny." Jo opened her eyes. The world was going by very fast. "Try not to kill me, will you?"

Trevor slowed the car enough to make a more or less successful turn off the main road. "I've only had a couple of pints, or three. And we're almost home now."

Jo stared at the sunlit London roads, the rows of houses with bicycles and dustbins on their front paths, the worn grass verges and littered pavements, the new-paint green of the trees. The unnerving brightness that had obliterated reality in Toby's garden had gone; now everything she looked at seemed extra-clear, as if, like Dorothy and Toto, she'd emerged from ordinary life into a Technicolor world.

"I'll be OK," she assured her father. "I haven't got food poisoning. I just felt..."

But she couldn't explain the panic in the garden, or the desperation now.

When Trevor had parked haphazardly in a too-small space, swearing under his breath, Jo opened the car door. "I'm going upstairs," she told him. "I'd better have a rest."

He leaned his arms on the steering wheel and looked at her with a troubled expression, blunted by alcohol. "Cup of tea might help, love."

"If I drink anything I'll be sick."

In the cool of the hallway, Blod slipped out of the shadows and curled herself round Jo's leg, but Jo ignored her, and Trevor picked her up. Jo watched them go into the kitchen. Her legs felt very tired, but she took hold of the banister and slowly climbed the stairs.

The light in her room was muted; the sun was round the other side of the house. Jo lay down on the huge bed with her face to the wall, burying her nose in the pink belly of an ancient rabbit who stood guard at the end of the line of cuddly toys. She tried not to think about Toby, or what he thought of her and her family. She tried to think about nothing.

Trapped under her body, her left arm throbbed. The blood supply to it was being restricted by her weight. She lay still for a few moments, thinking about her left arm. It was made of bones, and ligaments, and flesh, and arteries and veins and skin, like everyone else's left arm. No one but Jo would think there was anything special about it, or that it had any power beyond the usual things left arms do. It did, though; she knew that now.

She closed her eyes tightly, waiting for the red circles surrounded by the pulsing light. When she saw them, she opened her eyes again. The light was still there at the edge of her vision, white and insistent. She rolled over, liberating her arm, and closed her eyes again.

The fingers of her right hand locked themselves around the fleshy part just below her left elbow. She thought about the whiteness of the skin on the inside of her arm, the part where no one ever seemed to get sunburned. She began to press and release. Press. Release. Press. Release. Then she stopped releasing and just pressed, digging her nails in, clamping her teeth, willing herself not to gasp with the pain.

She opened her eyes. Where she'd pressed hardest, with her middle fingernail, a bluish-purple mark had appeared. She scratched it, hard. It produced a bud of blood. And it didn't take much more pressing and releasing for the bud to burst.

Jo scratched more and more with sticky, scarlet nails, smearing blood over her arm. It was agony. But when she stopped, in the place of agony came peace.

She lay there with her eyes closed, breathing steadily, unaware of any sensation except the absence of pain. But when she roused herself and looked at her arm, her heart gave a thud. The wound was bloody, as she'd expected, but there were also glistening patches of watery goo, like the pretend lacerations on the pretend corpses in *CSI*. Her nails, which must be sharper than she'd thought, had penetrated the liquid-producing layer of flesh which burns and blisters exposed. And which left a scar. Especially if you picked it.

She mustn't get blood on the duvet cover. She needed to clean the gouged-out place on her arm, and hide its ugliness. Slowly, she got up and opened her bedroom door. The murmur of 'Honky Tonk Woman' with the bass turned up came from the sitting-room. In the bathroom, Jo locked the door, leaned on the washbasin and ran warm water over her right hand. Pink water swirled down the plughole. She wetted some toilet paper and dabbed the patch on her arm where she'd scratched away her flesh. She said the words softly to herself as she worked.

*Patch. Scratch. My own little scratch-patch.*

She flushed away the bloody toilet paper and opened the medicine cabinet. The only plasters remaining in the box were the small ones designed for finger cuts, and Jo had to use two to cover the wound. Then she spread soap over the nailbrush. She felt nauseated, and her legs were wobbly, but she had to get the blood out from under her nails, and out of her sight. The soap went pink and frothy; her nausea grew, but she finished the job and felt her way unsteadily back to her room.

She sat on the edge of the bed and gazed at her 'Wonders of China' calendar on the opposite wall. Jo had no particular interest in the wonders of China, but the calendar was Sylvia the Chinese Cleaner's idea of a Christmas present. Sylvia came into her bedroom to clean every Thursday, so Jo had to have the calendar up.

The picture for June was of a little girl dressed in an elaborate costume with a huge headdress. Just like on every picture, for every month, there was a line of Chinese writing down the side, translated into English at the bottom. Under the picture of the little girl it said 'Be Free'.

"That's a joke", Trevor had said, "Considering how the Chinese might possibly be the most un-free people in the world." She read it again, and again. Just those two words. Maybe the English translation was done by a rubbish translator. Or maybe, she realized suddenly, the idea of being free is open to interpretation. Hadn't they learned in History that above the gate at Auschwitz 1, it even said, 'Work Will Set You Free'?

She looked at the pile of DVDs on the dressing-table desk, their plastic prongs and sharp corners concealed by a veneer of just being DVD covers. The sight calmed her. As she sat there on the bed, cradling her wounded arm, the panic, the desperation and the guilt – about Toby, about the press-release method and the scratch-patch – began to trickle away.

Her gaze landed again on the calendar. Being free wasn't about physically escaping, whether from China, or a concentration camp, or the rudeness of Mr Treasure's horrible secretary. It was about that line by some poet from ages ago, that Mr Gerrard had made them discuss. 'Stone walls do not a prison make, nor iron bars a cage'. By the end of the lesson they had worked round the idea that it was your mind that imprisoned you, and therefore it was your mind that freed you.

She wished that poet, whoever he was, could appear, right there in her bedroom. She wanted to tell him that although she'd left the English room that day feeling bemused, and wondering why poetry had to be so complicated, now she understood with luminous clarity what he'd meant. He'd meant that you make your own prison, and you find your own method of escape. Jo had found her way to escape.

# Chapter Six

At the end of each year Kingsgrove School held a Summer Ball. This year the organizing committee, of which Holly was chair, had decreed that the fancy dress theme was The Universe, and that everyone's clothes, make-up and hair had to reflect stars, suns, moons, planets, space rockets or whatever they could think of.

"Why have we got to have a theme at all?" Pascale moaned. It was the day before the second Maths paper, and Pascale had come round to help Jo revise. They hadn't done any revision yet; they were in Jo's room, sifting unenthusiastically through Jo's party dresses. "I mean, if it was just a party, without all this universe bollocks, you could wear this blue thing." She sat on the computer chair and smoothed Jo's blue dress across her knee. "The colour suits you, with your baby blue eyes."

"The universe *is* sort of blue," said Jo, trying to be helpful. "Or at least the earth is, in shots of it taken from space. You know, with clouds swirling around all over it."

Pascale pondered. "You mean you could fix swirly things to this dress, and be the earth?" She scrutinized Jo with narrowed eyes. "Might make you look a bit fat, though."

"Well, it's an idea." Jo took the blue dress from Pascale and held in front of herself. She'd had it last year for Trevor's fortieth birthday party. It did suit her, and she liked the twisted ribbon straps. But it wasn't exactly a *ball* dress – it wasn't even floor-length – and she didn't think Pascale's 'swirly things' would improve it. Also, it was sleeveless. A couple of weeks had gone by since Jo had stood in the bathroom swirling pink water round the washbasin. But the wound on her arm still festered. The desire to pick the scab every time it formed was impossible to resist, especially when she was in bed. Lying in quiet darkness was supposed to induce sleep, but lately, all it had induced in Jo was an awareness, both repugnant and delicious, of the plaster on the inside of her elbow, and the compulsion to rip it off. And then, the guilt, the necessity of keeping the blood off the bedclothes, the furtive trips to the bathroom.

She would have a scar there for ever. But in those moments of weakness, she didn't care.

She tossed the blue dress onto the pile of clothes on the bed. "I can't wear this. I'll have to get Trev to buy me something new."

Pascale studied her reflection in Jo's mirror. "Ed and I are wearing matching stuff," she announced. "His dad's got this silver jacket from his Rock 'n' Roll Nostalgia Nights, and silver boots. We thought if Ed wears those, and I wear a silver dress, and we both have glitter in our hair and do a zig-zag on our faces, we could be sort of Ziggy Stardust people. You know, seventies glitter rock. Sexier than dressing as aliens or astronauts."

"That's a really good idea!" Jo honestly thought it was. "But you can only do that sort of thing if you've got a boy to go with. You're lucky."

The question of who was going to be Jo's escort was a vexed one. Strictly, you could go to Summer Ball without one – lots of girls had to. But Jo couldn't stand the thought of being one of those girls. And Toby wouldn't be able to come because it was only for Kingsgrove students. Tom Clarke, the second most presentable boy in Jo's class, was also a committee member, and it was understood that he would be taking Holly.

"Hm," said Pascale. Jo knew she was only pretending to ponder. "Pity Toby can't come." She flicked Jo the look Jo had been expecting for a while. Curious, but full of superior knowledge. "So how are things going with the fit and delicious Toby?"

"Things are good," Jo said nonchalantly.

"Three weeks now?"

"About that."

"And how's it going?"

"I just told you, things are good."

"*Everything*?"

Jo wanted to tell her. It was next to impossible that Pascale would understand, but she longed to tell someone, and here was Pascale, asking.

"We haven't...you know, done it," she said in a rush. "If that's what you mean."

"Did I say anything?" said Pascale, her eyes wide and her hand at her throat. Then she dropped both her hand and the pretence of outrage. "Why haven't you, then?"

"Oh, I don't know. Probably because he'd rather do it with *you*."

Pascale could never tell the difference between real and sarcastic adoration. "*Really*?" she asked, flushing with pleasure. "Did he say that?"

Jo sighed. "No, of course he didn't say that! I know you think he's an arsehole for going out with me, but he's not *that* much of an arsehole."

"Oh." Pascale thought about this for a second. Then she added, bristling, "You know, Jo, you can sound really bitter sometimes. And it's not attractive."

Though Jo was used to such comments, generally from Tess rather than Pascale, this particular one enraged her. "Well, whoever said anything about me was *attractive*?"

Somewhere, deep inside Pascale's theatrical expression of shock, was genuine surprise. She put her hand on Jo's arm. "Oh, Jo, are you upset?"

Jo's anger dispersed as suddenly as it had appeared. Always, what Pascale did and said was authentic. She was incapable of calculated malice. Her brain-processes, except in Maths, were entirely engaged in plotting the best way through the maze between girls and their discarded, existing or prospective boyfriends.

"I just don't know what to do, Cal," Jo confessed.

Pascale had her bereavement-counsellor face on. She nodded sympathetically. "Is it that you don't fancy him?"

Jo had to think about this before she answered. Whenever she saw Toby she noticed all over again what she'd noticed the first time – that by any girl's standards he was good-looking. So she *must* fancy him. That's what fancying someone was. And yet, whenever he started to put his hands on her body, something seemed to stop him succumbing to the power which Pascale wielded so easily. Maybe the truth was that Jo simply didn't have that power. "Maybe he doesn't fancy *me*."

Pascale's eyes brightened at the prospect of guiding a lost soul through the relationship maze. "So why don't you just say, 'look, Toby, do you want me as a girlfriend, or a friend? And if you don't want me as a girlfriend, what are we doing?'" she suggested, making it sound very simple.

Jo was half horrified, half amused. "I couldn't do *that*!"

"Why not?"

"Because..." Because she was afraid he might reject her. And because she was even more afraid of where that rejection might lead her. "Because", she continued "however fanciable he is, I don't think I want to sleep with him." Then, seeing Pascale's confused expression, she added, "Yet, at any rate. Three weeks isn't that long."

"Three weeks will become three months, though," insisted Pascale, "and you still won't have done it, and both of you'll be wondering why not, and it'll just get ridiculous."

"All right," said Jo, glad to close the subject. She looked steadily at Pascale. "You won't mention this to Holly, will you?"

Pascale made a mock-offended face. "As if!"

"And thanks for the advice, Cal."

"Just ask Doctor Pascale!" said Pascale happily. "Now, talking of Holly and her insane ideas, we still haven't solved the problem of your escort. How about David Mathison?"

David, who was in the Lower Sixth, was one of Pascale's many rejects. "He and I had fun together before...we stopped having fun," she said. "He's nice, and he knows you a bit, and I bet he hasn't got anyone to go with. All those Lower Sixth girls are such dogs."

Jo laughed. "Is that why he went out with *you*, then?"

"He would have gone out with me even if every girl in his year was Miss Universe," smiled Pascale. She whipped round and stared at Jo. "There you are, you can dress as Miss Universe! Long dress, high heels, tiara, sash...my God, Jo, you'll look like a million dollars! And I'll be standing there with a zigzag on my face!"

Jo's heartbeat felt uneven. She sat down on the bed amongst the discarded clothes. "That's brilliant. Do you think anyone else will have the same idea?"

"Not if we don't tell them."

"Not even Holly?"

"*Especially* not Holly." Pascale giggled. "She's the one that's got us into this fancy dress crap anyway. I want to be there when you walk in and her jaw hits the floor."

"Can you ask David Mathison for me?" asked Jo. "You could hint that I'm doing something glamorous, without telling him exactly what it is. He'll need a tux."

Pascale raised her eyebrows. "God, he'd look amazing in a tux."

"But will you call him? I can't, out of the blue. *Please*."

"Well..." Pascale was pretending uncertainty again. "I suppose I could. And if he's already taken, there's Stuart Holt, and Max Can't-remember-his-other-name, and – "

"Oh, shut up! Just make sure you get me someone who'll be tall enough when I'm wearing high heels and a tiara. This is going to be *brilliant*!"

* * * * * *

Jo stared at the names on the list. There were still only five, though now there were six significant people in her life. She'd been putting off labelling Toby because it felt so underhand, having a secret from him. But if he didn't have a label, it wasn't fair on the others who *did*.

She turned over a few DVDs, trying to focus on one thing about Toby that set him aside from other people. But there were so many things. He was the only boy who had ever noticed her, pursued her, taken her out, kissed her, touched her body, comforted her when she was upset and tolerated her friends.

Well, she'd helped him along a little, with that phone call from the train. And she'd asked him if he had a girlfriend, which wasn't exactly subtle. But all girls did that sort of thing. It was part of the game. And hadn't Toby played the game too? Buying her that sandwich, helping her with the T-shirts, writing his number on her hand? Yet...her heartbeat wouldn't settle.

She had the biggest double bed in the world. Her mother lived miles away. And nothing would rouse Trevor from the alcoholic coma he fell into every night. Toby must be thinking he'd struck fantastically lucky. But somehow, he hadn't.

She flicked through DVD covers impatiently. This was stupid, stupid, *stupid*. But now she'd started it, she couldn't abandon it. She had to keep her place in the middle of them all. She had to be in charge like the ringmaster cracking his whip. She couldn't risk allowing herself to wobble.

U for Universal. 'Suitable for all', it said on the back of Disney's *Aladdin*. God, what was that doing here? She hadn't watched it in years. But maybe that was what Toby was. A 'U' person, who'd had lots of jobs and picked up lots of friends on the way. People in London he knew from when he was a waiter, he said. People who worked funny hours, so he met them late and stayed over. Mitch, one of them was called. Maybe Jo would meet them someday, but it was more likely that she wouldn't. Toby was one of those people who liked to keep his groups of friends separate. He didn't have a Facebook account. He wanted to segregate his social life, while plate-spinning his friends. All things to all people.

With a sigh, she typed 'Suitable for all' next to Toby's name.

She thought about what Pascale had said: *Ask him if he wants you as a girlfriend, or a friend*. What would happen if Jo did that? She imagined a scene in a film where the actress asked the actor that question. How would the script read? What would the director want? Long pauses, evident distress, or would he prefer the scene to be understated, leaving the audience to interpret the feelings?

Toby's smooth cheeks would sink slightly, and a nearly-hurt

look would come into his eyes. His eyebrows would sharpen at the corners; he would be alert for a trap, wondering what she *really* meant. Was she saying she didn't want him as a boyfriend? Well, why didn't she just go ahead and dump him? Suspicion and uncertainty would hover between them, taking up the space on the screen between the actor and the actress, arousing the audience's sympathy...or apathy. Such was a director's gamble.

Toby would hate her for asking the question. She knew it, and she knew she couldn't do it anyway. Like she'd told Pascale, they just had to wait and see what happened. She and Toby were sensible people, she reminded herself. Sex wasn't everything, though the way some people went on about it you'd think it was. Pascale's insistence on a trial separation from Ed, which was only a tactic of hers and had never really happened, had probably resulted in them doing it even more often than they had before. You could tell by the way she was always touching his leg.

The thing was, if Jo was ever going to do it, she wanted to do it with someone who made her feel that she couldn't *not* do it with him, and only him. So even if she broke up with him, whoever he was, she would still know that he'd been the one, in that world-changing moment.

But was Toby him?

"Jo!" came Trevor's voice up the stairs. "Jo-girl! Where are you?"

Jo pushed herself up and opened the bedroom door. The landing was so dark it was more like an evening in November than June. She could hear rain starting. Large drops thudded on the window pane, then more and more until all the thuds merged and became a power-shower. She went to the top of the stairs. "What?"

"I'm off to the pub," said Trevor. He was wearing his leather jacket, jingling his keys in his pocket. "You'll be all right, won't you?"

Jo nodded. "Got work to do. Maths exam tomorrow. You know it's pouring with rain, don't you?"

"See you later, then."

The front door slammed. Jo sat down on the top stair, gazing emptily at the place in the hall where he'd just been standing. In a movie there would be poignant music, or a cut to a lively scene, she thought. But in real life, there was just a space.

* * * * * *

Jo and Holly had just done their last exam.

"Come on!" Holly took Jo's arm and propelled her along the corridor. "After we've cleared out our lockers we're free to go. And look at this amazing weather!"

Mediterranean, they kept saying on TV. Pubs and restaurants were trying hard, with tables outside, to pretend they were in Spain. But even with its buildings throwing sharp shadows and heat haze rising off the tarmac, Jo thought Kingsgrove High Street still looked and smelled like Kingsgrove High Street – dusty, petroly, burger-and-chipsy.

"What are you doing tonight?" Holly asked. "Seeing Toby?"

"Don't know."

"But it's the end of exams!" Holly was shocked. "Cal and I are going to Press Gang with Ed and Tom and their mates."

"Oh, OK. Well, I'll see what Toby wants to do."

Holly was busy with her padlock. "How *are* things with Toby?" she asked. "God, this thing is so awkward! Why can't they design padlocks that work, for God's sake?"

Jo opened the door of her own locker, thinking about how things were with Toby, and wondering if Pascale had instructed Holly to ask her. "Things are OK." Her PE kit and an ancient copy of *Macbeth* nestled together in her locker. She picked up the book. "We did this in Year Nine," she said to Holly. "Do you think they want it back, or shall I chuck it?"

"Leave it on a desk. Not yours," advised Holly. She was doing her whole-face smile. "You like Toby, don't you? It shows in your face every time you talk about him."

"I'm sad, aren't I?"

"No, you're lovely!" She started to pack her bag. "I'm so lucky with my friends! Pascale's on the other end of the scale from you, Jo. And I get the best of both." She took a bar of chocolate from her locker and sniffed it. "Do you think this is edible? It's only six months past its sell by date."

"Throw it away," advised Jo, wondering about *the scale*. The scale of what? Attractiveness? Flirtatiousness? Ability to play a whole basketball match without going red in the face? With boys watching? Pascale could certainly do all of those things one hundred percent better than Jo.

It crossed Jo's mind how weird it was that Holly hardly ever saw her, just *her*, without Pascale, outside school. She never seemed to go to Holly's house any more, though she'd hardly been out of the place when she and Holly had been at primary school together. They'd gone to each other's parties and sleepovers, and Jo had become very attached to Holly's mum, who was so unlike Tess that nine-year-old Jo had once confessed to Holly that she wished they were sisters. She'd wanted a mum who had a serious job (Holly's mother was a senior nurse), but could act like a nine-year-old herself when she was playing dominoes or Pictionary with them. Tess *never* played games. Except golf, which didn't count.

Once Jo and Holly had started at Kingsgrove and met Pascale, they'd stopped going to Holly's house, maybe because it was a bus ride away, or maybe because her mum had to sleep during the day when she was on night duty at the hospital. Jo's house had quickly become headquarters. And whatever they did there, it involved either all three of them or Jo and Pascale.

"Why do you think Toby likes *me*, though?"

Jo had wanted to ask Holly this for a long time. She couldn't say it in front of Pascale, but Pascale did German instead of Sociology and she'd already finished her exams. Jo had to take advantage of this rare opportunity to talk to Holly alone.

"Why shouldn't he like you?" replied Holly.

This was a typical Holly tactic. Answer a question you don't want to answer with another question.

"I mean, what do you think he likes about me?" said Jo.

"How should I know? He's a bloke. Who knows what blokes like?"

Holly had done it again. Jo persevered. "I think you know what blokes like, Hol."

Holly removed her padlock and left the locker door open. "There," she said with satisfaction. "Sixth Form lockers next year! It's going to be so cool being in Sixth Form! Pick up that chocolate wrapper immediately! Where's your tie? God, I'm going to *love* it."

That was the other thing Holly did. When she didn't know what to say, she changed the subject, often so successfully that Jo never got back to what she'd asked. But today Jo was determined. "But Toby's so good-looking and I'm so ordinary."

"Why *is* he so good-looking?" asked Holly, interested. "I mean, what is it about his face that – "

"Stop asking me *questions*!" Jo's exasperation spilled out. "Can't you just *listen*?"

Holly's prettiness disappeared for a moment under the face she made when she was offended. It involved a wrinkling of the nose and a crumpling of the forehead, and a hooking downwards of the mouth. If Holly ever saw it in a mirror, thought Jo, she'd never do it again. "I *am* listening," she said testily. "I always listen. But what do you want me to say? That you're not ordinary, you're lovely? Well, I've already said that. Or do you want me to tell you that good-looking boys always go for girls who aren't as pretty as them? Why would you want me to do that, Jo?"

Some volcanic source of interior heat suddenly erupted inside Jo. Her ears buzzed. "Holly, you're *still* asking me *questions*!"

"Are you OK?" asked Holly, her eyes roving over Jo's face. "You've gone all red. Have you got heatstroke?"

When Jo didn't say anything, Holly shrugged. "Whatever."

Of all the people whose disapproval Jo couldn't bear, it was Holly's. But Holly had joined the ranks of the pain-makers without a second thought. How could *Holly*, her oldest, closest friend, with whom she shared so many memories, and whose inner workings she knew so well, turn on her?

Jo's breath shortened. Her temples pounded. The brain-numbing light began to invade the edge of her vision. Why did this keep happening? The plaster on her arm was itching, like it always did the moment she thought about it. She longed to pull it off and ambush the gouged-out flesh underneath it, but she had no fresh plasters with her at school.

"Holly, *please*," she blurted.

A light, almost-invisible film of impatience came over Holly's face, and there was impatience in her voice, too. "Please what?"

"Please don't be horrible to me," begged Jo. "I haven't done anything wrong."

"Oh, Jo..." Holly gave a small sigh, and looked out of the window for a moment, as if she needed time to work out how to explain something very simple to an imbecile. "I'm not being horrible to you," she said calmly when she turned back to face Jo. "I'm just trying to get you to see how it is."

"How *what* is?" asked Jo in genuine bewilderment. What had they been talking about, when Holly had become so hostile? "What do you mean?"

Holly sighed again, more exaggeratedly. "I mean *Toby*!"

"Oh." Jo looked at the floor. It was grimy at the edges where the cleaner's mop never reached, she noticed. She felt relieved. At least she could *see* the edges of the floor; the headache-inducing light had diminished. "Oh. Toby."

She leaned against the lockers and tried to meet Holly's eyes, but Holly wouldn't look at her. So Jo persevered anyway. "Look, Hol," she began, "Me and Toby, we're fine. I like him, and he likes me. I shouldn't have asked you why you think he likes me, it was a stupid question."

I'm not going to apologize, though, she told herself. All Jo had done was express her perfectly reasonable exasperation. It was Holly who had completely *un*reasonably put her claws out.

"All right," said Holly. The look she gave Jo was full of doubt. "All right. Let's just leave it." She paused, then she said, "So you'll be going out somewhere with him tonight, will you?"

"I don't know," said Jo truthfully. "I kind of never know what we're doing until the last minute. He's not even on Facebook."

"Ah," said Holly, nodding. "In that case, shall Cal and I just make plans without you?"

Jo heard something edgy in Holly's voice, but she was weary of this wrestling-match. She wanted to go home and lie in the garden with Blod on her feet. "Of course," she agreed pleasantly. "Have a good time."

"You too." Swinging her hair a bit, Holly put her bag on her shoulder and started down the corridor. "Come on, it's lunchtime. Pascale'll be at Burgerblitz with Ed. You coming?"

"Um..." Jo picked up her own bag. Sometimes, sacrifices had to be made. Friends were friends, after all. "OK," she said. "Lead on, boss."

# Chapter Seven

The dress was the most expensive thing Jo had ever owned, except for her computer. It was so beautiful that ever since Trevor had bought it she'd left it hanging on the outside of the wardrobe so that she could lie in bed and feel the tingle of ownership whenever she wanted.

It was a purplish colour, with a low neck, a low back, and a silk underskirt showing through the gauzy overskirt. It hung there in one classy line from the shoulders to the hem, waiting for its moment. Tess, not to be outdone by Trevor's generosity, had paid for a pair of high-heeled open-toe shoes, so well-made and comfortable that Jo thought that if only circumstances allowed, she would happily wear them for the rest of her life.

When Jo put on the dress its beauty glowed as if it were alive. It skimmed her body, millimeters away but streamlining and sculpting all the bits of her she didn't like, and showing off the bits she did. She had searched many, many shops for a dress with long enough, close-fitting enough sleeves. But when she'd seen it, she'd known it was the one. "Lovely," the assistant had beamed when she'd come out of the changing room. "A sort of medieval look, very flattering."

Pascale had helped her make the satin sash that said 'Miss Universe'. Jo slipped it over her shoulder, piled up her hair and sprayed it so that it wouldn't immediately fall down again, and secured in it the diamanté tiara from when she'd been a fairy in a Christmas play at primary school. Then she got out the expensive necklace and earrings that she'd had for her sixteenth birthday. She stood in front of the mirror, unable to stop herself trembling. She looked as good as a beauty queen, definitely.

Jo's escort was to be Stuart Holt. Pascale's first choice, David Mathison, wasn't going to the ball, as he and his parents had gone to South Africa for the summer. "I should have remembered," Pascale had told her apologetically. "His mum's South African. She once gave me a stick of dried zebra or something, when I went to his house. I didn't eat it, though. I just gave it back to her."

Jo was sure it couldn't have been zebra, but didn't argue. And Stuart, a friendly boy with curly hair and neat ears, was a pretty good substitute. He had been in Jo's primary school class. She remembered him coming to her seventh birthday party and refusing to eat anything but peanut butter and lemon curd sandwiches. Pascale had insisted that Jo mustn't let him in on the secret of her costume, but get him to wear a tuxedo. His uncle had produced one that fitted him, and his mum had bought him a dress shirt and a bow tie. "I'll have to wear my school shoes," he'd confessed to Jo. "They're the only ones I've got that aren't trainers."

"That's all right," Jo had assured him. She knew that no one would be looking at *his* shoes. "They'll be fine as long as you polish them."

It was a pity Toby couldn't come, but also in a way it wasn't. He was the same age as the Upper Sixth boys, but would have been out of place among them. Every time Jo imagined him with them, a vague embarrassment came over her, and she tidied the thought away.

"Are you ready, darling?" Tess's voice floated up the stairs.

"I've got the camera."

She and Trevor were in the hall, waiting to film Jo's departure for the ball. What was life like before video cameras? She supposed you just had to remember whether you felt nervous, or excited, or neither. Now, it was there on your face for everyone to look at, whenever they felt like it. And short of burning the house down, what could you do to stop them?

When Trevor spoke, Jo could tell by the thickening of his Welsh accent that he was feeling emotional. "Jo-girl, you look a-mair-zing. Dudn't she look fab-uh-lous, Tess?"

"Of course she does!" Tess's eyes were very bright. "Walk down, darling, and I'll film you."

The filming took so long, with Tess arranging Jo's skirt and taking the sash off and putting it on again, that it was ten past seven when they left, twenty-five past when they picked up Stuart, and a quarter to eight when Trevor dropped them at school and drove off happily, tooting the horn.

"This is a big night for my parents," Jo told Stuart by way of apology. "They've never seen their little girl all dressed up like this."

"You're an only child, aren't you?" asked Stuart. He put his hand self-consciously on her naked back and guided her towards the entrance. "I've got two older sisters. And," he added, looking sheepish, "a tuxedo can't compete with a ball gown anyway."

"Of course it can!" Jo didn't have to lie. Stuart's uncle's suit had transformed a boy of undeniable ordinariness into such an elegant figure that Jo wondered if he'd grown since she last saw him, or been hitting the gym or something. "I think you look really good."

"Thanks." Stuart went a bit pink, but controlled his features. "So do you."

Captain Holly and her soldiers, willing and unwilling, had been busy spending the PTA's entertainment budget. Every cranny of the school hall had been disguised with silver streamers and crêpe paper. The windows were festooned with paper planets, stars, moons, spaceships and signs of the zodiac. From the centre of the ceiling hung an enormous model of the earth, lit from the inside and spinning, a great deal faster than the real earth spins, but pretty impressively.

Jo and Stuart, like everyone else who came in with them, stared at the decorations for a few seconds before their gaze came back to ground level. And when it did, there were shrieks and gasps. Around the dance floor clustered paper-draped tables, each with a miniature version of the earth light in its centre. And there were garlands of silver stars across the front of the stage, where a professional band played arrival-of-the-guests music.

"My God," murmured Stuart. "We'd better give up on getting any new gym equipment."

"Who needs parallel bars when they can have a parallel universe?" quipped Jo. She knew she sounded over-excited, but, dammit, she *was* over-excited. "Hiya, Pascale!"

They rushed towards each other, leaving Ed and Stuart to approach more slowly, and, in Ed's case, with more embarrassment. Pascale's silver dress, the spray-on glitter on her skin and the painted zig-zag across her face did more for her femininity than Ed's costume did for his masculinity. Not even the famously cool Ed Samuels could look anything but weirdly androgynous in silver boots, greasepaint and spiked, silvered hair. Jo wondered if a guitar might have improved it. Didn't Ziggy Stardust play guitar?

"You look *incredible*!" exclaimed Pascale, air-kissing Jo. "Love the long sleeves – very sophis!"

"You look incredible too," said Jo. "That's definitely the word. Incredible. Where's Holly?"

"Telling someone what to do, I expect." Pascale's eyes, looking unreal behind the lightning bolt drawn on her face, roamed the room. "I saw her a minute ago. Do you like Ed's costume? His sister did our make up. Clever, isn't she?"

Without waiting for an answer she drew Ed to her side. "We've got to stay together, Ed," she told him bossily, "or the costumes don't make sense. Keep hold of my hand."

The plains and hollows of Ed's normally sculpted face had been obliterated by the make-up. He looked like someone impersonating him, but missing, as lookalikes do, the essential charm of the real thing. His eyes, which usually held a serious, watchful expression, looked glassy. "Next year I'm wearing a tux," he said moodily to Pascale. "No arguments. I mean, Stuart looks way better than me."

Pascale nestled nearer to him. "So you're thinking we'll still be going out together next year, then? I wish you'd tell *me* these things!"

Stuart and Jo laughed obediently. Then Ed said, "You look really good, Jo." Although Pascale had tight hold of one of his hands, he extended the other one and touched Jo's forearm lightly. "You could be Miss Universe any day, that's all I can say."

And that's all you're going to be *allowed* to say, thought Jo. "Thanks, Ed!" she said airily. "The costume was Pascale's idea."

"Clever me!" Pascale tugged at Ed's hand. "Come on, the dancing's starting."

Before she dragged him out of earshot Ed addressed Stuart over his shoulder. "You can't dance with Jo all night, can you, mate? Let me in there, will you?"

Jo could hear Pascale protesting that no one dances *with* anyone, and can't you just keep your hands to yourself, and Jo's got a boyfriend, you know. Jo didn't care. She couldn't calm herself. Her heart was actually thudding.

"Wow! Who's this hot chick?" Said a voice from the crowd.

Holly was making her determined towards them. The skirt of her dress, which was made of stiff, glittering material, reached Jo before its wearer did. Behind Holly, struggling with a bunch of balloons, came Tom Clarke. Holly's face, as Pascale had predicted and Jo had hoped, registered middle-scale shock and top-scale awe.

"Hello, you two." Jo returned Holly's hug. "Stuart, do you know Tom?" The boys nodded to each other.

Holly, being Holly, had wiped her initial reaction to the sight of Jo off her face, and replaced it with her usual Golden Girl of the West shimmer. Eyes, lips, blusher-enhanced cheeks and freckle-strewn nose were all back on duty and working hard. "What a great idea!" she exclaimed. "Miss Universe! And Stuart, you look gorgeous!" She twirled. "What about me? You like?"

Jo noticed that the material of Holly's dress wasn't glittery after all. The blue taffeta had been painstakingly appliquéd with tiny sequined stars. "It's fabulous," she told Holly, meaning it. "Did you do it yourself?"

"As if! No, my mum did it. And Tom's suit, too. Show them, Tom."

Tom held the balloons away from his body to display a black tuxedo like Stuart's, but with the lapels and a blue cummerbund covered with the same twinkly stars. Jo couldn't help laughing with pleasure at the sight. If she'd been a few years younger, she thought, she'd have clapped her hands. Not only did the costume look great, but the fact that Holly's hardworking mum had produced it, Tom had been persuaded to wear it, and was now showing it off with such obvious contentment, made her feel indescribably happy. "Oh, Holly, you're amazing!"

"No I'm not," said Holly, though Jo could tell she thought she was. Then, unexpectedly, Holly got self-conscious. She surprised Tom by taking the balloon strings from his hand. "These are supposed to be tied in each corner of the room," she told him briskly. "We'd better get on with it before more people arrive."

"Why?" asked Tom. "The room's already decorated."

A perplexed crease appeared between Holly's eyebrows. "But people spent so long blowing all these up, I can't let them down – the people I mean, not the balloons." She began to follow her skirt away, then turned back with an anxious look at Jo and Stuart. "Have you found our table yet? Don't let anyone else sit in your places, will you?"

"We'll go and find it now," Jo reassured her. "See you later."

It started out just a pretty good party. There was some desultory dancing and a lot of screaming with laughter and 'going out for some air' onto the school field. But at some indefinable moment, when the air was getting dusky and the fairy lights in the trees had been switched on, the ice broke. People forgot who they didn't look as nice as, or whose table they wished they were on. They just got on with having a great party.

Holly's position on the committee had ensured that her friends had a well-placed table, near the stage and in view of the other diners. By the time supper was over Jo felt as if she'd never done anything in her life except sit at this grease-stained paper tablecloth, with Stuart's black sleeve on one side of her long purple sleeves, and Ed's silver one on the other. Once, a long time ago, she took some exams, though she couldn't remember doing it. And at some time in the future, something else was going to happen, but she couldn't remember what that was either.

After the meal the band disappeared and a DJ took the stage. "Don't worry," said Holly, "the PTA didn't book him. He's Grant Cox's brother, and he's really good. Tom's been to another event where he's played, haven't you, Tom?"

"Yep," said Tom, nodding wisely. "Trust me, he's really good."

He was. Within seconds the floor was filling. "Come on, Ed," said Pascale, dragging his arm. "Here's our chance to show off."

The prospect of this didn't seem to impress Ed much. But the dance floor was too crowded for anyone to show off anyway. If Pascale was disappointed, she didn't show it. She tossed her hair and writhed about, reminding Jo of a champagne-sodden Tess on Trevor's fortieth birthday. Ed did his usual half dancing, half standing still. Jo hoped that no one would notice her watching him.

"Aren't you two dancing?" asked Holly over her shoulder as she and Tom passed on their way to the dance floor.

Stuart and Jo looked at each other. "Oh, OK," said Jo.

It was hard to dance in such a crowd. Jo's tiara loosened itself and her hair started to escape its pins. She feared for her bare toes among the boots and spiky heels. Then someone fell against her and almost knocked her over. She felt Stuart grab her round the waist, but when she righted herself it was Ed who appeared in front of her, smiling through his sweat-smeared make up. "We said we'd have a dance, didn't we?"

"*You* did," corrected Jo. She had to shout to make him hear her. Her voice squeaked against the booming music. "Watch out for Pascale!"

"Oh, Pascale..." he said, rolling his eyes. "Look at her, she's all over Grant Cox."

Jo looked. Between the heads bobbing around her she

recognized Pascale's silver-sprayed hair and Grant's cornrows. "She's such a groupie," said Ed, "and he's only the DJ's *brother*!"

Jo giggled. "Didn't she want you two to stick together because of your costumes?"

"That only applies if *I* want to go off somewhere." He was smiling, and looking at Jo approvingly. "You're taller than I thought, you know."

"Got heels on," she gasped as someone's elbow landed between her shoulder blades.

"Come here," said Ed. He took both her hands and pulled her towards him. "Can't have you getting knocked over."

They couldn't really dance much. Jo was very aware of Ed's arms around her, and the texture of the silver lamé jacket he wore. She locked her hands behind his neck, feeling the little ring of bone sticking out at the top of his spine. She tried to remember what that ring of bone was called. They'd learnt it in Biology. Axel? Axis? Atlas?

Ed's belt buckle – God, don't think about it – was digging into her stomach. She adjusted her position, but he moved too. He must have thought Jo's little wriggle was encouragement. She took her arms away from his neck and pushed her hands against his chest, trying to make a space between them. "I feel a bit crowded," she said.

He relaxed his hold on her. "Sorry."

"Oh, no, don't be!"

They swayed about in silence for a minute. Jo closed her eyes, trying to imagine she was dancing with someone who wasn't Pascale's boyfriend. It didn't work, because she couldn't conquer the guilt.

The music never ended. That was the problem with DJs – they just segued one track into another to keep the dancing going. But how did you ever get an opportunity to stand still, especially in such a crowd? Jo wondered inanely if she and Ed would have to dance together for the rest of their lives.

"Better?" shouted Ed in her ear.

She nodded, and they went on dancing. She could feel Ed's hipbones, and his spine through his jacket and shirt. Even though he'd loosened his embrace, the side of his face was sweating silver greasepaint into her hair. She turned so that her forehead touched his sticky cheek. She realized that he was taller than Toby, because when she embraced Toby their foreheads touched. And she was wearing high heels, too. He must be *a lot* taller than Toby.

Pascale's voice entered Jo's meandering thoughts, as piercing as a police siren. "Ed Samuels!" She emerged from the crowd of dancers, her silver make-up shining surreally under the lights. "Are you going to dance with me or not?"

"What about laughing-boy over there?" asked Ed in his geezer voice.

"Who? Grant Cox?" Pascale seemed unwilling to notice that Ed still had his arms around Jo. Standing on tiptoe, she grabbed his shoulder and kissed him on the mouth. "Oh, Ed! You are funny!"

Jo had no choice but to squirm out of Ed's arms. "See you later," she said to no one in particular. By the time she sat down, Ed and Pascale were snogging energetically. Stuart, Holly and Tom had vanished.

Jo tried to shake off the memory of the dance. So far in their relationship Toby had always touched her tentatively, as if he were hardly doing it at all, but Ed's touch was really *there*. Being close to him didn't seem the same as being close to Toby at all. But why was she comparing them? She'd even compared their heights, as if she were shopping for a date on the Internet.

She took a gulp of diluted apple juice, wondering vaguely

what Toby was doing tonight. Not something he'd tell her about, that was for sure. She took another gulp, thinking about what was hidden by the plaster on her arm. The truth was, she was as devious, secretive and – what was that word she and Holly had been so struck by when they'd studied *Cat on a Hot Tin Roof* ? They'd slipped it into every conversation for about a week. Mendacious. It meant that you lied. It was a great word, definitely. And Jo was as mendacious as Toby.

* * * * * *

Fridays were always busy at Rose and Reed. This particular Friday, Gordon had also called a staff meeting after closing time. And it was a hot day. When the shop closed Jo was exhausted, and longed to go home. But Gordon sent Sophie, a part-timer even newer than Jo, out for sandwiches, Eloise brewed a pot of coffee and they all crowded into Gordon's office.

"Why are we in here?" muttered Jo to Eloise. "Can't we have a staff meeting in a café or something?"

Eloise stopped licking mayonnaise off her fingers and gave Jo a surprised look. "But we need a TV, don't we? Gordon's got the recording."

"What recording?"

"Oh sweetie, did no one tell you?" Eliose took a bite of her sandwich. "We've had a visit from the mystery shopper."

"What mystery shopper?" Jo was beginning to feel very stupid.

"It's how Head Office checks up on the branches," explained Eloise, "to see if the employees are up to scratch. Gordon wouldn't have been told about it – they just send this ordinary-looking person with a concealed camera to film what the assistant who serves them does. Or doesn't do, more like."

Jo began to understand. "So is Gordon going to show the film this person took of one of us?"

Eloise nodded, her mouth full of sandwich.

"It's me, isn't it?" Jo's heart jumped about in her chest. "Come on, Eloise, tell me."

Eloise raised her eyebrows, but said nothing. Then Gordon came in with his sandwiches in one hand and a DVD in the other, followed by Toby with a box of strawberries, a pile of plastic sundae dishes and a packet of plastic spoons. He filled two dishes and brought them to where Jo sat.

"Thanks." She took the strawberries, but she didn't start to eat them. Her stomach felt clenched up. "Did you know we've got to watch a mystery shopper film?"

He shrugged, propping himself against the windowsill as there was nowhere left to sit. "Something like that."

"I bet it's me," said Jo.

"Why? It might be me, or Sandy, or anyone. Maybe even Gordon himself. Relax."

Jo couldn't relax. She hardly listened to Gordon's preamble. Her eyes were fixed on the DVD lying on his desk. When he put it into the player a rustle of expectation went round the room. Everyone thinks it's them, thought Jo.

The TV screen leapt into life. There was the ground floor of the shop. There was Tasha at the cash register. And there was Jo, standing by the door, looking bored. The person with the hidden camera approached her and asked if she could show her dresses suitable for wearing to the office, in a 12 or a 14, long sleeves please.

Jo, who had gone very hot, remembered the woman. About thirty, with an educated voice and bobbed hair, she'd come in only about a week after Jo had started to work at Rose and Reed.

The mystery shopper trailed around after Jo, filming her haphazard selection of four dresses. The woman picked out the only one they didn't have in a 12 or a 14.

"Will you be getting any more of these in?" she asked.

"I don't know." Jo's recorded voice sounded like a little girl's. Everyone laughed. Toby put his strawberries down on the windowsill and nudged Jo's back with his knee. Jo had stopped *looking* at the recording, but she couldn't escape *hearing* it.

"Well, could you get one from another branch?" asked the mystery shopper.

"I don't know," said the little girl's voice quietly.

"Or could I get it mail order? You have a catalogue service, don't you? What would I have to pay for delivery?"

"I don't know," said the even quieter little girl. "But if you'd like to wait a moment, I could ask."

"No, I think I'd better leave it." The mystery shopper thrust the dress into Jo's arms, which were already full of the rejected dresses. "But I also need a jacket. Could you show me some?"

Again the camera followed Jo's back view as she led the woman to the Formalwear section. Jo took a brief look at the screen. Her hair looked its usual limp self, and it had separated at the back like it always did by the afternoon. She looked away.

She didn't do much better with the jackets. The woman wanted the sleeves altered, and Jo didn't know what whether, or how, this was possible. After the woman told Jo she didn't want to buy anything there was no more dialogue. Wondering if the film had finished, Jo took another peep at the screen. It hadn't. Because she had forgotten to put back her armful of dresses before she attended to the search for a jacket, she had left them draped over a rack of suits. The last thing the camera recorded was Jo scooping them off, catching one of the hangers in the collar of a suit jacket, and dropping all four dresses on the floor in her scramble to extricate it.

The film ended. Gordon stood by the TV, his hands in the pockets of his trousers, surveying his employees. "I think you'll all agree that wasn't good."

He waited while people murmured and looked at the carpet. Suddenly ravenous, Jo filled her mouth with strawberries.

"What do we learn from this unedifying sight?" asked Gordon.

He wasn't looking particularly at Jo, but she knew the question was for her. She was about to apologize for getting him into trouble with Head Office, but before she could speak, Toby pushed himself off the windowsill. "What's the point of this, Gordon?" he asked aggressively. He took the disc out of the player and held it up. "You know what I'm going to do? I'm going to throw this piece of garbage away."

He threw it into the waste bin under Gordon's desk, where it clanged satisfyingly. Taking no notice of Gordon or anyone else, Toby gently removed Jo's strawberry bowl from her lap and set it on the window sill beside his own. Then he put his arm under her shoulder blades and pulled her up. "I'm taking Jo home now."

Eloise looked stricken. "It's my fault, Toby. I obviously didn't tell Jo everything she needed to know."

"But that's exactly why this exercise is useful," Gordon told her. "We *all* learn from it."

"But it's not fair!" protested Toby. "If they filmed Jo today she'd be miles better. Why humiliate her?"

"It's not humiliation, it's staff improvement," insisted Gordon grimly.

"It's bollocks," said Toby. He still had his arm around Jo. "And if you try and do it to me, I'll tell you to stuff your job."

"Toby," began Jo, "you really don't need to – "

"And *you* can shut up, too."

Jo didn't mind him being rude to her in front of everybody. In fact she was proud of it. It showed they were a proper couple. He'd stood up for her by putting his own job on the line and saying what everyone was secretly thinking. She wished there was a 'Strong heroism' label she could slap on his forehead, right there in front of everyone.

"You're crazy," she told him as he bundled her out of the office and up the stairs. "They'll sack you. They'll sack *me*."

He didn't let go of her until they were outside on the pavement. "No they won't," he said, pulling the shop door behind them. "But they might think again about their moronic mystery shopper idea."

Jo's heart was doing a tap dance. Toby looked the same as he always did, but he *wasn't* the same. Jo reached for his hand. "This is where I thank you for rescuing me."

He smiled. "Go on, then."

She put her hands behind his head and pulled his face down to hers. He didn't resist. She kissed him for a long time, and felt his lips and tongue respond, and his arms snake round and clasp her against him. Neither he nor she was wearing much. She knew he could feel her bones and her skin and her flesh as plainly as she could feel his.

When she pulled away and saw his familiar face with its tufty hair and the shadow that showed he hadn't shaved since last night, the self-consciousness she usually felt with him flew away.

"I love you, Toby," she said. "Not because of what you did in there. I just do."

He pulled her towards him again. She couldn't see his face, but his heart under his T-shirt felt like a pneumatic drill. He

112

kissed her on the top of her head, pressing her skull hard.

Then he drew away, lifted his chin and looked up and down the street. "Those sandwiches Sophie got were rubbish. Do you want a pizza?"

# Chapter Eight

This weekend, Jo decided, they'd do it. Even if Toby didn't want to, she'd *make* him want to. It's the only power girls have got, Pascale said. And it's the most powerful power in the world. Sexual desire has brought down great men and elevated great women. It's at the source of everything that's ever happened in history, Pascale said. Jo doubted this, but she was beginning to think that maybe she *did* have the power, after all.

She thought of nothing else all day Saturday. Her standing with Gordon actually seemed to have gone *up* since the events of yesterday. Eloise had obviously been instructed to allow Jo to work on the till instead of leaving her to sweat in the stockroom like she usually did.

"Maybe we'd better go over some things again," said Eloise when Tasha had had to come to Jo's rescue at the till for the twentieth time. Humiliating though this was, since Tasha was no more experienced in shop work than Jo, she didn't care. She couldn't concentrate enough even to *think* about caring.

She decided to wear the new underwear Trevor had bought her to go under her Miss Universe dress. Little lacy knickers, and a skimpy bra to match. She'd shave her legs when she got home, though she'd only done it a couple of days ago. She'd wear that musky perfume of Tess's that Toby liked, and experiment with curling her hair and sweeping it off the nape of her neck like Pascale's. Jo had heard somewhere that boys found the napes of girls' necks sexy.

Since last night, everything seemed clear. Her confession to Pascale about not knowing if Toby fancied her was irrelevant now. They were a couple, she and Toby. He must really, really like her, or he wouldn't have risked confronting Gordon like that. And the way he'd kissed her outside the shop last night was different from any kiss he'd given her before. He had kissed her as if she was important to him.

She knew what she had felt when the compulsion to tell him she loved him rushed over her. It wasn't passion, or sexual desire. It was just that at that moment, she knew she loved him. All of a sudden, her course of action had sprung into clarity, as brightly as a computer screen. Her virginity was a weight she'd been carrying around too long. It was dragging her back into childhood instead of allowing her to go forward into adulthood. Now that she'd realized she loved someone, she really did have to get rid of it.

Toby was working upstairs that Saturday, and Jo didn't see him much. Their lunch breaks were at different times. But at closing time he came and leant on the cash desk where Jo and Tasha were tidying up.

"Where shall we go tonight?" he asked Jo, smiling with no teeth showing. "Up to town?"

"You sound like Tess," said Jo, hanging up plastic bags. "You'll be saying 'my club' next."

"Town's just another way of saying London," said Tasha, who didn't know Tess.

Toby was watching Jo patiently. "We could go for a meal in the West End if you want. There's a place on Frith Street I sometimes go to."

Jo and Tasha exchanged a look. "He sounds keen," said Tasha.

"I just want to have a nice night out!" protested Toby.

"What train shall we get?" Jo looked at her watch. It was ten past six. "By the time we both go home and get ready..."

"Listen, Jo," interrupted Toby, looking at his own watch, "I've got to go up there early, to do some shopping. Why don't you meet me at Waterloo? About eight thirty?"

Jo was disappointed, but couldn't say so in front of Tasha. Once again, Toby had plans he hadn't told her about. She was tempted to say, "What sort of shopping?" but then she realized he might be going to buy her a present.

"Oh, all right. I won't bother to get dressed up, then, if you're going in your work things."

"Tell you what," he said unexpectedly. "Why don't you wear a skirt? You never do." He nodded towards a rail of short cotton skirts. "And you've got better legs than most of the women who are trying those on."

Tasha giggled. "He's really out to please tonight, Jo!"

"I might," said Jo. She had to concentrate very hard on not going red. Toby's suggestion had made it very clear that his plan for the evening was exactly the same as hers. She came round the cash desk and kissed him on the cheek. "You'd better go and get your train, then. See you at eight thirty."

\* \* \* \* \* \*

Trevor, wearing an apron, opened the front door before Jo could get her key out. "I've heated up a shepherd's pie, made by the loving hands of Mr Marks and his good friend Mr Spencer," he announced.

"Sorry," said Jo, rushing past him and taking the stairs two at a time. "Must have a shower. Toby and I are going out for a meal in the West End."

"Celebrating something?" asked Trevor peevishly.

"No." Nothing I'm going to tell you about, anyway, she thought. When she'd showered, she wound her hair round rollers and dried it. Then she put on the only skirt she owned. It was made of washed-out denim, and came about half way down her thighs. With no tights underneath it was cool enough for August. But she wished she had a flouncy, semi-transparent skirt like the one Pascale often wore, which looked sexy and properly summery.

The denim skirt didn't look bad, though. Jo model-posed in front of the mirror. Toby was right. Her legs, though not in the same league of brownness, smoothness or length as Pascale's, were pretty good. She sat down on the bed and inspected the plaster on her arm. The shower had loosened a corner, so she ripped it off. The wound had stopped weeping yellowy water, but it hadn't started scabbing over either. She prodded it gently, wondering if this would be the last time she'd touch it. Toby, mendacious or not, couldn't be her boyfriend – her *proper* boyfriend – if she never let him see her naked, could he? Somehow, by a serious effort of will, she had to *make herself* leave it alone.

She opened her bedside-table drawer and reached right to the back, where she kept an empty crisp packet. She folded the used plaster and placed it in the crisp packet with all the others, and the papers they came wrapped in. It wasn't Sylvia's business if she found used plasters in the waste paper basket or the bathroom bin, but Jo couldn't stand the idea of her inspecting them, wondering. The soiled plasters would stay in the crisp packet until the day came when Jo would put it in her bag and nonchalantly, on the way to the bus stop, screw it up and throw it into a public litter bin.

When she'd put on another plaster and dressed in a long-sleeved top, she took the rollers out of her hair. But when she pinned up the curls, the result was more 1970s starlet than sophisticated wanton. Pascale's hair must be more receptive to curling than Jo's. Swearing softly, she heated up the straighteners.

Her phone rang; it was Holly, asking what Jo and Toby were doing tonight. Jo rushed through the conversation, afraid she'd miss the train.

"Let me know what happens!" said Holly.

"Will do!" replied Jo.

She left the house without saying goodbye to Trevor and walked to the station as quickly as the effectiveness of her deodorant would allow. She didn't get a seat because a lot of other people were going to Waterloo Station on a Saturday night. Swaying in the carriage, she thought about Trevor sitting alone with his shepherd's pie. For a moment she felt guilty, but then she remembered that he still hadn't made an appointment to see Mr Treasure. Every time Jo reminded him he said, "Can't Tess go? Teachers frighten the pants off me. And anyway, I'm going to Wales."

She sighed. On TV and in movies, and even in her class at school, people's parents just got divorced. Kids said, "my parents are divorced, and I live with my mum and see my dad every other weekend." But it seemed to Jo that her own parents' separation just got muddier and muddier. If anyone asked her to explain, what would she say? "Well, my mother's living with her parents and I'm living with my dad in a house my mum and dad both own, and he wants to sell it and spend his half on another house, but my mother doesn't want to live in a flat, she'd rather come back and live in our house, with him paying for it even though he's just been made redundant and wants to go and live in Wales anyway. Still with me?"

And where was *Jo* in all this uncertainty and vagueness? Did Trevor or Tess ever think about that?

The train arrived late at Waterloo. Jo saw Toby before he saw her. As she walked across the concourse she watched him jittering from foot to foot. He looked nice, in his usual loose-limbed way, neatly groomed despite not having been home after work. He greeted her with a relieved hug. "Thought you weren't coming!"

"Train was late. What have you been doing? Where's your shopping?"

"Didn't buy anything." He saw her face. "Sorry, couldn't find what I wanted. I booked the table, though, so come on."

The restaurant wasn't like the golf club, or any of the pseudo-rustic pubs on Jo's grandparents' dining-out circuit. It was a proper restaurant, with starched tablecloths and discreet waiters who pulled out her chair and spread her napkin on her lap for her. Jo and Toby even ordered cocktails.

Jo watched him, trying to gauge his mood. It was different from how he'd been in the shop. He seemed nervous, as if it was their first date. Of course, he could be nervous about what was going to happen later. But if that were the reason, why didn't Jo's willingness, which she was making as obvious as she could, make him feel at ease?

They drank almost two bottles of wine with the meal. Although Toby had more of it than Jo, she still felt very drunk. It was more wine than she'd ever had all in one go. She wondered, not for the first time, how Trevor could get through bottle after bottle and still stay upright. Well, almost.

The wine didn't seem to relax Toby. In the end, Jo encouraged him to have another cocktail, and she had one too. Leaning on each other, they left the restaurant.

"You're drunk," said Toby amiably.

"So are you."

"I'm going to get a taxi," said Toby, flailing his arm at the nearest one, which didn't stop.

"Why can't we go on the Tube?" asked Jo.

"Because I want to go in a *taxi*." He scanned the traffic. "There's one!" They scampered between the lines of cars. "Waterloo, please!" said Toby, opening the door.

Nestling with his arm around Jo in the corner of the cab, Toby seemed to make a decision. He put his hand up her skirt, almost as far as her knickers, and left it on her thigh. Jo was so drunk that she watched without protest as his eyes got a dreamy, unfocused look, and he breathed faster. She let him put his tongue in her mouth, and even arched her back so that his other hand could locate the fastening of her lacy bra. She was aware that her own breath was shortening, and that she wanted to swallow, but couldn't. Holly said that happened all the time, but Pascale said that when you *really* want to do it you get a feeling inside you like a period pain, though not so bad. In fact, quite nice.

Jo waited, there in the taxi, for the nice pain. But all that happened was that the constriction in her throat increased as Toby went on kissing her. He smelled of alcohol. The hand that was up her skirt had found the top of her knickers and was trying to pull the elastic away from her body. The other hand had undone her bra and was kneading her left breast uncomfortably.

Things were going wrong. Jo didn't feel nice. She felt ill, partly from the unaccustomed alcohol, and partly from plain, old fashioned shame. What was the taxi-driver thinking? Although it didn't matter, because she would have felt the same even if she and Toby had been doing this at home.

She clamped Toby's knicker-hand with her own hand.

"Tobe, we can't do this in a taxi."

"You want to, though, don't you?"

"Not here," Jo said as forcefully as she could. But registering outrage was hard because Toby's face was still all over hers.

"Don't worry," he insisted. "I've got some – "

"Toby!" She tried again. "I don't want to do this *here*."

He took his hand out from under her skirt. He looked agitated and sweaty, as if he'd set himself a task he was regretting embarking on. "What the hell is it with you?" he asked aggressively. "You were all over me in the restaurant, and then you come on like I'm a criminal or something because I want to have a bit of fun in a taxi."

Jo tried to wriggle free, but Toby's bra-arm was still clamped around her, squeezing her against his chest.

"I'm sorry," she muttered.

"Why is it such a big deal?" he persisted. "I thought, after what you said last night – "

"Toby..." She had to stop him. The 'If you loved me you'd do it' argument was too painful to hear. It made him sound like a hormone-crazed fourteen-year-old. "Maybe what I said last night...I mean, people say things..."

"So you didn't mean it, then."

She tried not to hear the petulance in his voice. "I don't know *what* I meant, Toby. I was...look...it didn't feel right." Then she added something she wished she hadn't, "maybe you're not...you know, the one."

He slid his free hand under her cheek, lifted her head and looked at her with exasperation. "Christ, Jo, who *is* 'the one', then? One of those wetheads at your school?"

"No, of course not!"

The taxi was crossing Waterloo Bridge. It was only two more minutes to the station. Jo wished she could get out and walk.

"You just don't fancy me, do you?" Toby had clamped her head onto his chest again. His heart hammered against her cheek. "You're saving yourself for Mr Wonderful. Well, when you meet him, be sure to introduce me, so I can be as dazzled as you are by his wonderfulness."

Jo knew he was being mean, but felt too weak to argue. Pascale's theory was that if you did anything at all to bruise a boy's ego, even something as small as observing that your uncle's got the same jumper as him (this had actually happened to Pascale), the boy would get back at you by equally small, but very noticeable acts of meanness. You had to feel sorry for them, really. And how many times had Toby bruised *Jo's* ego, without even noticing?

"Look, Toby..." Already, before she'd even got to the end of the sentence, Jo was beginning to regret her next words. "My mother says – "

"Oh, your *mother*! How old are you? Twelve?"

Through her alcohol fuelled haze, Jo realized that Tess, for all her shortcomings, understood about boys. Jo believed her when she said that they can separate sex from love, but girls can't because they don't see why they should. But it was impossible to say the L-word to Toby now. She shouldn't have said it in the first place.

"It's all right, Tess doesn't think I'm saving myself for my wedding night," she told him. "But she's always said I should be really, really sure before I commit myself." What Tess had actually said was that Jo must trust someone. But she couldn't say the T-word to Toby either.

He seemed to be thinking about this. After a few moments he let go of Jo's head, and she sat up, looking at him warily. His face bore no expression. He didn't speak, but sat with his hands folded on his stomach, as if he were watching TV, until the taxi stopped. He looked out of the train window all the way to Kingsgrove, and they walked home in silence. At her house they exchanged a chaste kiss. They didn't arrange their next meeting, and Toby didn't say he'd call her. The effects of the wine were receding, but Jo still felt helpless, unsure of what to do. She watched him walk down the street for a few moments, then she put her key into the lock and pushed the door.

Trevor was watching a movie, his armchair surrounded by half-empty beer bottles, half-smoked cigarettes and loose pages from *The Guardian*. He put up his hand in case she spoke. Jo could see that the film was almost over. She knew the last scene of *Fight Club* pretty well. As soon as the credits started to roll, she asked, "What's happening with you and Tess?"

Trevor gestured to the cooler beside his chair. "Want one?"

"No, thanks."

"Mind if I do?"

"Are you serious?"

"All *right*." He opened another bottle of beer. "Tess is pissed off because I'm not letting her have the house, that's all."

Jo looked around the living room, wondering how much longer it would be hers, and Blod's. "Well, do you *have* to sell it?"

"All my money's tied up in it, Jo-girl, and I need money to start this thing with Mord." He glanced up, and when he saw her face his expression softened. "Look, love, if Tess's dad's prepared to give her the money to buy out my half, he's welcome, and then you can go on living here."

"With Tess, though?"

"'Fraid so. I'm going to be in Wales, where your mother is always telling me I belong, and should never have had the presumption to venture out of. But all I can say to that is...hah bloody hah!"

123

This struck him as intolerably amusing. Jo watched him for a minute, shrieking and coughing, and fumbling for a cigarette and dropping the pack and picking it up again, and then she went upstairs and sat down in her computer chair.

She tried to make herself think. She wanted to work out what had happened tonight, consider it and deal with it, like a sensible person. But it didn't happen. She sat there with her hands at her sides and her legs stretched out under the dressing-table desk, and the movie that ran inside her head folded into darkness, like the black screen at the end before the credits roll. *That's all, folks, go home now.* There were no thoughts and nothing in her imagination. She was besieged by first-take, un-edited emotions, on which her brain had no influence. Unnamed, untamed, they twisted in her stomach, impossible to separate.

She pictured Toby's watchful eyes, the way he looked at his reflection in shop windows and fiddled with his hair, the space his long limbs and shambling walk took up, the feel of his skin, the smell of his shower gel. She remembered how his heart had practically jumped out of his chest when she was kissing him in the doorway of the shop, and what she'd said, and her eyes began to burn.

Panic rose. Her right hand closed around her left elbow, but then she released it again. The scratch-patch wasn't what she needed. She tried to breathe. The room was full of light. It shouldn't be – it was the middle of the night – but Jo stood up and walked into the brightness, conscious suddenly of what she *did* need. She sat down on the window seat that ran around the bay window. Her make-up lay all higgledy-piggledy in a glass tray on the window-sill. Beside it stood her make-up mirror. And beside that, in its usual place, was the little china box she'd brought back from Delft.

The china box contained her eyebrow tweezers and hairpins, as well as something that looked perfectly innocent, but would be confiscated at an airport. Jo knew it was there, underneath the hairpins and the tweezers, small, but powerful enough to be considered a threat to air passengers. She thought about it *hard*. She shut her eyes and rocked backwards and forwards, eyes shut, humming softly to herself, letting the thought possess her. When she was sure the thought had *become* her, and no longer existed as a thought at all, she opened the lid of the china box.

Her fingers closed around the tiny pair of nail scissors. Each blade had a point like a little knife. Without needing to open her eyes, Jo carefully ran her fingertips over one of the blades.

She could do it, she was sure. She could do it in her leg, high enough for her knickers to hide. Toby would never know. No one would know. And in that nanosecond of physical pain, the endless mental pain he had made would recede.

Still blind, she took a tissue from the box on the windowsill, pulled up her skirt and the side of her knickers, and stiffened the muscles of her leg. First there was the cold of the metal, then a bright heat. Jo gasped. The moment of release. And then there was warmth, and the wetness of the little spurt of blood.

She opened her eyes. Perfect. Not too much blood to cause a fuss, not too little to fail to do the job. And it *had* done the job. Instantly, unlike the scratch-patch method, and more sensationally, with a more exquisite stab. She pressed the tissue to the wound. It hurt a lot now.

Her heart thudded, fatigue deadened her limbs, her body felt weak. But she got up, and, still pressing the tissue to her thigh, went to the computer chair. She deleted Toby's 'Suitable for all' label, and examined the white space it left behind. Tentatively, as if the keys were burning her fingertips, she typed

'Scenes of sex or violence' in it.

The digital clock by the bed read 00:36. She stuffed the bloodstained tissue into the crisp packet and put a plaster on the wound. Then, too feeble to undress, she lay down on the bed.

She would have to live with tonight for ever. It would never go away. Many nights from now, perhaps years and years into the future, the picture of herself and Toby tangled up on a taxi seat, and the sound of her stupid little-girl voice saying, "I just don't think you're the one," would rise up and hover in her brain. And Jo would let out a little yelp at the memory.

But tonight, the scissors' tiny point had put the pain in its place. *She* was in control. She pulled the duvet around her ears and put out her bedside light. And very soon, with a peace all around her more profound than any she had felt since Tess had left Trevor, she fell asleep.

* * * * * *

When she woke up she lay in bed for a long time, looking at the frame of light around the curtains, thinking about last night. She also thought about the exam results.

The trouble was, if she did really badly no one would employ her, maybe not even Rose and Reed. Though of course if she did really badly, how would she show her face in Rose and Reed or anywhere else? After the build-up Mr Gerrard, Miss Balcombe and even Mr Phipps, who considered her an also-ran as far as the race for grade A Maths was concerned, had given her, the humiliation would be intolerable. The vultures would pounce, stabbing her with, "Oh, you must be so disappointed, Jo! After that essay you did that Mr Gerrard thought was so *brilliant*". Or, "Aren't you supposed to be quite good at French?"

126

And as they gloated, Jo would remember that she was better at almost everything than almost all of them, and want to kill them.

But there was another even worse scenario. If she did really *well*, the pressure to do A Levels would become intolerable. Different vultures – Trevor and Tess – would stab her repeatedly. Peck, peck, peck. And because of her good results, her case against staying on would be in danger of collapse.

She tried to remember the English exams, the Maths, the French. She'd worked hard for them, and all the other subjects, except Art, which she hated with the white-hot hatred only a project involving wire, glue, bits of net and dry leaves could induce. Why had she worked so hard, and bent for hours over a too-small desk, her wrist stiff, her head throbbing from lack of air and late nights?

Because she couldn't let herself down. And that was the whole point, surely? To do her best because she *could*, not because she had to in order to achieve some goal involving anybody else.

She stripped off the lacy knickers and inspected them for bloodstains. They seemed OK.

She put them and the matching bra in the laundry basket. She'd probably never wear them again. Then she spent a long time in the shower, washing again and again. She shampooed her hair three times, too. Then, still wearing her dressing gown, she put a fresh plaster on her leg and sat down at the computer.

It was Sunday. Toby's day off was Monday this week, so he'd be at work today. After work, though, maybe he'd call her. Or maybe she'd call him. And if neither of them called the other, she'd see him when he came into work on Tuesday. By that time, surely something would have to happen.

Jo didn't know what she *wanted* to happen, though. If this

was Toby's opportunity to dump her, and he took it, would she care? If she dumped him, would he? If not, why were they together in the first place? And if they *did* split up, how would they go on working together in the same shop, day after day for the rest of the holidays, or longer?

She studied her reflection for a few moments, then she got dressed in jeans and an old top. After sitting on the edge of the bed for five minutes, fingering her phone, she called Pascale.

"Can I come round?" she asked. "I want to talk to you about something. Not on the phone."

"Of course!" said Pascale happily. "Hope it's scandal!"

"It's not," said Jo. "See you in half an hour."

Pascale lived in a boxy white house in a row of boxy white houses between older, redbrick villas. Some residents had trained flowers round their doors, or put up fancy shutters. But Pascale's house remained unadorned. Jo always thought it looked like a square igloo.

"Hiya!" Pascale, barefoot and looking like an artist's model in a flounced skirt and with her hair unbrushed, took both of Jo's wrists and dragged her into the hallway. She examined Jo's face critically. "Are you sure you're not ill? Even *you* aren't usually this pale."

"Maybe I need some sun," Jo reassured her.

Pascale's hands moved to Jo's elbows, and she shook them gently. "Come on, cheer up!" Her fingers found the plaster on Jo's left arm. She pushed up the sleeve of her blouse. "What's this? Have you hurt yourself?"

"Mosquito bite," said Jo.

Pascale frowned. "Must be a *huge* bite."

"I picked it and it got infected."

"Silly!" scolded Pascale, releasing her. "Let's go in the garden."

They went through the house to a tiny lawn on which two sun loungers and an umbrella had been set up. "Where are your parents?" asked Jo.

"Shopping. We're going to Spain tomorrow remember. Got your sunblock on?"

Pascale plumped herself down on the more comfortable of the two loungers and pulled her skirt up almost to where her knickers ended. "Must get my legs brown. I'll get us something to drink in a minute when Poisonous is out of the kitchen."

Pascale's brother was called Poins. Jo often wondered how Pascale's parents, people apparently so unimaginative that they couldn't even put a pot plant beside their front door, had come up with their children's exotic names. She felt rather sorry for Poins, who was a cheerful boy of about eleven. The sort of boy who played with Meccano. He had once told her proudly that his name was in Shakespeare, though he didn't know which play. Jo had been determined to find out for him, but only remembered this when she happened to see, or hear about, Poins.

"Did he ever find out which Shakespeare play his name is in?" she asked Pascale.

"What do you mean? He's always known. It's in *Henry IV Part 1 and Henry IV Part 2*. Dad told him that when he was really small, and he's always trotting it out. He used to say it to strangers on the bus."

"Oh," said Jo. Perhaps she had misunderstood.

"Now, shoot." Pascale folded her arms and put on her what-seems-to-be-the-trouble face. "Hol and I thought you and Toby might be having...you know, The Night. West End restaurant and all that. So did you?"

Jo lay back on the lounger. "Nope."

"Why not? Was there some problem?" This was what Doctor

Pascale liked to diagnose, ponder, and treat.

"Well, only the same old one," said Jo.

Pascale made an exaggeratedly horrified face. "You mean you still don't know if you want to? Jo, it's been *months*!"

"Two months and one week."

"What's been going on, for God's sake?"

Lying on the sun lounger was making Jo feel too much like a patient on the psychiatrist's couch. She sat forward, her hair swinging over her face. "It's been OK, Cal. You know, kissing."

"Proper kissing?" asked Pascale sharply.

Jo sighed. "Yes, a bit of tongues. But last Friday, something happened that changed how I felt. I suddenly realized how much I like him, and he was kissing me, and everything just seemed really nice. Last night, though, when he'd taken me out to that posh restaurant, and he wanted to do it, I just *couldn't*. I felt such a cow."

Pascale put her mouth into a line. "Last Friday, when everything seemed so nice, you didn't tell him you *love* him, did you?"

Jo said nothing.

"Don't you know *any*thing, Jo?

"Look, I just did it," said Jo, exasperated. "It felt right at the time."

"What did he say?" said Pascale in a prosecuting-counsel voice.

"He...well, he was pretty nice about it."

Pascale's eyes were ablaze. "No, what did he actually *say*?"

"He kind of changed the subject."

"Oh, *Jo!*"

"I know, I'm stupid. It's just that – "

"It's just that he's doing what blokes always do and you're sitting there *letting* him. Put up a bit of a fight, for the sisters.

130

Girl Power!"

Jo looked at Pascale, expecting her to run her hands through her hair, like actors when they had to show frustration. But she was sitting very still, her face in the shade and her legs in the sun, frowning and thinking.

"You're too soft, little Jo," she said. "You need to toughen up and play the game a bit. I bet when he thought he was going to get it and didn't, he was horrible to you, wasn't he?"

Jo didn't say anything for a moment. Pascale was right on both counts. She *was* too soft, and Toby *had* been horrible to her last night. But it wasn't as clear-cut as Pascale thought. "I don't blame him, though, Cal," she said quietly. "It was my fault."

Pascale let out a strangled shriek. "I don't believe I'm hearing this! Of course it wasn't *your* fault! *You* weren't horrible, *he* was! Jo, you really have got to be a bit more hard-nosed!"

This was insane, thought Jo. Two girls sitting in a garden discussing how to be hard-nosed. Did boys do this? Jo doubted it. "So what do I do?" she asked obediently.

"Right." Pascale sat forward. "Don't contact him. No call, no text, no email, nothing. If he contacts you, ignore him. When do you next see him at work?"

"Tuesday."

"Well, get there early, before he does. When he arrives, pretend to be talking on your phone. End the call fast when he sees you, as if you're talking to someone you don't want him to know about. Then bustle away as if you've got something really important to do."

"But he usually gives me a kiss when he comes in."

"Jo, you're not going to get *near* enough for him to kiss you! And ignore him while you get on with your work."

"He's upstairs in Menswear most of the time, anyway," said

131

Jo, imagining the scene. "But he might corner me in the stock room."

"If he does, don't let him *ask* you anything. You know, the 'have I got the plague or something?' questions they always ask. Especially don't let him get away with that 'wrong time of the month, is it?' bollocks. The trick is to start talking before he does."

"What do I say?" Jo wondered if she should be taking notes.

"You say 'If you want to apologize, Toby, I'm listening. If you don't, then piss off."

Jo laughed in spite of herself. "Like a teacher! Well, not the last part, but – "

"But nothing. Just *do* it. If he cares the smallest bit about you, he'll come up with some pathetic excuse. Or perhaps a good one. It depends what level of bullshitter he is. Some boys can bullshit for England."

Jo said nothing. She was thinking about the DVD labels. Toby, with his vague ambitions and nameless, faceless friends did have the makings of a top class bullshitter. But there wasn't a label to describe that.

"Come on," Pascale said, getting up. "Let's get drinks."

"I'll forget all this stuff the moment I see him, you know," said Jo as they went into the kitchen.

Pascale opened the fridge. "Look," she said, leaning on the door, "just remember that *you're* asking questions, not him. Of course, you can let him ask when he can see you again, and of course you say you're busy and you'll call him. *Don't* let him be the one to call you, and *don't* be the one to suggest seeing him again. *He's* the one in the wrong. Now, what do you want, Coke or apple juice? Or just water?"

"Apple juice." Jo was still dubious. She knew from experience that even when the other person was in the wrong she'd end up apologizing. If you liked someone, that's what you did in order to keep them liking you. "What if he dumps me?" she asked, taking the glass from Pascale, trying to control the wobble in her voice.

"He's not going to," said Pascale with decision. "If there's any dumping to be done, *you're* going to do it." She smiled gleefully. "You, me and Hol have got a one hundred percent record on not getting dumped, Jo. And you're not going to be the one to spoil it, are you?"

# Chapter Nine

Jo tried to get to work early on Tuesday, but the bus got stuck in traffic. She'd only taken one-and-a-half steps into the shop when she found her nose buried in Toby's T-shirt. He held her so tightly against his chest she couldn't move.

"Snog on your own time, you two," said Gordon airily as he passed.

Jo slid her hands between her chest and Toby's, and pushed. He didn't move, but he got the message. When he released her, his expression was a mixture of a hard frown and a timid smile. "What's the matter?"

Jo didn't know what to do with her own face. If she smiled, it would look as if she wasn't upset any more, which she was. But if she didn't smile, she would look like the humourless martyr she put so much effort into *not* being. In the end, she settled for raised eyebrows. "What do you think?" she said coldly.

Put up a bit of a fight, Pascale had said. Be tough and play the game.

Toby followed her down to the Staff Room. Her fingers shook as they searched her bag for her identity tag. She untangled the ribbon and put it round her neck. As she flipped her hair out from underneath it she saw that Toby was staring at her, his face muscles loosened by surprise.

"Is this because I didn't phone you?" he asked. Then he

seemed to register something, and his eyebrows collided in a frown. "Did you phone *me*? Because if you did, you wouldn't have got me. Someone stole my phone."

"Really?" Pascale had suggested Toby might come up with an excuse. "And no, I didn't phone you."

"Oh. Well, I had no note of your number, or your landline. In fact, you've never given me it, have you?"

His voice had become reproachful. Jo forced herself not to apologize.

"I never even thought about it," she told him. "But you could have called a directory. You know my address, don't you? Trevor's listed under Probert, T., funnily enough. Or if you were really clever you could have asked Gordon when you got to work yesterday." She tried to keep her voice calm, though being sarcastic made her feel sweaty.

Toby fiddled with the side of his hair. "I bet even if I *had* got your number, you wouldn't have picked up." He made a faint attempt at a smile. "But anyway, I didn't come to work yesterday."

Jo was surprised. "Why not?"

"I was sick."

"What was the matter?"

His face tightened. He was bracing himself either to lie, or confess the truth. "I...um...I got my drink spiked."

Jo let out an unamused laugh. "Toby, it's *girls* that get their drinks spiked."

"Not necessarily. I was in this club in the West End, and I just sort of fell asleep."

"In the club?" she asked incredulously.

He nodded, still fiddling with his hair. A sure sign of a liar. "And when I woke up my phone was gone."

"And then?" This was getting stupider and stupider.

"I don't remember. I was drugged. My mate Mitch must have got me out of the club, because I woke up yesterday on the floor of his flat. I used his phone to call work."

Jo was scornful. "So you know Rose and Reed's number off by heart, but you don't know mine?" Her voice almost cracked, but she tensed her muscles and tried to breathe evenly.

Toby was regarding her sorrowfully. "I'm sorry, Jo, I just like clubbing, and you're too young to get in."

Jo couldn't look at him any more. She opened the cupboard where they kept their possessions while they were in the shop. Toby's wallet lay in its usual place. "They didn't take your wallet, then?"

"No." Toby's voice was small and unconfident, the unrehearsed lines sounding very different from the prepared ones he'd come out with about the spiked drink. "They only seemed to want my phone."

Jo deposited her bag and turned round. "Hardly seems worth going to the trouble to drug you, does it? Did you go to the police?"

"Of course not. What could they do?"

"They could tell the management of the club to watch out for people 'falling asleep' on their premises, couldn't they? Maybe catch the guy at it?"

"Or the girl," said Toby with a flash of inspiration. "I bet it was a girl. Less suspicious."

"Yeah, maybe. What's the name of the club? I'll phone and tell them that some girl's spiking men's drinks to steal their phones. I'm sure they'll believe me."

Toby's patience was thinning. "Look, Jo, this isn't fair. Why can't – "

"*Fair*?"

She put all the outrage she could muster into her stare. Her eyes smarted. Toby didn't speak. He just went on looking back at her, and after a few seconds some force buzzing between their brains made him realize. He slumped against the wall, closing his eyes and opening them again. "Oh, God. You're really pissed off about what happened on Saturday night, aren't you?"

Jo noticed the pink rims around his eyes, and the bruise-like smudges underneath them. Hangover? Insomnia? Tears? Don't give him the chance to ask anything, Pascale had advised. Answer a question with a question, like Holly does. "What gives you that idea?" she asked testily.

Toby was silent. He took a brand-new phone out of his pocket and pressed some keys. "Give me your number again," he said steadily. "And your landline."

Jo ignored this. He'd got away without an apology, either for Saturday night or for not phoning her. She felt like she'd been horrible to him for the sake of her pride, and Pascale's instructions, but she also felt mildly pleased that she was able to do it. Suddenly, what she had to say next took shape.

"Please don't lie to me any more, Toby. I can't stand it."

The grey of his eyes looked dark against the pallor of his face. "What does that mean?"

She didn't answer. He fingered the phone in his hand, turning it round and round, not looking at Jo. Then he seemed to come to a conclusion, and took in some breath. "Jo, if there's something you want to say to me..."

He was interrupted by Eloise coming downstairs from the shop. "Come on, you two," she urged in exasperation. "Gordon's going nuts up here!"

Toby fingered the phone a bit more, then thrust it into the cupboard and started up the stairs. Eloise gave Jo a meaningful look as Jo locked the door behind them. "What's up with him?"

"Hangover."

Eloise laughed. "I like to see a bit of loyalty in a girlfriend! You know he threw a sickie yesterday, don't you?"

"Yep," smiled Jo. "And if you didn't already know, I'd tell you."

Eloise laughed again, and squeezed Jo's arm. "You go, girl!"

* * * * * *

When Jo got home from work Trevor was playing chess with Ken at the dining table. She expected her father to nod without looking up from the board, but he surprised her by raising his head and addressing her.

"I'm off to Wales tomorrow," he announced, "to see Mord. I'm not sure when I'll be back, so Tess'll be staying here."

"*Why*?" asked Jo in frustration. She sat down. "I'll be fine on my own."

Trevor moved a bishop. "She doesn't think so."

"And what do *you* think? You know what she's like."

He looked at her from under uncombed hair. "The only way to stop her nagging you, Jo-girl, is to give in on this nonsense about leaving school."

"Trevor, *please* don't call me Jo-girl." She looked at Ken, who gave a self-conscious smile. "Hello, Ken," she said.

"Hello, Jo."

He went back to studying the chess board. Jo knew he was embarrassed, and felt sorry for him. She gave Trevor a hard look. "So you're definitely doing this thing with Mord, then, are you?"

"We're discussing it," he told her. "I can't make any definite plans until your mother calms down a bit, and you know..."

"...what she's like?"

Trevor shoved his hair off his forehead with the back of his hand. It fell forward again immediately. Jo tried to observe him objectively, as if he were a stranger. If she saw him on the Tube, or sitting in the corner of a café reading a newspaper, what would she see? A forty-ish man who looked like he could do with a good meal, a good wash and a haircut? Would it even cross her mind that he might be someone's dad? "Trev," she said tolerantly, "I don't think living with me is exactly going to calm Tess down."

"Checkmate," announced Ken, moving pieces busily. "Want another match, try to even things up?"

Trevor shook his head. His bony shoulders drooped, as if they couldn't support the disappointment of losing the chess match, which was the latest piece of shittiness in a pile that had been building up for a long time. "I'd rather go to the pub," he suggested. "Winner buys the first round."

"So that'll be a triple whisky and chaser, then, will it?" asked Ken cheerfully, getting up and taking his jacket off the back of the chair.

They both looked at Jo. "Revision to do, Jo-gir...ah, Jo?" asked Trevor.

Jo sighed. She almost couldn't be bothered to tell him. "My exams finished *ages* ago. That's why I've been at work today, in the shop." She looked up at him, knowing she was being irritating but not caring. "I haven't got to go to school, you see. There's nothing to do there. It makes sense really, when you think about it."

She saw Ken give Trevor a nervous look, half-smiling, as if he were expecting a fight to break out, of which he would be the unwilling referee. But the weight on Trevor's shoulders, or his longing for a drink, was preoccupying him. He didn't notice Jo's sarcasm. To Ken's evident relief, all he said was, "See you later, then. Be good."

When they'd gone she went on sitting at the table for a few minutes, wondering what she actually *was* going to do with the evening. She glanced at the clock; seven minutes past seven. She didn't want to watch TV all alone in the sitting room, or play a computer game upstairs, or chat on Facebook to people she saw all the time anyway, or trawl the internet, or read a magazine, or a book...A *book*? After five solid years of enslavement to books?

She thought about Toby, who had made his escape from books, apparently without opposition from his sweet-faced mum or his shadowy, absent dad. All day, she'd been troubled by the uneasy look in his eyes as he'd stood there in the Staff Room, turning the replacement phone over and over. They'd avoided each other, Toby upstairs, Jo downstairs. At lunchtime she and Sophie had gone to a coffee shop without telling him, and at six o'clock Jo had made sure she got in and out of the Staff Room before Toby came down. It was childish, but Jo didn't know what else to do. One of them would have to approach the other eventually, but she was sure – almost sure, anyway – that it shouldn't be her.

What had he been looking for, when he'd asked her if she had anything to say to him, and Eloise had come in? Did he want Jo to dump him, so he wouldn't have to dump *her*? She chewed the inside of her cheek, pondering anxiously. What would a screenwriter make his characters do at this point? The girl would get kidnapped, or trapped by an earthquake or something, and the boy would rescue her, and they'd realize they were made for each other and all the stuff about meeting other friends, getting drinks spiked and having phones nicked would be forgotten. No, not forgotten. Re-assigned as the necessary growing-pains of the relationship, yadda, yadda, *bleurgh*.

Romance and psychobabble, all in one movie.

*Bleugh*, she thought again. And no amount of babble, psycho or otherwise, would help her decide what to do about Toby. Or stop her feeling horrible about being horrible to him. Or wondering if he was, indeed, being horrible to her, or did she just think he was because Pascale had said he would be?

When her phone rang, she jumped. It was Holly, sounding distant and tinny. "We're on our way to Press Gang," she told Jo. "Me and Ed. Cal's gone on holiday. Do you want us to call for you?"

Jo tried to breathe evenly, calming her heartbeat. She obviously wasn't going anywhere with Toby tonight. And even if Holly's invitation didn't solved the long-term problem he presented, it got rid of this home-alone evening. "Why not?" she said. There was a tiny tremble in her voice, but Holly didn't notice. It wasn't a very good connection. "Listen, Hol," she went on, "my dad's just told me that he's going away tomorrow and Tess is going to be staying here till further notice."

"OhmygodlittleJo!" Holly was understandably horrified. Tess had once told her that she should get her tooth fixed, or she'd end up uglier than the Hunchback of Notre Dame. Holly had avoided her ever since. "We'll be there in ten minutes."

It was Holly who pressed the bell. Jo saw her from the window, and opened the door. Ed was waiting on the path near the gate. He was wearing a tight T-shirt with distressed seams, like the ones Toby had approved of in Rose and Reed. It showed how flat Ed's torso was. The thought flashed through her mind that it must be weird, not having a chest that stuck out in any way, that in fact was almost concave. She realized furtively that Toby, with his contoured muscles, would have looked much better in the T-shirt.

Ed, who hadn't seen Jo since the Summer Ball, nodded at her. She nodded back.

"Hiya!" said Holly. "Oh, you've got my favourite trousers on! I love that logo, the way the two Rs wind around each other. "Will you give them to me when you've finished with them?"

"Hol, you're much taller than me." Jo looked down at the trousers with the Rose and Reed logo on the pocket, noticing they weren't very clean, and that she should have changed when she got home from work. She still had her jacket on, too. But it was too late now. "You can put them in a glass case and admire them, if you like, but you'll never be able to *wear* them."

Holly smiled her crooked-toothed smile and took Jo's arm. "I might wear them as cut-offs, if that didn't make me look like my mum. Come on."

The garden at Press Gang was crowded for a Tuesday evening. Jo, Ed and Holly ordered Frappucinos. Jo had a piece of pineapple cake, too. There were no garden tables free, but they found an abandoned bench with some spilt ice cream on it. Holly wiped it with a tissue and they sat down in a row.

"How am I going to survive?" Jo asked them. "It'll be like Chinese water torture. Drip. A Levels. Drip. A Levels. Drip. A Levels."

Ed looked bored. But Holly sipped, put the cup down carefully and looked seriously at Jo. "Well, don't bite my head off, but I think your mum's absolutely right."

Ed started to say something, but Holly suppressed him.

"I mean," she went on, "Sixth Form is so cool! You get to be a prefect, and sit on School Council." She turned to Ed. "You agree with me, don't you? Jo just *can't* go and work in that horrible shop while we're swanning around at school being fabulous, can she?"

Ed laughed. Jo thought he looked older since she last saw

him, only a couple of weeks ago. That couldn't be, surely, but there *was* something different about him. "That's what you think Sixth Form's like, do you?" he asked Holly. "Being fabulous? They make you do this thing called *work*, you know."

"Oh, Jo won't mind that," said Holly, with enthusiasm. "She's really clever, except at Maths, but since she wouldn't do Maths A Level anyway – "

"Can I speak?" interrupted Jo sulkily. "For a start, in Sixth Form you're still in prison, when you could be off doing something in the real world. And also, if I do leave, I'll still be friends with you all, won't I? After all this time, do you think I'd just abandon you two, and Pascale, and Tom, and Stuart and everyone else?"

There was a pause, which Jo couldn't quite read. She nibbled a corner of the pineapple cake. It wasn't embarrassment that was silencing them, and it certainly wasn't amazement at her brilliantly persuasive argument. Ed was looking into his coffee and tapping his foot lightly on the grass. It suddenly came to Jo that he looked different because there was no gel on his hair. He'd stopped being a wethead.

Holly's expression was as fervent as an evangelical preacher. "Oh...*Jo!*" The words were a long, strangled sigh, loud enough for the couple at a nearby table to turn and stare. She lowered her voice. "Even if we *do* all stay friends," – she saw Jo's expression – "which we will, of course, it won't be the same without you. Look how great Summer Ball was this year, and we've got two more to come! And when you're in Upper Sixth you get to be voted Kingsgrove or Queensgrove, and you might be chosen to be Head Girl." She noticed that Ed was grinning and Jo was frowning. "Only if you *want* to be, of course," she added.

Jo could feel her spirits sinking. She put her plate down on the grass. The cake felt like a stone in her stomach, and that thing inside her was doing its theme-park ride again. "Holly," she said as unaggressively as her plunging mood would allow, "I don't want to be voted Queensgrove at next year's Summer Ball, and I don't want to be Head Girl. I never want to see any of the teachers again. I don't want to hear Tess and Trevor moaning at each other on the phone about whose turn it is to go to Parents' Evening, or Speech Day, or the Christmas play, or the Carol Service." She watched Holly's blank expression become animated again; she knew what she was about to say, and stopped her. "And I don't want to do a single freakin' A Level, and I *especially* don't want to go to freakin' university!"

There was a silence. Ed, who had stopped grinning, cleared his throat. "Are you going to eat that, Jo?" he asked.

Jo looked down at the unfinished slice of cake. An ant was exploring the rim of the plate. "Help yourself."

Ed picked up the plate and stuck the fork into the creamiest bit of cake. "Thanks."

During this exchange, Holly had evidently been re-thinking her tactics. She looked sympathetically at Jo. "Look, we understand, don't we, Ed?"

Ed, munching, made no response.

"I mean, we've *all* just done exams. We're *all* fed up with Miss Balcombe's attempts to be a teacher. We're *all* glad to see the back of the National Sodding Curriculum. But we've got the summer to forget all that, and we can start again in September with courses we've *chosen*."

Jo sipped her coffee silently.

"No Triple Science?" encouraged Holly, squeezing Jo's arm. "No PE?"

Jo sipped a bit more. "I'm not going back, Hol."

Holly drew breath to protest, but she was stopped by the

sound of Ed clanging the fork onto the empty plate. He held it down with his thumb and picked up his coffee. "Sounds to me like Jo's made up her mind," he said, with no approval or disapproval, or judgement, or irony, or loading of any of the words.

Jo could feel her neck going pink. Ed understood. No-nonsense Ed, willing to obliterate every argument Holly had mustered with one sensible stroke.

It was too much for Holly. "Oh, *Ed*, what's the matter with you?" She seized Jo's right wrist, pinching it uncomfortably "Come on, Jo, let's go down to the river and look at the ducks, shall we? Just you and me."

"I don't want to look at the ducks," protested Jo. "What about my coffee?"

"We'll be back in a minute." Holly was raising and lowering her eyebrows like someone in a sitcom, trying to send a silent message. Jo knew she wanted to talk about something not for Ed's ears.

"Let me finish my coffee first," she insisted.

Over the rim of the cup Jo caught Ed's eyes. They were smiling. "What if I just don't listen?" he suggested to Holly. "I've got my earphones with me."

"It's all right, Ed," said Jo before Holly could speak. "I haven't seen those ducks for at least a month." She drained her cup. "Lead on, boss."

She followed Holly between the parties of drinkers down to the riverbank. The water was low, and most of the ducks were sitting on the grass hoping for scraps from Press Gang's customers. They usually only got cigarette packets and chocolate wrappers, but being ducks, they never learnt.

Holly pulled Jo out of earshot of everyone except the ducks. "Now *listen*," she said sternly. "You're not going to want to hear this, but I'm going to say it anyway. Ready?"

Jo didn't have time to respond.

"This stupid nonsense about leaving school is all because of Toby Ferguson, isn't it?" demanded Holly, frowning so hard that the open-eyed prettiness she usually displayed had disappeared completely. Her face was one big mass of concern.

Relief made Jo want to hug her. "Jeez, Holly, is *that* what you think? It's *ages* since I decided I was going to leave – long before I met Toby!" Around the time Tess left, she thought. The fifteenth of February. By the end of that month Jo's mind had been made up. She'd mentioned it to Mrs Bull, who had tried to persuade Jo to consider A Level Computer Studies, and Mrs Bull had obviously told Mr Treasure.

"But when you *did* meet Toby," continued Holly, undaunted, "and he started showing off about having his independence, and getting a car, and being a fashion buyer and all that, you thought you could do the same, didn't you?"

Jo was offended. "I don't want to be a fashion buyer," she said, though she knew this wasn't what Holly had meant. "I just want to leave school."

"And do *what*?" persisted Holly. "I mean, *has* Toby got his independence? *Has* he got a car? *Is* he a fashion buyer? Well?"

Holly's eyes looked shiny. This was really important to her. Her chest was going up and down as she tried to control her breathing. Her anxiety as she waited for Jo's words was certainly flattering. But somehow, it was annoying, too.

"You know he hasn't," said Jo coldly.

Holly's tears, precariously balanced on her lower lids, escaped. She was looking pretty again, though, even with her nose going pink. She sniffed. "Exactly. Without decent GCSEs you can't do anything – everyone knows that, which is why people never shut up about it, and get slaughtered on vodka and God-knows-what on Results Day. But you *will* get decent GCSEs, because you worked hard for them." Her eyes filled with more tears, and she sniffed again. "But why do all that work, Jo, then throw the results away, because of a *boy*?

"It's *not* because of a boy!"

People nearby turned to see who was shouting. Jo didn't know she had shouted. With an effort to calm herself, she lowered her voice. "I couldn't give a toss what Toby has or hasn't done," she told Holly. "But at least he made the decision to leave school when he was sixteen, and did it. And if I want to, so will I."

Holly looked stricken. She wiped her cheeks with her palms. "Right."

Jo thought for a moment that she'd won, and Holly had given in. But the word wasn't a surrender; it was a decision. Holly had one more round of ammunition to fire. She wiped her nose with her fingers and raised swimming eyes to Jo's face. "Has Toby ever told you exactly *why* he left St Bede's?"

Jo's heart began to jerk about. This wasn't fair. This was a blow below the belt.

"What's this about, Hol?" she asked suspiciously.

"He was expelled."

"*What*?" Jo wasn't prepared. She'd had a few seconds to prepare a scene involving a job offer he couldn't refuse, or terrible GCSE results. But she hadn't considered this.

"It's true, Jo, I promise."

"And how do you know?" asked Jo indignantly.

Holly looked very uncomfortable. "I found out through my mum's friend Liz."

Jo was so surprised she felt her mouth slacken. She knew she was staring at Holly, but couldn't stop. "And how the bloody hell does this Liz know anything about Toby?"

"She's the school nurse at St Bede's."

Jo struggled to digest this. Some phrase like 'professional confidence' hovered in the back of her mind. "And she's been gossiping to your mum? What a bitch!"

"Jo!" Holly was horror-struck. "It was *me* she told, not Mum. It came up by accident. Liz was at our house and we were just talking, and when I heard where she works I asked her if she'd known a boy called Toby Ferguson. I had no idea what she was going to say – I was as shocked as you are. He was expelled two years ago, when he was sixteen. Before he even took his GCSEs."

Jo felt weak. He had never done his exams. No wonder he hadn't got very far into art school, or fashion buying. "What was he expelled for?"

"Liz didn't know. Or maybe she did know, but she realized by then that she shouldn't have said anything." Holly slid Jo a nervous glance. "I know she was wrong, and maybe I was too. But I'm just so worried about you."

"I bet you are." Jo couldn't help sounding mean. She felt like a world class dickhead. She began to walk back up the riverbank. "Thanks for your concern."

"Jo..." Holly hurried after her. "Wait a minute."

Jo stopped, and the two girls faced each other. They were near enough now for people to hear. Holly was almost crying again. "Please, little Jo," she pleaded. "You can shoot the messenger if you like – I don't care how angry you are with me. But for your own sake, just do what's right, will you?"

# Chapter Ten

Trevor loaded his car with as many of his belongings as he could, and he and Jo stood self-consciously on the pavement beside it. Suddenly Trevor lunged forward, grabbed Jo's shoulders and kissed the top of her head like he used to when she was little.

"Be good, now, Jo-girl," he said, his breath damp on Jo's scalp. "Don't let her get to you."

"I'll be fine," Jo reassured him. "Don't worry about me."

He stood back and looked at her. The late afternoon sunshine showed the colours in his hair, and the criss-cross lines beside his eyes and mouth. Jo wondered if, when he was eventually free, some other woman would make him happier than Tess had.

"Send me a text or something?" he asked.

"Course," said Jo. Tears nearly came, but she stopped them, and flapped her hands at him. "Go on, just go, before this gets like the last scene of *The Return of the King*."

"What happens in the last scene of *The Return of the King*?" he asked, opening the car door.

"They're saying goodbye to each other," explained Jo. "You know, the hobbits. But it takes so long, most people have left the cinema and are half way home before the credits actually roll."

Trevor laughed. "Edited by Joanna Probert – ruthlessly.

That's a credit I'd like to see."

"Maybe you will, some day," said Jo. Producer, screenplay-writer, director, actress, editor. And finally, censor.

Trevor drove away, honking the horn and probably waving, though there was so much stuff in the car Jo couldn't see what he was doing. Jo waved anyway, then she went back into the house.

Tess was leaning into the mirror by the front door, painting her lips with a lip brush. "Has he gone?" she said to Jo's reflection.

Jo nodded.

"Well, he'll soon be back. His little enterprise is guaranteed to go belly-up." Tess stood back and scrutinized her handiwork. "Is this colour too dark for me?"

"Nothing's too dark for you," said Jo. *Moderate Horror*.

"It's just that this make-up has got to last all evening, but I don't want it to look too...you know..."

"Tarty?" suggested Jo.

"...showy. I mean, it's only teatime now, but I won't have the chance to take off my daytime face and put on my evening one, so I was just wondering..." – she pursed her lips, as if she were about to kiss the mirror – "...if it's a bit OTT."

Jo felt as if she'd walked into the wrong studio in the multiplex. What was going on in front of her was so banal, so inane, and so wrong, wrong, *wrong*, it should never have got the funding in the first place. And now that it had, why was she wasting precious eyesight watching it? "It's fine," she told her mother.

"Right." Tess seemed satisfied. She put the lipstick and brush in her make-up bag and closed it with an emphatic click. "I'll just get my shoes on, then I'll be off."

"Where are you going?"

"Oh, here and there," said Tess, starting up the stairs. "You can get your own supper, can't you, darling?"

Jo didn't even bother answering this. She thought about Trevor heading for the motorway with the window open and the fan full on, because Tess wasn't there complaining about her hair getting messed up, or demanding to know why he didn't have a car with air conditioning like any normal person. He'd probably be singing, too. 'Rhinestone Cowboy', or, if he was especially pleased with himself, 'Copacabana'.

Her throat constricted. This was *stupid*.

Tess clonked downstairs in very high heels. "If you go out, remember to lock up the house," she instructed Jo, giving herself one last inspection in the mirror. "And feed Blod."

Jo knew there was no point in mentioning that for months and months *she* was the one who had managed the locking up of the house and the feeding of the cat, along with many other things, while Trevor had been in the pub. She didn't say anything. She didn't even nod.

Tess whipped round. "Are you sulking?" she asked sharply. "Because if you are, let me tell you, young lady, that cuts no ice with me. Trevor's gone and that's that."

Jo still didn't speak.

"I mean it!" After she'd said this Tess set her mouth in a shiny line, checked she'd got her keys, opened the front door, strode out and slammed it behind her.

"*I'm* sulking!" said Jo to the space where Tess had stood.

Into her mind came an image of the nail scissors, which hung there, glittering, like the ghostly dagger in *Macbeth*. She saw Holly's blue eyes, pleading with her to be sensible and weeping when Jo had refused. And she saw Toby's grey eyes, getting darker and darker as he stood there lying to her.

It was insanity, but it *worked*. In that split-second of relief, the little spurt of blood, the mark on her skin, everything would disappear. Trevor's desertion. Tess's uncomprehending unkindness. Toby's fingers grasping the top of the lacy knickers she'd so knowingly put on, fumbling for the secret place, filling her with panic and revulsion. The little scissors would cut out her pain.

She pictured the scarred, scary girl she'd seen in a scandal-mag Pascale had brought into school. The patch on Jo's arm where she'd picked and picked the flesh, destroying the scab every time it formed, had already scarred, quite noticeably. It was a secret scar though, hidden by all but the shortest sleeves.

Jo didn't want to look like the girl in the magazine. She'd stop before it got anywhere near that. But not now. She grasped the banister she could no longer see, hauling herself up, step by step.

The scissors were in their place. She opened them and stared. Two blades. More pain, more relief. It had been a hot day, and she was wearing a short cotton Rose and Reed skirt. She caught hold of the hem to pull it up, then paused. Would two points cause twice the bloodshed of one? It was Wednesday today; Sylvia the Chinese Cleaner was due tomorrow. She wouldn't have said anything about a tissue in a bin, especially not to Trevor, but if she found a larger bloodstain in Jo's room, on the window seat cushion, or the carpet, she would wonder what it was, and perhaps mention it, cautiously, anxiously, to Tess.

Jo remembered with relief that she was alone in the house. She didn't have to hide in the bedroom. Clutching the open scissors, aware that their points were digging into her palm, she went downstairs.

The garden lay under the low light of a warm, early-August evening. Jo remembered the white brightness that had drenched Toby's garden, obliterating everything in it. Her behaviour that day had been unforgivable; she hadn't encountered Mrs Ferguson since, and didn't know what she would say when she did. *If* she did. But what she'd felt was panic. Desperation, like you'd feel if you were drowning, or someone was trying to strangle you.

But this numbing, half-blind compulsion was a different desperation. She just *had* to do it.

She went down the path and plunged into the green gloom under the bushes near the shed, ducking as a pair of wood pigeons flapped indignantly away. No one could see her. Her heart pumping hard, she pulled up her skirt and the edge of her knickers, tensed her leg and stuck the twin blades into her groin. Then she pulled them out again and sank to her knees on the leaf-strewn earth under the laurel bush. Eyes closed, she knelt there, breathing softly and regularly until she calmed. She opened her eyes, her wounded flesh burning, and inspected what she had done.

Two blades hadn't caused twice as much damage, or twice as much blood, as one, but they had made an untidier cut. She'd forgotten to bring a tissue. As the blood oozed up, startlingly red and thick-looking, like cheap jam, she pulled off some laurel leaves and pressed them to the spot. Her hand clamped to her groin, she crept into the darkness of the shed. Gratefully, like an animal finding a place to give birth, she sat down on a stack of rodent-ravaged newspapers in the corner, her back against the wall, dizzy with still-hot pain.

Through the open shed door the house looked abandoned, uninhabited except for a prowling Blod. Later, when it was too dark for any neighbours to notice her blood-streaked leg from an upstairs window, Jo would slip furtively across the lawn, and let herself back into the empty house.

\* \* \* \* \* \*

The next morning, Jo turned from the cupboard in the Staff Room, her identity tag dangling round her neck, to find Toby blocking the doorway. He stood with his hands in the back pockets of his jeans, his shoulders hunched. It was a while since he'd got his hair done, she noticed suddenly, and it sprang up in tufts. Her heart was stirred by the apprehension in his eyes. "Hello," she said.

They still hadn't spoken since their uncomfortable exchange on Tuesday morning. Neither had called or texted the other. Jo had thought Toby would come in this morning, ignore her and go straight up to Menswear. But here he was.

"I can't stand this" he said.

He came towards her, giving her a modified version of The Look, with more sexy and less funny. She could hear Eloise greeting Sophie upstairs in the shop. They'd come down soon. Whatever Toby was going to do, he'd better do it quick.

He rubbed the tops of Jo's arms with the palms of his hands. "I just couldn't go on with the 'I'm offended' act."

"Me too," said Jo. Wondering if this was the truth, she decided to say something she had no doubts about. "I mean, I didn't do so great myself on Saturday. I must have sounded like...I don't know, some sort of – "

"Some sort of *you*." He gave up on The Look, gathered her to his chest and put his face in her hair. His heart beat steadily underneath her right ear. "That's the thing about you, Jo. You can't be someone you're not."

His words resonated through Jo's skull. In a sudden rush of understanding she realized that she liked him putting his chin on her head like this, simply because it was something he did. If she could be some sort of *her*, then he could be some sort of *him*.

She felt relieved, and grateful to Toby that he'd been the one to give in. It didn't matter what he'd been doing in that club. It was all childish and distant now. Now, it felt right to be squashed between him and the cupboard door, with her arms round his waist and her head on his chest.

He took a breath and released it. "Would it help if I said I know I acted like an idiot, and that's the reason I went out clubbing and got too drunk to know my phone was being nicked?"

"It might," said Jo.

Toby took hold of a strand of her hair and began to wind it round his finger. "Are we cool?"

"We're cool."

He kissed the top of her head. "I thought you'd dumped me."

"No, you didn't." Jo smiled, though he couldn't see her face.

"Shall we go out on Saturday? For a curry?"

"I'd rather go to a movie."

He stepped back and looked at her with his head on one side. Jo gazed at his arms coming out of his short sleeves, and his wristwatch nestling among the hairs on his wrist. He was so familiar that she couldn't remember a time when she didn't know him. It seemed like hundreds of years ago, in some ancient, forgotten time. BT. Before Toby. "Come on," she coaxed. "I promise I won't criticize the editing, or the direction, or the writing. And *you're* the one that always criticizes the clothes."

He smiled a proper, toothy smile. Jo hadn't seen the smile for so long it sent a jolt of pleasure through her.

"All right, then," he agreed. "But only if we can go for a curry afterwards."

* * * * * *

Tess came in the back door, weighed down with yellow and purple plastic bags from Oxford Street stores. Without saying hello, she gave Jo a look. "So have you been thinking about which subjects to take next year?"

It was Friday night. Jo, exhausted from the week in the shop, was trying to eat a bowl of pasta she'd cooked herself for supper. She wasn't very hungry, and she suspected the half-used jar of pasta sauce she'd found in the fridge had been there too long. "Tess, I haven't even got my results yet," she said patiently. "I might fail everything."

Tess put her load down on the kitchen floor. "No you won't," she said airily. "And anyway, that's irrelevant. They'll take you back whatever happens. Alan Treasure is a personal friend of mine."

"Really? Poor him." Jo's mouth was full of spaghetti, some of which landed back in the bowl when she said the 'p' on 'poor'.

Tess's voice took on an accusing tone. "You are such a rude girl! Who taught you to be so rude? Not me, I'm sure."

"Must have been Trevor, then."

Tess took off her jacket, hung it on the back of a kitchen chair and sat down. "Haven't seen much of Tony recently. What's up?"

"For God's sake, Tess, his name's *Toby*."

"Cracking at the edges, is it?" asked Tess, putting her chin on her hands. "How long's it been? Couple of months? Well, time for a bit of structural damage to show through."

"It's *two and a half* months." Jo picked up the bowl and

156

tipped the rest of the pasta into the bin. "You don't know anything about him, and you couldn't care less. You can't even be bothered to remember his name."

"Trevor says he's a very personable young man."

Jo slung the empty bowl into the sink. "I don't care what Trevor says. Or you, for that matter. I can see Toby or not see Toby without sharing the information with *you*, thanks very much."

"Oh, don't be such a sourpuss," said Tess, with exaggerated scorn. "When the wind changes your face will stay like that if you're not careful, and you'll end up as ugly as..." She abandoned the sentence, preferring to lean towards Jo with a listen-to-this look. "You know, my lunch crowd were *very* interested to hear that my little girl's got a boyfriend. They can't believe you're so grown up, darling!"

This, of course, was because Tess didn't look old enough to have a sixteen-year-old daughter. "Really?" said Jo from the sink, clattering the plates. "Did you tell them I'm grown up enough to have a job in a shop, too?"

Through the kitchen window she watched Blod stalking a bird under the rhododendron bush. Life must be simple if you're a cat, she thought. You wouldn't have to put up with Trevor going off to Wales and leaving you with an incurable, ingrained, permanent, unchangeable *snob*. "No, of course you didn't," she added lightly. "But you'll have to tell them when I leave school and work there permanently, won't you?"

"You're *not* doing that!" Tess stood up. She picked up a tea cloth and twisted it between her hands. "What would people say? Everyone I know sends their children to university. None of my friends will ever speak to me again if you leave now."

"Well then, you haven't got to worry about what they'll *say*, have you?"

Tess wound the tea towel tighter. "Oh, Jo, why are you being so stubborn?"

"I'm not being stubborn, I'm being practical. And if you keep repeating the same arguments, so will I. How come the shop's good enough for Toby but not good enough for me? Because I'm cleverer than him? How do you know how clever he is?"

"Don't browbeat me, darling!" wailed Tess fretfully. "I'll get a migraine."

"It's all this moaning about A levels that'll give you a migraine," replied Jo, unrelenting.

"Don't be so disagreeable, darling," pleaded Tess. "It makes you look so horrible, and you can look quite nice when you try. I do wish you'd smile more and not sulk so much."

Exasperation surged through Jo. Tess was talking, but she only heard a sort of bleating noise, underpinned by that strange 'r' sound like the droning of a wasp. "Tess!" She slammed her fists down on the table. "Just shut up, will you? Shut *up*!"

Tess stopped twisting the towel and looked at Jo in astonishment. "You can't speak to me like that!"

"I just *have*," said Jo, breathing heavily through her nose.

All the misery of the last few days gathered behind her eyes. Her mother's red lipstick, heavy mascara and bobbed hair blurred like a reflection in a distorting mirror. Jo's eyeballs burned, but the tears didn't fall. "Will you just *listen*?" she wailed. "For the millionth time, *you can't make me do something I don't want to do!*"

Tess put her hands over her eyes. Her small nose, pink with emotion, protruded from between them. A shock wave passed through her gym-toned, expensively dressed body, and she began to shake. Standing there, drawing quivering breaths, striving for control, she looked like an abandoned child. She sobbed quietly for a few moments. Then she wiped her nose on the towel. "I just can't bear the thought of you throwing away your chance to..." She sighed heavily. "It's such a *waste*."

Jo breathed in, held her breath for a moment, and let it out again. "Tess, there is nothing more to say." She stood up. "I'll be upstairs if you want me."

In her bedroom, she opened the DVD labels file and looked at Tess's 'Moderate horror' description. She wondered what sort of daughter goes upstairs and judges her mother as if she were a silver disc slotted into a machine. The same sort of daughter who inflicts pain on herself, and likes it, while loathing herself for it at the same time? The sort of daughter who has a panic attack in her boyfriend's house, in front of his mother?

Stupid, stupid, *stupid*.

She deleted 'Moderate horror', and studied the empty space beside her mother's name. Suddenly, she felt hot. From the depths of her brain, or perhaps her heart, came a spurt of vitriol. The shininess of Tess's shopping bags, the pinkness of her nose, the fatuousness of her attempts to engage Jo in girl-talk – all of it enraged her beyond endurance. She began to flip through DVD cases.

Here was a good one: 'Strong, violent horror'. She typed it in, half-wishing it could be 'Weak, violent horror', which described Tess better. But part of the game was using *real* DVD guidelines, not made-up ones, and she had to stick to the rules she'd made for herself. That was what it was all about – being in control. She sat back, satisfied.

But in the next instant her satisfaction vanished. Regret, as futile as Miss Balcombe's French lessons, took its place. Venting her fury on Tess had achieved nothing. She thought about the slow-to-heal wound in her groin. Had that achieved anything? Really, tangibly improved anything, except her reluctant, recurrent, ever-rising desperation? She was still confused about Toby. Trevor was still a drunk. Tess was still Tess. The computer screen still stared back at her. And she still felt desperately, incurably useless, as if everything she did seemed OK at first, but then wasn't.

Sighing, she pushed the keyboard away. If her life was a movie, she decided, the audience would have left by now.

# Chapter Eleven

In the cinema, Jo put her hand on Toby's leg as a sort of experiment. He was so deep in concentration on the film that he didn't notice. She pressed her hand into his thigh a bit harder, and he put his hand over hers. But after a few moments, when both their hands got sweaty, he took it off again. Feeling a fool, she did the same.

"Hello lovebirds!" trilled Tess when they got back from the Indian restaurant. She was sitting at the kitchen table with half a bottle of wine in one hand and a full glass in the other, while Blod circled her chair. "I'm as drunk as a skunk, and as happy as a hatstand!"

"I thought you were going out," said Jo, opening the fridge. "Toby wants a beer. Did Trevor leave any?"

"Hello, Toby darling!" called Tess, raising her glass to him as he stood in the doorway. Jo almost laughed at how embarrassed he was.

"Hello, Mrs Probert," he muttered.

"Mrs Probert? Who's she?" Tess's voice rose to a near shriek. She leaned closer to Toby. "My name is Thérèse Pratt, Tess to my loved ones, and that includes *you*."

"Um..." said Toby.

Jo retrieved a bottle of beer from the back of the fridge. While she searched the drawer for the opener she tried again to make Tess talk sense. "Why aren't you out?"

"Little me on my little ownsome tonight," said Tess. She gulped down the glass of wine without taking breath and poured another. "We decided not to go."

"Who's we?" asked Jo, raising her eyebrows at Toby as she handed him the beer.

"Me and my friend."

"Who, Erica?" asked Jo. To Toby she said, "The one with the lilac sports car," and he smiled. He still looked self-conscious, though.

"*Not* Erica," said Tess decisively. "*Definitely* not Erica."

"Oh Tess, have you fallen out with her?" asked Jo in mock-dismay.

"None of your business, Miss Nosy Parker." Tess had put the bottle and the lipstick-smudged glass down, and was pushing herself up from the table. "I'd better make myself scarce, hadn't I?" She picked up her handbag and slung the strap over her shoulder, but left her high-heeled shoes where she'd discarded them. As she passed Toby in her bare feet, she didn't even come up to his shoulder. "Nighty night, you two," she said. "Don't do anything I wouldn't do!"

When she'd gone Jo picked up Blod, who miaowed discontentedly. "She didn't feed you, did she?" she murmured into the cat's fur. As it was Saturday, Jo had been at work all day. "Why didn't you scratch her with those lovely claws of yours?"

Toby watched while Jo put down food and water for the cat. Then they went into the sitting room and put the TV on, and Jo went round drawing curtains and putting on lamps. No-one had used the room this evening. Tess obviously *had* been out, and come in earlier, and more in need of alcohol, than she'd intended.

"Your mum's scary," said Toby from the sofa.

"You think?" Jo thought about the 'Strong, violent horror' label. On Results Day, she might have to change it to '*Extremely* strong, violent horror'.

Toby seemed to have read her mind. "I was wondering about something. After your results, shall we go away?"

Jo's insides leapt. She stopped tugging at the stubborn curtain over the French windows. "On holiday, you mean?"

"Ye-es," he said with a little frown.

"Tess would never let me go."

"Because of the money?"

"No, not because of the *money*!" Abandoning the curtain, she flopped down beside Toby on the sofa and put her chin on his shoulder. She could feel his collar bone, and the pad of muscle where his neck began. She could smell his shampoo, the curry he'd eaten and the beer in the bottle he held. She could see his chest moving up and down as he breathed. In her head, she strove for the truth. When she had it, she smoothed it, so that Toby wouldn't be hurt by it. "She'd say I don't know you well enough to go on holiday with you, and I'm too young anyway."

"Oh," was all he said.

Between his body and Jo's an unspoken message was being transmitted. What do people do on holiday? They spend the day on the beach then they go back to the hotel room and make love. Then they go out for dinner and come back and make love again. They even make love in the morning before breakfast. They're miles away from parents, work, husbands, wives, whatever they want to get away from. What they do in that hotel room is a secret between them, to be remembered for years – perhaps forever. But she and Toby weren't going to do any of that.

"I'm always forgetting you're only sixteen," he said, and took a mouthful of beer. When he'd swallowed it he squeezed Jo more tightly against him. "You act older than me most of the time."

Jo sighed. "I get a lot of practice," she told him, "with parents like mine."

"But they'll still refuse to let you go on holiday with me?"

"Of course."

He finished the beer and set the bottle on the floor beside him. Jo thought he'd start to kiss her, but he disentangled himself and stood up. "Think I'd better get going. Work in the morning."

Jo stood up too, somehow feeling relieved. She wondered if it was relief that he hadn't started to put his hands on her – she was wearing her new skirt again, and she didn't want his fingers to encounter the plaster at the top of her leg – or that she wouldn't be going on holiday with him. "You're not working Sunday again, are you?" she asked. "That's about four weeks running."

"Gordon needs the help." At the front door, he bent to kiss her. His lips felt wet and tasted of beer. "And I'll get Tuesday and Wednesday off."

Monday was Jo's day off. "So I won't see you in the shop till Thursday, then?"

He blinked. "Guess not. Take care." And before she could reply he turned and strode to the gate.

Jo shut the door behind him and leaned against it.

*Guess not*?

Her breathing felt shallow, and she noticed that she was trembling a little, like she sometimes did in the winter when she was waiting for the bus in her blazer and skirt. It wasn't cold in the hall, though. In fact, it was hot. It was *shock* that was making her tremble – shock that Toby could ignore her hint even more blatantly than she'd dropped it.

Thursday was five days away. Why didn't she have the courage to ask what he did on his days off, or insist he took her out more often than Saturday nights? If Pascale, who at this moment was doubtless being drooled over by some flashy-looking Spanish boy, had witnessed that throwaway *Guess not*, what would she have done?

She pushed herself off the door and went back to the sitting room. It was gloomy, full of shadows, the people on the silent TV screen mouthing pathetically. Jo lunged for the remote, and suddenly, overwhelmingly, an intolerable weight began to press on her from every direction. She collapsed on the sofa, clutching her stomach. What the hell was this?

The feeling increased. It wasn't panic, or confusion, or despair. It was something wilder than any of those; something violent. She thought about the sticky flesh under the plaster on her arm. Then she stopped thinking about it. Mastering this new, crushing opponent needed more than an assault on the scratch-patch. But there was no time for, and no possibility of, going upstairs and getting out the nail scissors. Jo sat there, her eyes roving the room, searching for a weapon.

On the table lay her school pencil-case, a legacy of those far-off days when she used to sit here and revise while Trevor was in the pub. Jo hauled herself up and seized it, rummaging with purposeful fingers until she found her compass. She couldn't wait the few seconds it would take to pull her skirt up and her tights down to expose her upper leg where she'd driven the scissors in on Saturday night. She had to do this *now*, or the enemy, whatever it was, would overcome her.

She was still wearing her jacket. There was no time to take it off. She pushed up the left sleeve with her right hand. It wouldn't go any further than halfway up her forearm, but that would have to do. Holding her breath, she drove the point of the compass into the fleshy part just above her wrist. She drove it in hard, much harder than with the scissors.

There was quite a lot of blood. Swallowing, striving for control, she stumbled into the downstairs toilet and grabbed a handful of paper. She had to flush several gory wads away before she could return to the sitting-room, her jacket sleeve hiding the toilet-paper bandage, her heartbeat slowing. In her right hand she still held the compass.

She looked at it carefully, turning it over and over in her hand as if it were a cherished object. It *was* a cherished object. It was a trophy, evidence of a conquest. She suddenly felt light-hearted, as if nothing could ever matter, in the whole world, for the whole future. She knew that all these people – the ones she had secretly labelled, as if they were movies – couldn't just trample over her without causing actual, running-down-the-arm bloodshed.

A noise, a kind of buzzing, started in her head. She sat down shakily at the table, wondering if this was, at last, the onset of insanity. Then she realized that it was the sound of her phone, ringing in her handbag. Grabbing it untidily, she managed to answer it before the caller rang off. There was no caller ID, just a number. "Hello?" she said warily.

"Jo? It's Ed."

"*Ed*?" she repeated inanely. "Ed Samuels?"

"Yeah, same old Ed."

What was Ed doing, phoning her? He didn't even have her number. She was too nonplussed to speak.

"Look, can I meet you somewhere?" He sounded nervous. "Tomorrow? I just need to talk to you about something."

Jo's brain began, slowly and wearily, to work. "What about that coffee shop on the corner? With the awning?"

"Gino's?"

"That's the one."

"Eleven?" suggested Ed. There was relief in his voice. "I've got to be at work for twelve."

"See you then," said Jo.

"Thanks, Jo."

He hung up. Jo stared stupidly at the phone for a moment. Gino's, with its plastic plants and grubby striped awning, was a place no one from school ever, *ever* went. That's why she'd suggested it, and why Ed had been relieved at her suggestion. Obviously, as Pascale was in Spain, he didn't want anyone to see him with someone else. But why did he want to see her at all?

* * * * * *

He was sitting at the corner table farthest from the door. When Jo saw his expectant, embarrassed face, the feeling she'd had when they were dancing at the Summer Ball revisited her. He was just so straightforward; he wore his insides on the outside.

She sat down opposite him. "What is it?"

"I expect you can guess." He really *was* embarrassed. His face, and what she could see of his neck above the collar of his Burgerblitz shirt, had gone perfectly pink. He pushed back his hair, which since he'd stopped gelling it fell over his forehead in a clump. "It starts with a P."

"Ah." Any boy who risked going out with Pascale, even if he lasted as long as Ed, had to accept that he'd eventually suffer for it. It was a natural hazard of life. "Look, I'm not sure I can help much," said Jo, beginning to be embarrassed too.

He pulled his unzipped jacket closer around his body, twisting sideways on his chair so he wouldn't have to look at Jo. He planted his feet and stared between them at the floor. "I think she's seeing someone else."

The milk-frothing machine suddenly began to roar. At the same moment, a girl with a notepad appeared at their table and looked at Jo expectantly.

"Oh...a latte, please."

Ed's coffee was only half drunk, but he ordered another. He probably had to stay awake, flipping burgers until midnight. Jo waited for the noise to end, then she said, "Ed...why are you telling *me* this?"

Unexpectedly, Ed looked straight at her. It wasn't The Look – he'd never consider bestowing that on Jo – but it was meaningful. Suddenly, its meaning came to her, and a miniscule shift in his gaze showed that he knew she'd understood. They looked at one another for a long moment, then Jo got up, pulled her chair nearer to his, and sat down again. You couldn't be too careful, even in Gino's. "You think she's seeing *Toby*?"

He nodded miserably.

Jo's blood-vessels had contracted, every one of them. Her body shuddered with a cold, mean spasm. Under her cardigan she could feel the hairs on her arms sticking up. "What makes you think that?" she whispered.

"She's kind of gone cold on me."

"Toby's gone cold on me too," said Jo before she could stop herself.

Ed was immediately alert. He looked at her with bright eyes. "It's bloody obvious who they're *hot* for, then, isn't it?"

Jo strongly wished her words unsaid. "No, I didn't mean that, exactly." She tried to say what she *did* mean. "Um...it was ages ago that...well..." Nothing she could think of was suitable for Ed's ears. Girls didn't go around telling boys about the stuff that had gone on, or rather hadn't, between Toby and herself. She tried again. "I just get the feeling he's not really concentrating on me."

Ed didn't say anything. He was leaning his elbows on the table, his head in his hands. He looked very dejected.

"Have you actually *seen* her with Toby?" asked Jo gently.

"*I* haven't, no."

"Who has, then?"

"Poins."

For Pascale's brother Poins to be a witness, Toby must have been in the little igloo house. Jo felt dismayed. "*Poins?*"

Ed leaned back and put his hands in his trouser pockets. "I was round at Pascale's on the Friday night before they went to Spain, waiting for her while she was getting changed. I was playing cards with Poins. You know what he's like, always wanting to play some game. Then he asked me if he could do some card tricks on me, but I refused because I hate all that crap, and he said that the other bloke that called for Pascale the other day let him do card tricks so why wouldn't I? And when I asked what bloke, he realized, and went all shy, and said he didn't know his name. So I asked him what he looked like and believe me, Jo, it was Toby."

The waitress brought their coffee. Jo spooned some of the froth off the top of her latte, her brain busy. "What did he say about him?"

"Are you sure you want to hear it?"

"Just say it, Ed."

"He said the bloke had jeans on with 'RR' on the pocket. Like Rolls Royce."

Jo tried to think rationally. Poins, who liked cars and planes, *would* notice that. "Lots of people buy Rose and Reed jeans," she said.

"And this bloke had dark hair, and he looked done up, Poins said. I guess he meant sort of well-groomed. Like Toby." Ed's

169

brown eyes were watching her nervously. "What do you think?"

Jo's brain was still busy. That Friday was the day of the staff meeting at work. The day she'd said that stupid thing to Toby. The next day, he'd tried to have sex with her in a taxi. And the day after that, Sunday, was the day Jo had gone round to consult Doctor Pascale on what to do about Toby. She put down her spoon. She felt sick.

"Oh my God," she said in a small voice.

"Are you all right?" asked Ed, his expression sharpening.

"Oh my God," she said again. "I talked to Pascale about Toby...personal things..."

"When?"

"The day before she went on holiday. The Sunday. And I had a pizza after work with Toby that Friday, the day he..."

She swallowed. She was sure she was going to be sick.

"The day Poins saw him at Pascale's later on?" supplied Ed.

Jo's heart began to thud. "Why didn't you say anything sooner?" she asked, trying not to sound as if she was accusing him. "I mean, this is more than a week ago."

"I've been thinking about it," he confessed. "You know, wondering." He gave her one of his candid looks. "But she's coming back from Spain tomorrow, and I couldn't stand it any longer."

Jo picked up her coffee and sipped it. Her nausea diminishing, she tried to sound businesslike. "What are we going to do?" She took another sip. "If we confront them, they'll just deny it."

He went on looking straight at her, his mouth in a line. Then he laughed. The way he looked when he laughed reminded Jo of the moment when he'd pulled her towards him when they'd danced. The thing with Ed, she decided, was that he didn't mess around. If he wanted to dance with you, he did it. If he wanted to know what his girlfriend was doing with your boyfriend, he asked. And if he wanted to laugh, he laughed. "Christ, Jo, we're a right pair!"

"I think it'll just have to come out of its own accord," she said, realizing this as she said it. "They'll tell us eventually. They'll have to."

Ed nodded. He seemed receptive to this idea.

"And don't forget," went on Jo, "it may be a load of nonsense. Poins might have been making the whole thing up just to get back at you because you wouldn't let him do his stupid card tricks. Pascale doesn't call him Poisonous for nothing."

Ed shook his head. "I *know* she's cheating on me."

"Well, if you get proof, dump her," she told him decisively. Someone had to be the first to fail the never-been-dumped challenge, and if there was any justice in the world, it should be Pascale.

"Don't worry, I will."

Jo knew he would. No messing around. "What time tomorrow does she get back?"

"About three in the afternoon."

They were both silent, thinking about this. "We need to arrange some way of getting them together, with us there," said Jo. "Then they won't be able to hide it."

Ed's eyes brightened, though there was still anxiety in them. "We could go on a double date, to Press Gang, maybe, tomorrow night?"

"Toby won't go to Press Gang."

"Why not?"

Jo couldn't admit that Toby refused to tell her. "He just doesn't like the place. In fact, I can't say I'm very keen on it myself."

"Somewhere else then," said Ed, frustration creeping into his voice. "Toby can choose where, if he's so picky."

Jo was dubious. She sipped her coffee mechanically. "I'll try to fix it, but the next day we're both at work is Thursday."

Ed looked at her, not understanding. "Get hold of him on Facebook, then. Or on the phone, or email him or something. I mean, he's your *boyfriend*, Jo."

"OK, but last night I said will I see you before Thursday and he said guess not."

Ed drank a lot of his coffee and clattered the cup back onto the saucer. "God, he *has* gone cold on you, hasn't he?"

Jo felt the beginning of a flush on her cheeks. She couldn't tell him that it wasn't so much that Toby had gone cold on her, it was more like he'd never warmed up. "I'm glad you told me," she said, and put down her cup. "It makes a lot of things clearer." She rested her chin on her hands and stared into the cup, trying to keep her face and voice normal, so that Ed wouldn't realize how profoundly depressed this conversation was making her. "Trouble is, Ed, I feel such an *arse*."

"It's not *you* that's the arse," said Ed, "it's Pascale. She can't act like this and expect to keep her friends. She'll end up such a famous bitch no one will speak to her."

Jo looked up at him. "No she won't. Kingsgrove's not exactly short of bitchy girls. And there'll always be another sucker waiting in line."

"All right," conceded Ed. Then he smiled sarcastically. "But I'd like to be a fly on the wall when Holly finds out. She's going to go ballistic."

It was true. Holly's morality was ingrained. A sudden rush of affection flooded over Jo. "I love Holly," she told Ed. "She was my friend before Pascale ever was. We were in Reception together."

Ed was unimpressed by this admission. He pushed his empty cup away and crossed his arms on the table. "So will you call Toby and fix to meet tomorrow night? Then call me and I'll get Pascale."

Jo bent down and took her phone out of her bag, letting her hair swing forward over her cheeks in case he was watching her. "What's your number?"

He recited it and she put it in her phone. Then she said, "Actually, how did you get mine?"

"Off Holly. I told her that Pascale had tried to phone you from Spain, but it wouldn't connect, so she wanted me to give you a message. It was lame, but you know Holly, always ready to help."

Jo looked at him. His ears had gone pink. He's as dopey as I am, she thought. "If she asks, I'll pretend that's what happened."

"Thanks." He looked at Jo awkwardly for a second, then pushed back his chair. "I'd better get going. I'll pay for your coffee."

"No, it's OK, really," protested Jo, but he'd already got the money out. "And call me, about the double date," he reminded her.

She nodded. "Thanks for the coffee."

He paid at the counter, collected his change, stuck his hands in his pockets and set off towards Burgerblitz without looking back. Jo went on sitting at the table, cradling her coffee cup, looking reluctantly at the phone that lay beside it. Call Toby, Ed had said. But Toby would be at work, and she'd have to leave a message which he probably wouldn't pick up until this evening. She could call his landline and leave a message with his mum, but he might not go home after work. Sunday was one of his clubbing nights. And she didn't particularly want to speak to his mum.

Stolen mobile phone, indeed. A blade of fury stabbed Jo's insides. He could, conceivably, have been with Pascale on that Sunday evening when he said someone had spiked his drink in a club. It was unlikely, though, as she and her family had to catch an early flight the next day. On the Monday, when he'd thrown the sickie, at least Pascale was in Spain so he couldn't have been with her. But wherever he was, Toby still hadn't been with *Jo*.

She called his mobile. "Hi, it's me," she said to the messaging service. "I miss you! Can we meet tomorrow? Call me after work."

She hung up, but her phone rang immediately. "I'm on lunch hour," said Toby. "You called me. What's up?"

"Nothing." Her heart jerked around in her chest. Mendacity made her nervous, even when she was lying to such an uncaringly mendacious person. "But we just didn't arrange anything last night, and I want to see you." Her voice really did sound unnatural. Surely he'd notice?

"Well..."

Here it comes, she thought. Lie number one thousand, two hundred and sixty-three. "Look, Jo, I'm going clubbing tonight." His voice didn't sound natural either. Or maybe it never did when he was lying, but she hadn't realized until now. "And tomorrow night I'm busy too."

"Oh." She tried to sound suitably disappointed. "Well, Tuesday?"

She waited. Toby was calculating silently. "OK, then, where?"

"You choose."

There was another silence. "Er...look, can I get back to you?" he asked. "It may not be Tuesday, but I'll try to make Wednesday. I'll call you. Bye."

When Jo hung up, her armpits felt clammy. Liar, liar, *liar*, she murmured to herself. She pocketed her phone, picked up her bag, and, abandoning the almost-cold coffee, opened the swing door and went out into the midday sunshine.

# Chapter Twelve

The double date idea hadn't worked, but the following day Jo and Ed made a new plan.

Pascale had phoned Ed from the airport earlier to say she'd had a stomach upset in Spain and was still feeling queasy. When Ed had pressed her further, she'd said she was very tired after the journey and wanted to go to bed early.

"She said in this little-girl way, 'You can wait till tomorrow if I can, can't you?'" Ed had reported.

They decided that later that evening Jo would show up unexpectedly at Toby's house and that Ed would do the same at Pascale's. If neither of them was at home, the game, as they say in old gangster movies, would be well and truly up.

"Don't worry, we'll catch them," Jo had assured him.

At five to eight in the evening, with her feelings swinging between anger and dread, Jo walked from the bus stop down Whittaker Road to Keats Close. She knew that on the other side of Kingsgrove, Ed would be on his way to the igloo.

When she got to the zebra crossing she turned to check the traffic. Then she saw something so unexpected that her heart did a somersault. Dawdling along Keats Close consulting her wristwatch, was a blonde girl who looked so much like Holly it had to *be* Holly. Jo saw her produce her phone, press some keys and put it to her ear.

Jo, who had gone hot and cold and hot again, didn't cross the road. She hurried down the alley between the dry cleaner's and the kebab shop. Holly hadn't seen her.

She waited for about five minutes, leaning on the wall of the kebab shop. The hammering in her chest slowly subsided. Stupid, stupid *moron*. She tried to calm herself, reasoning that Holly hadn't been going to see Toby at all, but just happened to know someone who lived in Keats Close. But Jo's common sense told her that after eleven years of friendship, she knew everyone that Holly knew.

Why was *Holly*, not Pascale, on her way to Toby's?

Her brain reeled. Could he actually be cheating on her with *both of them*? In fact, cheating on each of them too? Everyone knew that boys were either the loyal type who had one girlfriend or the serial cheat type who had lots. Why hadn't it occurred to her before that Toby was a prime example of the second type?

She tried to think clearly. She hadn't seen Holly for almost a week, since the scene last Tuesday at Press Gang. They'd had a couple of non-committal phone conversations, Holly sounding a bit strained. Jo had assumed that she was worrying about approaching the subject of Sixth Form again without upsetting Jo. *But she hadn't been worrying about that at all, had she?*

Blood surged through Jo's veins, making her ears sing. She wanted to run away, but she knew she should go straight to Toby's house and confront him with the news that she knew Holly was there. She mustn't let him get away with it. Ed wouldn't mess around, and neither would she.

Breathing unevenly, she left the alley. Long shadows fell across the street, and a breeze tugged her hair across her face. Slowly, she walked down Keats Close and up the path of Toby's house.

"Jo!" he said when he opened the front door. He was wearing a new-looking, ironed shirt with the Rose and Reed logo on the breast pocket. His face looked as if someone had just told him he hadn't won a million pounds after all. "Um...I'm about to go out, but come in."

As Jo stepped into the hall her nose detected his familiar going-out smell – shower gel, shampoo, aftershave. Robson was barking somewhere at the back of the house. "Anybody in, apart from you and Robson?" she asked, reaching up to kiss Toby's cheek.

"Um...my mum's gone to Scotland for a couple of weeks, in fact, but – "

At that moment Holly came out of the sitting-room. "Hello, Jo! How are things?"

Jo pretended surprise, then bafflement. "What are *you* doing here?" Then suspicion. "Er...am I interrupting something?"

Toby held up his hands. "Not guilty, Your Honour."

"Of course he's not *guilty*." Holly slapped Jo's arm lightly. She sounded her usual self, but Jo could see that at the very back of her eyes, behind the self-confident brightness, she knew that she was guilty, Your Honour. And she knew that Jo knew that. "We're just hanging out, aren't we, Toby?"

They were both looking at Jo. Holly was twisting a tendril of hair around her finger, which she only did when she was nervous. Jo thought the better of protesting that Toby was *her* boyfriend, so *she* should be the one hanging out with him. She wanted to lull them into a false sense of security. And she certainly didn't want to sound like the kind of girlfriend she despised – possessive, paranoid and pathologically uncool. "I *see*," she said ponderously. "You're just..." – she made speech marks in the air with her fingers, something that Holly always said only brainless saddos do – "'hanging out'. O...K..."

A small frown appeared between Holly's eyebrows. Jo knew it meant that she was embarrassed by what Jo had just said, but was prepared to tolerate it because Jo was only an artless little thing, and *Holly* was in charge here. "What does that mean?" she asked carefully, as if Jo were hard of hearing. "Don't you trust us?"

Jo's strategic intentions vanished. She felt hot with rage. She felt like her six-year-old self, who used to make scenes in toyshops, and had to be dragged out, kicking. She felt like she'd felt just before she'd driven the compass into her arm, and stabbed herself with the nail scissors, first one blade, then both.

"*Toby*!" she said, so sharply that Holly actually jumped, and Toby blinked. Jo pushed Toby with all her strength. There wasn't much room in the hallway, and as he took a step backwards he caught the banister post with his ankle, stumbled and sat down heavily on the stairs. Jo stood over him, shouting. "You *bastard*! If you want to hurt me, why don't you just beat me over the head with an iron bar and have done with it?"

Holly had caught hold of both Jo's arms. Struggling to free herself, Jo shouted at Holly too. "And *you're* supposed to be my *friend*!"

Toby got to his feet. He was stronger than Holly. He caught hold of Jo and pressed her to his chest. To her shame she began to cry, not with lung-wrenching sobs, but pitiful, poor-me tears, like Cinderella in the ashes.

He loosened his grip enough for Jo to look up at him. She knew her face was blotchy, but she didn't care. She pushed him away. "You, and Pascale, and *you*..." – she gave Holly a venomous stare – "I wish I'd never seen any of you. I wish you were all *dead*, and in *Hell*."

Through blurred vision she saw that Toby and Holly were exchanging stricken looks. "It isn't how it looks, Jo. Honestly," said Holly. The false brightness and the accusation had disappeared from her voice. She sounded like the Holly Jo loved, and had imagined loved *her*. "Toby and I are just friends, that's all. And what's Pascale got to do with it?"

Of course. Holly didn't know about Pascale. Toby had deceived her as ruthlessly as he had deceived Jo. She took a tissue from the pocket of her jacket and wiped her eyes. The tears kept coming, though. She couldn't speak, and the only thing she could hear was her own jerky breathing.

Holly was framed by the sitting-room door, her hair silvered by the light behind her. Blonde strands, some of them ringleted where they'd been wound round her finger, fell round her face. The desire to be forgiven made her bright eyes even brighter. But Jo couldn't forgive her. She knew an important scene was being played out here by these three characters on this little stage. And it wasn't over yet.

She struggled to calm herself. "Just friends?" she repeated sarcastically.

"That's right," said Toby.

Jo looked at him. Automatically she began one of her if-this-was-a-scene-in-a-movie fantasies. The director would want Toby to do The Look, filmed in soft-focus, and then the camera would show Jo's face, attractively tear-stained with the help of the make-up girl and half an onion. She would gaze imploringly at him, then turn to Holly, who, looking even more gorgeous than her real self, would smile an actress's smile, lips perfectly lipsticked, teeth fixed and whitened. She would have some line like, "How could you think anything else, Jo? Don't you know I love you?" And then she and Holly would hug, and the camera would show Toby looking deliriously happy, and the music would have a lot of strings in it.

But the audience, if they were bothering to watch Jo

carefully enough, might pick up what she was feeling. Patronized – she was sure she could act that if she tried. Distrustful? Easy. Actresses did that all the time, employing the lowered chin, raised eyes, prettily-puckered brow method. Most of all, though, she felt liberatingly bloody-minded.

"So, Holly...*you're* going out tonight with *my* boyfriend?" she asked slowly, pretending not quite to understand.

Holly flicked Toby a what-the-f... glance.

"No, I'm going clubbing," explained Toby patiently.

Jo's eyes were dry now. She put the balled-up tissue back in her pocket. Holly tried to put her arm around her shoulders, but she wouldn't let her. "Why's Holly here, then?" she asked Toby, "If you're going clubbing?"

Toby's expression was wary; Holly's was panicky. "I just came round to tell him about something," she said awkwardly.

Jo couldn't read the truth in either of their faces. What was Toby afraid of? What was making Holly panic?

"Well, *fine*," she said decisively. She opened the front door. "Isn't that just fan...tas...tic?"

"For God's sake, Jo – " began Toby, but Jo ignored him.

"I'm leaving now," she said. "So you can just shag each other's brains out in peace, can't you?"

She walked quickly up Keats Close and into Whittaker Road, where she sat down on the bench outside the library. The white light threatened, but she shut her eyes and breathed, and it retreated.

What the hell was she going to say to Ed when she phoned him? Oh, Toby's not with Pascale tonight, he's with *Holly*. He hasn't only stolen your girlfriend, he's stolen my oldest, closest friend too. He's turned them both into liars like him, and I'll never trust anything either of them say, ever again.

No, she couldn't say that. The words would sound pathetic

to Ed, who would have no conception of the enormity of Jo's loss. Trevor. Toby. Pascale. Holly. All of them had gone. The only person she had left was Tess. Selfish, stuck-up Tess.

When she was calm enough, she took out her phone and dialled.

"Pascale was in," Ed hurried to say before she could speak. He sounded relieved. "When I got there her mum told me she'd gone to bed early and was fast asleep."

Jo *wasn't* calm. Her grip on the phone tightened. She could feel her breath condensing against her cheek. "So you just believed her mum, did you?" she asked meanly.

"Christ, Jo," he said, not hearing – or pretending not to hear – Jo's hostility, "you're as bad as me. I'm such a suspicious bastard, I said I'd left my keys in her room and had had to manage for a week without them, so her mum let me go in, and there she was, fast asleep."

Jo could picture Pascale, suntanned, peaceful, sleeping in the dusk of a bedroom curtained against the light of the summer evening. She felt defeated. "Oh," she said.

There was a pause. "So what happened at Toby's?" asked Ed.

"Um..." There was no point in pretending. "Well, Toby was there. And Holly was with him."

There was another pause while Ed processed this. "*Our* Holly?" he said eventually.

*No, some fantasy Holly you wish had been there instead. Me, too.*

"Yes, our Holly," she said. At the back of her throat, tears threatened. She swallowed uncomfortably. "They pitched me some stupid story about how they're just friends and Toby's going clubbing tonight, and Holly had come round to tell him about something."

Ed chewed this over. "So why couldn't she tell him on the phone, then?"

"What?" It came out as a whisper. Jo concentrated on overpowering the tears, trying to sound normal. "How should I know?"

"Look," he said. "Let's get this straight. That night, with the card tricks, Toby was waiting for *Pascale*, not Holly. Am I missing something?"

"For God's sake, Ed!" gulped Jo. She swallowed again. "He's seeing *both of them*!"

He didn't speak

"Are you still there?" asked Jo.

"Sorry, I was thinking."

Jo's exasperation defeated her tears. "What is there – " she began.

"I don't buy it, Jo," he interrupted. "I mean, when he said he was going clubbing, he meant alone, because Holly's only sixteen, right?"

"But he *isn't* going clubbing," said Jo, wondering if flipping burgers all day was affecting Ed's brain. "He's going somewhere with Holly, or else why would she have been at his house?"

"OK," said Ed. "So they were dressed to go out, were they?"

Jo pictured the scene in Toby's hallway. She saw his ironed shirt and clean jeans. But what was Holly wearing? Dirtier jeans, and her red top with the button missing that she'd had for ages. Jo could see her standing there, winding strands of unwashed hair around her fingers.

*Boys*, she thought. Burger-flipping hadn't affected Ed's brain at all. He was using it to approach the situation logically, instead of using his emotions like Jo herself had done. "Actually," she admitted, "Toby was, but Holly wasn't. She looked a bit scruffy."

"You mean...as if she'd just called in, as a friend, to tell him about something she couldn't tell him on the phone?" suggested Ed.

Jo knew he didn't mean to incense her, but she was incensed nevertheless. "Ed, he's *my boyfriend*!" she protested. "She can't just go round and see him whenever she likes, and have secrets with him, can she?" She hoped she wasn't whining, but knew she probably was. "It's not fair! It's not even normal!"

"You sound well pissed off," observed Ed, with something between admiration and trepidation.

"Pissed off?" The whining had become a screech. "I wish they were both *dead*!"

She could hear his hesitation – an intake of breath, a moment's decision-making, the application, perhaps, of more logic. "But you were telling me yesterday," he said, "how much you love Holly, and you were in Reception with her and all that. You don't really wish she was dead, you just need to sort this out."

Jo's throat closed up. She couldn't speak.

"Look," he said, "forget trying to work out what they're doing for a minute. When will you see him again?"

"Thursday." The word emerged squeakily, as if she had to force it out.

"Well, it's only Monday today," said Ed. "Anything can happen by Thursday. You know Holly, she's so bloody moral, she's probably emailing you a full confession right now. If there's anything to confess," he added reasonably.

Jo was sure there was. Ed hadn't seen the looks that had passed between Toby and Holly, or felt the shock-waves coming from them when she – harmless little Jo – had lost her temper and pushed Toby over.

"OK," she said meekly. She might as well let Ed think he was right.

He picked up the meekness. "Are you all right?" he asked. "I mean, I'm not trying to, you know, dismiss this like it's nothing. I just think it might be more innocent than you think, and you shouldn't beat yourself up about it."

"Thanks," said Jo. "I'll try not to."

"And you don't have to worry about fixing a double date with me and Pascale any more, either," he added. "I'll deal with her."

He was right. The discovery of Toby's little liaison with Holly, innocent or not, had changed the plan. Jo recovered a nearly-normal voice. "What are you going to do?"

"Short of murdering her?" Ed gave a little laugh. "I'll think of something. It'll give me something to occupy my mind when I'm on my three hundredth burger-flip."

* * * * * *

After work the following evening, Jo opened the list of DVD labels. It had to change, obviously, after recent events. Pascale was leaning more towards horror than sex. And Ed's honesty had complicated him. He wasn't Pascale's drooling poodle any more. In fact, Jo had begun to realize this at the Summer Ball, though she'd left his label as 'Strong sex references' for other reasons then. There *was* more to him than that. But did it have a label?

That was the problem with DVD guidance labels. The pithy, direct phrases appealed to her because they were so simple. Yet they were too simple for subtlety, and Ed had turned out to be a bit more complex. Equally, how could Holly go on being 'Fairly adult'? 'Extremely puerile' just about summed up her behaviour last night. But that wasn't a phrase you were likely to find on a DVD case, even *Jackass – The Movie*.

And what about Toby? 'Suitable for all' couldn't appear on the same DVD as 'Scenes of sex and violence', but they nestled together convincingly in Toby. Jo wished there was a label to show you that the film contained barefaced, criminal betrayal. A sort of heartbreak indicator. Instead of three stars, three broken hearts.

She went back to Ed's name and deleted 'Strong sex references' from beside it. She searched the pile of DVDs, first with her eyes then with her hands. Then she went downstairs and pulled out every DVD Trevor had left and every one Tess had brought. *Sleepless in Seattle* – romance between Meg Ryan and Tom Hanks. *You've Got Mail* – romance between Meg Ryan and Tom Hanks. *Proof of Life* – romance between Meg Ryan and Russell Crowe. Maybe Tess wished she was Meg Ryan. But none of Meg's films turned up a suitable label for Ed.

Jo looked at the clock above the mantelpiece. It was fourteen minutes to eight. Tess had been upstairs getting ready to go out, and was now bustling in the kitchen. The smell of her perfume filled the sitting-room even though the French windows were open. Discontentedly, Jo returned to the DVDs.

Trevor's little collection of left-behinds looked more promising. She turned over *The Deer Hunter*, *Patriot Games* and *Casino Royale*. Nothing. Then *Enemy of the State* caught her eye. Rated 15, nothing new there. But its Theme/Content listing was 'Conspiracy'.

The word stunned her. That was *exactly* what the Toby-Pascale-Holly thing was. An anti-Jo conspiracy. Her heart constricted, like a fist clenching. Why would they want to conspire against her? What had she ever done to them?

"Jo-oh! Where are you?" called Tess.

"Sitting room!"

Tess opened the door and swung it a little as she spoke. She had her car keys in her hand. "I'm just off, darling. There's some cold chicken and a pack of salad in the fridge for your dinner. I won't be late."

"Where are you going?"

"Erica's having a little gathering." She held up a bottle of wine. "This is my contribution, but I promise I won't drink too much to drive home."

Jo smiled weakly, unsure if this was a dig at Trevor. She imagined Tess's friends with their blonde highlights and crimson claws, nodding sympathetically as they listened to Tess's account of the hell of living with a teenager, ready to cap her stories with stories of their own. "See you, then. Have fun."

"Don't forget to lock up with the mortice key when you go to bed," said Tess. This, Jo knew, was code for, "I'll be very, very late."

The front door closed, and Jo heard the over-revving that was Tess's method of starting a car. She was hungry; chicken and salad sounded good. But just as she reached the kitchen door, the front doorbell rang, and she swerved back to answer it. Through the decorated glass she saw the blurred dark shape of Pascale's tumbling hair.

*Pascale*?

When she opened the door the sight of her friend's inscrutable smile disturbed her. Pascale was so smooth, so knowledgeable and confident, it seemed impossible that she could deceive Jo. She had, though. And she still was. Clearly, Ed hadn't yet done anything.

"Hey, little Jo!" Pascale held up a bottle of wine, cheaper and bigger than Tess's. "God, the *lads* in Marbella! You and me and Hol have *got* to go there next year, on our own. Strictly no parents."

She strode into the hall, put her jacket over the banister

post and turned to Jo with a can-you-believe-it face. "What about Holly and Toby, then? I nearly wet my pants when Ed told me. Jeez, how much scent are you wearing? It smells like a bloody brothel in here."

So Ed *had* done something. He'd told her about Toby and Holly, in the hope of extracting both outrage and a confession from Pascale. But he hadn't succeeded. Bewilderingly, Pascale didn't even suspect them. "Must be Tess's," said Jo weakly. "She's just gone out."

Pascale flopped down on the sofa. Jo didn't sit beside her, but took Trevor's armchair instead, with her feet drawn up underneath her.

"I sometimes think Holly's a sandwich short of a picnic," declared Pascale. She blew out some air between pursed lips. "I mean, you'd think she'd tell you if she's been having jolly little get-togethers with your boyfriend. And how could she keep it from *me*?"

Keeping it from Pascale would constitute mental instability, certainly. Faint with astonishment, Jo tried to process what she was hearing. Pascale was surely scaling new heights of shamelessness. To arrive uninvited at Jo's ready to gossip about Holly's questionable behaviour, when all the time *she* was guilty too, was beyond belief.

Jo tried to take control. She decided to make Pacale sweat a little. "You don't think they're...you know..."

"Toby and Holly?" snorted Pascale. "For God's sake, Jo, Doctor Pascale can smell a two-timer a mile off, and believe me, Toby's fine. And you know what Saint Holly's like."

Jo's astonishment increased. She looked at Pascale carefully, noticing how beautifully her newly-tanned skin glowed, and how glossy her hair was. "But it *is* weird," she persevered, "Holly being in his house like that. You just said, you nearly wet your pants when Ed told you."

"I was so amazed at Holly going round there without you! She's not exactly the world subterfuge champion. Ooh!" Suddenly, her face brightened, and she sat forward eagerly. "Maybe they were planning something to do for *you*!" Her face fell again. "It's not your birthday till April, though, is it?"

"Pascale..." Jo had come to the end of her patience. "It's obvious that Toby's cheating on me with Holly. Why can't you see that?"

Pascale's brown eyes focused sharply on Jo's face. "Because it isn't happening. Holly doesn't do things like that." Her expression became sympathetic. "Oh, Jo, if you suspect he's cheating on you, it must be with some other girl!"

Jo didn't trust herself to reply. Hearing Blod mewing on the front windowsill, she went and pulled the window up. "Come on in, you silly old sod. The back door's open, you know."

"Jo..." persisted Pascale. She rested her head on the sofa cushion, looking at Jo from between eyelids half-shut with suspicion. "What's up?"

"Nothing's *up*," said Jo, stroking Blod methodically. "Forget it. Maybe I shouldn't try to work out what Holly's doing or why she's doing it. I just mean that...well, you know what Toby's like. It's not very easy to trust him."

Pascale nodded wisely. "He's always been a bit slippery, that's true."

"In fact..." said Jo uncertainly. She had suddenly realized that the way to the truth was through Pascale's self-appointment as resident Agony Aunt. "Toby's been so peculiar lately, I just don't know what to do. And you always help."

Pascale sighed. "Actually, I'm not sure I can help this time."

Jo's heartbeat quickened. She put Blod down on the carpet. "Why not?"

"Well..." Pascale looked sheepish. "I can't seem to sort my own boyfriend out, let alone yours."

"Has something gone wrong with Ed?" Jo managed to ask.

Pascale looked into the middle distance and screwed up her nose. "Not sure, to be honest. I think he's gone off me." She smiled knowingly at Jo. "But I'm not going to dump him just yet."

"Never throw out dirty water until you've got clean?" said Jo. The beating of her heart was actually making her voice shake.

"You're learning, little Jo."

"Anyone on the horizon?" Surely *this* would make Pascale blush?

"Well..." Pascale didn't blush. She picked up Blod and held the cat on her chest, ready to bury her face in its fur if she needed to hide confusion. Jo almost admired her. She really was a professional. "I shouldn't really talk about it, but yes, there is someone."

Jo felt ill. Pascale's nerve was more than astonishing; it was nauseating. "Is it anyone I know?" she asked.

"Oh, no," said Pascale decisively. "I mean, it's no one at school." She was still clutching the cat. Jo could hear Blod's contented purring. "In fact, I think I've given up with schoolboys," added Pascale. "I'm going to go for someone older in future. Ed can be such a tosser sometimes."

So can older boys, thought Jo. Her stomach was still trying to climb into her throat.

Swallowing, she tried to make her tone neutral. "So am I allowed to hear about this other guy you're interested in? Or am I the person you *especially* can't tell?"

Pascale stared at her. Jo could hear the muffled sound of the radio Tess had left on in the kitchen, and Blod's purring.

"What?" asked Pascale, frowning. "What have *you* got to do with it?"

"Stop pretending to be so innocent!"

"What?" asked Pascale again. She was gazing at Jo in bewilderment, her hair spilling around her suntanned face and her eyelashes spread out. "Jo, are you sure you're all right?"

When she thought afterwards about what happened next, which she did often, events always fragmented in Jo's memory and refused to put themselves into a recognizable order. In fact, the whole episode seemed irrefutably, irredeemably mad.

She put both her feet against the coffee table and pushed with all her strength. The table slid across the thin carpet and struck Pascale's shins very hard. Pascale's face expanded with shock. She let out an eardrum-shattering shriek which sent Blod scurrying for cover behind the curtains.

Pascale couldn't move. The edge of the coffee table was pinning her legs against the sofa. With Jo kneeling on it, it was immoveable. She began to cry.

A tsunami of fury unleashed itself over Jo. She grabbed Pascale by the shoulders, pushing the squashy flesh of her upper arms backwards until her head landed with a thud on the back of the sofa. Pascale tried to defend herself, but rage made Jo strong. The tsunami had been gathering for a long time. It was unstoppable. And that's when the madness really started.

Jo's most vivid memory afterwards was Pascale's teeth. When Jo demanded the truth, Pascale's weeping turned to sobbing. She protested that she didn't know what Jo meant. When Jo, forced to make things plain, said, "Who are you cheating on Ed with?" Pascale seemed to lose control of her face. Her teeth showed white against the squared-off 'O' made by her lipsticked mouth, forced open by the paralysing grimace of hysteria. "No one you know," she gasped, breathing noisily. "I swear, Jo, no one you know. Please, please don't tell Ed!"

But Jo didn't give in. "What about the card tricks?" she demanded without sympathy.

Pascale's hair was plastered to her face by tears and spit. She still couldn't close her mouth, and her nostrils quivered as her lungs tried to draw in enough air. Jo, staring at those teeth and that damp, blotched face, knew she was inflicting a greater punishment than she needed to. But knowing this didn't make her stop. Now that the usual power balance between her and Pascale was reversed, her superior position intoxicated her. She grabbed Pascale's chin and tried to push her lower jaw up. She couldn't stand to look at those white, lipstick-smeared teeth any more. "Just admit it, will you?"

Pascale's eyes, wide with fright, rolled back and looked at the ceiling as the pressure of Jo's hand forced her mouth shut. Her chest heaved. Her features were so swollen with crying that she didn't look like Pascale any more. Jo let go.

"Please, Jo, *please*," implored Pascale as soon as she could speak. Her voice was croaky. "What have I done?"

"You know what you've done!"

"No I *don't*! Why won't you believe me?"

"Because no one ever tells me the truth!"

The panic drained from Pascale's eyes. Still tear-filled, they gazed at Jo with tenderness. It was such a familiar expression that it overrode the wreckage of her face and made her look like Pascale again. "How can you say that? I'm always straight with you. You're my best friend."

Suddenly, Jo wanted to cry. She wanted to be a little girl again, who could cry and cry until things got better. But there wasn't any point. No amount of crying could make this awfulness better.

She was still kneeling on the coffee table with her T-shirt

round her armpits. Pascale must have grasped it during their struggle. Pascale half sat, half lay on the sofa, exhausted, and gazed at Jo with sorrowful eyes. "What's wrong with you?" she asked, her voice trembling. "How did you turn into someone who can do this?"

Jo didn't move to comfort her. Someone who can do this, she thought. Commit violence against Pascale. Commit violence against Toby. And Pascale didn't even know about the violence against Jo's own flesh. What would she say if she did? She'd look at Jo with that mock-innocent gaze and say, "You know you're a *whole basket* short of a picnic, don't you?"

Pascale pushed the coffee table away and stood up. Without looking at Jo she collected her jacket and the bottle of wine, sobbing and sniffing. Then she half-walked, half-stumbled out of the front door and pulled it shut behind her.

Jo pulled down her T-shirt and looked out of the sitting room window. It was getting dark. Only half way through August, and the summer seemed almost over. She thought about the results coming out next week. She thought about the sharp nails on her right hand, the short-bladed scissors in their china box and the compass in her pencil case. She must have used these things on purpose, though she didn't know it at the time, to preserve her secret. If they had been razor blades, people would have found out, because there would have been more blood than she could hide.

She sat down, closing her eyes against the bright, hammering light in her head. Inside her, intolerable rage stirred again. She clenched her teeth, grinding them into each other, making her jaw hurt. But the rage didn't go away.

Her phone said 20:26. Incredibly, it wasn't even half an hour since Pascale had rung the doorbell. Through the open door she could see Blod in the kitchen. She watched the cat's tiny pink tongue lapping the water in the bowl. Everything was silent. As Jo walked through the house it was so still that she felt as if she were walking through a painting. The corners were full of shadows; the dusky light made a square of dark blue between the sitting-room curtains; the air bore the heavy scent of lilies from the vase in the hearth. Tess wouldn't be back for hours.

She couldn't stay in this creepy, silent house, with its memory of Pascale's tears and snot and spit, and her own vicious jealousy. She couldn't do any more about getting the truth out of Pascale and Holly. But she could get the truth from Toby. Now, tonight.

# Chapter Thirteen

Toby's house was dark and blank-faced. Disappointment gnawed at Jo as she approached. But then she saw that the bathroom window at the side of the house was open. Of *course*, the rooms at the front, where the curtains were open, were the sitting-room and Toby's mum's room. Toby's mum was away, and Toby himself must be in his own bedroom at the back. Jo pressed the bell.

Nothing happened for a few moments. Jo pressed the bell again. She heard it ring inside the house, but still nothing happened. She cupped her hands around her face and looked through the glass panel. Darkness. All the doors off the hall were closed. It was pathetic, but tears tore at the back of her throat again. Was *nothing* going to go right, ever again?

There was a noise from inside the house. At first Jo couldn't identify it. She put her ear to the glass and listened carefully. It was coming from the back of the house. The ground floor, maybe the kitchen. There it was again. Suddenly she recognized it: someone was banging something hard.

Without allowing herself to think, she set off down the side of the house, under the open bathroom window and round to the back, her trainers making no noise on the path. When she looked through the glass panes of the kitchen door, the sight she saw was not the one she expected.

Holly was standing on a chair in the centre of the room,

looking up at the ceiling. In one hand she held a sweeping brush. She was wearing jeans and had her hair in a ponytail like she sometimes wore it to school, and looked exactly like the usual Holly. But on her face was an expression Jo had never seen there before. Deep, desperate panic covered her features like a mask. Her eyes had almost disappeared under her tightly-drawn eyebrows. Jo could see her sticky-out tooth, along with the other top ones, chewing her lower lip. The hand that wasn't holding the brush was flailing beside her in a gesture of impatience. She was muttering something which Jo couldn't hear. Again and again, she hit the ceiling with the end of the brush handle.

A hot feeling, as if all her blood had rushed to her head, came over Jo. Holly was here, just like last night, and she was doing something very suspicious. "Holly!" she called, knocking very hard on the glass of the kitchen door. "Where's Toby? I want to talk to him!"

Holly's face seemed to collapse, as if she had no strength in the muscles needed to keep it looking like beautiful Holly. It didn't look beautiful. It looked very troubled. She climbed off the chair and came to the back door. "You can't!" she called through the glass. "I'm sorry, but you can't!"

"Open this door or I'll get a stone and smash the glass!" threatened Jo, with the conviction of someone who knows they're being lied to. Then, as Holly's face began to crumple, she relented. "It's all right, Hol," she said more quietly. "But I *must* talk to Toby."

Holly leaned against the inside of the glass door. She'd managed not to cry, but her face was pale and her eyes were red. "I'm sorry, but I can't let you in. It's beyond my control. I just can't."

Realization flooded over Jo. What Holly had said in Toby's

hallway was true – she *had* come round to tell Toby about something. Something she couldn't say on the phone or by text. Well, now Jo knew why. With desperate, breath-shortening certainty, she knew that Holly was standing guard while Toby and Pascale were upstairs in his bedroom. A secret like that was too big to risk it being recorded by an electronic device. That incriminating *Inbox*, that *Received Calls* list; the downfall of any plotter who underestimated the power of the mobile phone.

"Christ, Holly, how *could* you?" Jo could hardly speak; the words were scarcely above a whisper.

Holly shook her head. The tears came, but Jo had no sympathy. When she had rung the doorbell, Holly had started pounding on the kitchen ceiling to warn Toby and Pascale. At this very moment, they were probably tiptoeing down the stairs and out of the front door, marveling at the stroke of luck that had sent Jo round the back.

It was like a comedy film. But it wasn't in the smallest bit funny. Everyone Jo had trusted had betrayed her. In comedy films, things like betrayal didn't come into it. But in real life, farcical situations like this weren't comic, they were tragic. "*Please* open the door," she implored Holly. "They've probably gone by now, anyway."

Holly, her eyes brimming, stared at Jo for a long moment. Then she seemed to make a decision. She unlocked the door, flung it open, caught hold of Jo and hugged her tightly. "I'm so sorry!" she blurted. "I've been so miserable! You don't know how awful this has been, and it's been going on so long, and I didn't know how to make it go away once it had started."

Jo let her cry a little longer, then gently unwound her arms from her neck. "It's gone away now," she said. Her voice seemed to be coming from somewhere far away, like an echo in a cave. She felt as if everything she had ever learnt, understood, memorized, valued, believed or defended had fallen in a heap in the middle of Toby's mum's immaculate kitchen, and lay there like an unlit bonfire, waiting for destruction. "You don't have to worry about it any more, Hol."

Holly drew breath to speak, but at that moment there was a thud in the room upstairs, and the sound of a door opening.

They both froze. Jo didn't know what to do. She longed, overwhelmingly, for everything to be out in the open at last, but she didn't want to experience the moment when that happened. She didn't know if she wanted Toby to kneel and beg forgiveness, or just disappear somewhere very far away, so that she never saw him again. And although she couldn't avoid seeing Pascale again, before she did she needed longer to have passed since their last, violent meeting.

"I'd better go," she said to Holly. "I *really* don't want to see them."

But it was too late. Jo heard masculine laughter in the hall, and the kitchen door opened. But it wasn't Toby who stood there. Framed by the kitchen door, wearing his usual tight jeans and T-shirt, and carrying his pointy-toed shoes in one hand, was Gordon.

Close behind him came Toby, without his shoes or his shirt, smiling. "What was that – " he began. Then he saw Jo, and stopped. His smile vanished. "Shit," he said.

Jo's body felt suddenly electrified. The sudden realization of what was going on struck her like a million tiny flashes of lightning. She could hear Holly sobbing miserably. A tremor went down her legs; she felt as if she might collapse. She lurched against the worktop, her heart shuddering like a pile-driver. It was hard to speak, but she knew she was the one who must. And suddenly, she found her voice.

"*Shit*?" she repeated, fixing Toby with the most venomous

stare she could muster. She wished Mr Gerrard, who hadn't chosen her for Lady Macbeth in the Year Nine Mini-*Macbeth* because he said she didn't look evil enough, was there to see it. "How about 'Sorry'?" She let go of the worktop and advanced on Toby, registering dimly that she'd never seen him without his top before. Their amateurish attempts to be lovers had never reached that level. "Do you realize you've never apologized to me, ever?" she demanded. "Even when you were the one deeply, *deeply* in the wrong?"

No one spoke. Out of the corner of her eye Jo saw Gordon perch wearily on a stool at the breakfast bar, still minus his shoes, and put his head in his hands.

"Do you know what 'deeply in the wrong' even *means*?" Jo asked Toby. She could hear her tone getting spiky. She must control it. She mustn't start to sound like Tess. "Or have you never actually bothered to found out?"

Gordon and Holly both began to speak. Gordon proved the stronger. "Jo, he *is* sorry. He's given me hell this last few weeks, moaning about how bad he feels." He looked at Toby, who was leaning despondently against the sink, his head down, his arms folded across his naked torso. "In fact, he was going to tell you tomorrow, weren't you, Tobe?"

Holly leapt at her chance. "That's what I was going to say, Jo!" She was sobbing and sniffing so vigorously, Jo almost didn't understand her. "We were talking about it earlier tonight, and I said he had to tell you, after you came round last night and found me here. I felt so bad, I didn't know what to do, I – "

"*You* felt bad!" Jo practically spat the words at Holly, then turned on Gordon. "Toby's been giving *you* hell!" The same rage that had made her kick the coffee table into Pascale's legs – poor, innocent Pascale, whose latest conquest, whoever he was, certainly wasn't Toby – possessed her. "What about *me*!"

At last, Toby raised his head. In his face Jo saw anguish. It was the scene, about ten minutes before the end, when everything hangs on a tough decision. The actor emotes, his eyes doing the business. The actress, transfixed by the enormity of his sacrifice, wails, "No! Don't do it!" But a man's got to do what a man's got to do.

Toby pushed himself off the work surface and stepped towards her. He didn't touch her. He just stood there, the same old Toby with his thin-lipped almost-smile, his neat hair, his far-apart eyes with their watchful expression. But not the same old Toby.

"You can hate me if you want," he said solemnly. "But listen, I always really liked you, and I still do. And if things hadn't been the way they are with me, you'd have been..." He paused, and drew a breath as if he was going to say more. But then he let it out again, and without looking at anyone, opened the kitchen door and went out. A moment later, Jo heard his bare feet padding up the stairs.

Holly had started crying again. Over and over, she mumbled, "I'm sorry, I'm sorry..."

Jo felt as numb, and as dumb, as a doll. "whatever, Hol," she said. Then she looked at Gordon. "I'd like to hand in my notice," she said. "I don't want to come back to the shop any more."

She opened the door into the garden. While she'd been in Toby's house it had got a lot darker outside. She slammed the door behind her and began to run.

\* \* \* \* \* \*

When she got home, breathless and sweaty, Tess was still out. Jo turned off her phone and sat in the dark at the side of the house by the dustbins, where Tess wouldn't see her when she came in.

Blod came round the corner, padding across the concrete path, inclining her head, beseeching Jo with yellow eyes. Jo picked her up and crouched at the bottom of the wall, the cat draped against her chest. She could feel Blod's bones beneath her fur, and her tiny wet nose nudging her cheek. The cat began to purr contentedly.

It didn't matter what Toby, or Gordon, or anybody said. It was all Jo's fault. *She* was the one who had told Toby, stupidly, that she loved him, and then, equally stupidly, that he wasn't 'the one'. *She* was the one who had quizzed him fruitlessly about his friends and his ambitions, but was too spineless to demand to know why he'd been expelled from school. The fact was Toby had never really wanted to be her boyfriend at all. He was just playing some lunatic game with himself, using her to show himself, once and for all, that he only liked men. He'd more or less admitted this. "If things hadn't been the way they are with me..." he'd said. Well, things *were the way they are with him*, weren't they? And because of Jo, he knew it, once and for all. And all the time he was playing his sordid little game with her, he was going clubbing with his friends in London. He was sleeping at Mitch's place, but not on the floor, of course. And the reason he wasn't having sex with Jo was very simple. He was having sex with Gordon.

*Gordon.* Jo was back in what-the-hell's-Holly-doing territory. Blod squawked and struggled, so Jo set her down. She watched the white underside of the cat's tail disappear into the darkness, remembering how Holly, such a so-called loyal friend, had evaded her questions and patronized her suspicions about Toby. But that had been *ages* ago, on the day of their last exam. Jo had hardly known Toby then, but even so, Holly had refused to discuss him in more detail than her casual "how's it going?"

enquiry had demanded.

Had Holly known something Jo didn't know?

Why hadn't Jo *seen* it? It was obvious that Gordon was gay, so why not Toby? The 'friends' in London. The clubbing. The clean-shaven chin, the neat clothes and sharp haircut. The prospective career in fashion. And what jobs had he done before he was a shop assistant? A waiter, and a hairdresser, for God's sake! She unclasped her hands and covered her face with them.

It was cool in the night-time garden, but suddenly she became almost unbearably sweaty. Her T-shirt was clinging to her back below her shoulder blades, and the waistband of her denim skirt seemed to be melting into her flesh. She'd pulled her hair back into a clip, but all over her scalp sweat was cooling as it touched the air. And something was driving her heart faster and faster. She pressed her nails into her palms, willing herself to fight it as if it were an invisible sparring-partner. But its very invisibility made it too fearsome an opponent. Invisible like The Force. *Help me Obi-Wan Kenobi, you're my only hope.* Or like Frodo when Gollum bit his ring-finger off at the top of Mount Doom. No one could fight what they couldn't see.

Her hands still clenched, Jo pushed them into her eyes, so hard that coloured circles chased each other in blackness. She had to shut up about *movies*, for Christ's sake. She had enough to deal with in the real world, and no one to help her do it.

She blinked until her vision cleared, then went back inside. The curtains were open, and moths gathered at the lighted windows. Jo pulled the French windows shut behind her and leant her damp forehead against the glass. She couldn't see the garden. All that was out there was a black tunnel that ended nowhere. But when she shut her eyes again, the darkness disappeared and the brain-piercingly brilliant light took its place.

As helpless, and as determined, as a moth, Jo backed from the window and stumbled into the kitchen. She paused in the middle of the room, blinking and swaying. *Liars. Stinking, filthy liars, the lot of them*.

The kitchen was full of metal things. Electric things. Sharp things.

*You're a liar too, Jo.*

Necessary lies. She looked down at the large square plaster on the inside of her elbow. An infected mosquito bite, she'd said to Pascale. Just above her wrist was another plaster, where the compass point had gone in. How long ago had she done that? Three days? Four days? The wound had begun to heal, though there was still yellow stuff on the plaster whenever she changed it. No one had even asked about that, though she was ready with an excuse about burning her wrist on the oven shelf. The marks on her legs – one higher up from the scissors' single blade, one lower down from her two-pronged attack in the garden – were easier to hide; no bikini, no questions, no made-up answers.

She opened the cutlery drawer, hazily recognizing the long-bladed scissors, the carving knife in its sheath, table knives, the narrow boning-knife Tess had never learnt how to use, smaller knives, kebab skewers. She took out the vegetable knife. The one with the comfortable, familiar handle. The blade was short, but not too short.

She stared at the knife for a long time, her heart jack-hammering in her chest, sending her blood sprinting round her body, ready to spill out all over the kitchen floor. She put the knife back and slammed the drawer shut.

Then she took it out again and put it up her sleeve, in case Tess came back and saw her in the hall. Upstairs, she hid it at the back of her knicker drawer. Then she lay down, spreadeagled on the enormous bed, staring at the algebra formulae she'd taped to the ceiling and forgotten to take down after the exam.

Her fists were clenched; her eyes burned. The vision in her head glowed so brightly that the dark room seemed full of light. It was a vision of release from terror, like when Tess used to hear her having a nightmare when she was little, and would come in and cuddle her until she opened her eyes. There was a buzzing in Jo's ears, but she couldn't tell if it came from inside or outside her skull. The feeling of wanting to run around and scream was intolerable. She pressed her jaws together. So much noise, so much light.

Then she was moving. Off the bed. Over to the chest. The underwear draw was opened. She glared into the mirror. Was this the person who'd caused all the pain? The person she needed to hurt? She felt as if she were moving in a ball of light, like a spotlight on a stage. Maybe what she assumed to be a nightmare was reality. Maybe, she thought as her fingers found the knife handle, if she inflicted this punishment upon this person, upon herself, she could forgive herself.

The knife didn't seem all that sharp. Her leg didn't hurt much. But there was blood. Jo sat on the edge of the bed, looking at the bright red ooze seeping out of her body and making its way across her thigh.

Reaching for a tissue, she dabbed and pressed the wound. The blood hadn't stopped. It looked very red. But there was no pain. Absolutely none. The light all around her had gone, too. She sat there on her bed with the bloodstained tissue in her hand and blood running down her leg onto the carpet. She felt very, very tired – she'd walked to Holly's and run back, which was quite a long way. She felt cold, too, though the bedroom was warm. So cold she was beginning to shiver. And her heart felt odd, swelling and contracting irregularly, as if it couldn't make up its mind what to do.

She lay down. Her eyes closed themselves. Empty, soothing darkness enveloped her. What a mentally deficient way to behave, she thought, sticking a knife into your leg because your boyfriend is gay.

The duvet cover felt wet underneath her. Good grief, had she peed without knowing it? The wetness did feel warm, like pee. She had no strength to sit up and inspect it. She'd just have to let the bed get wetter and wetter, and brave Tess's disgusted scolding.

*Oh. Hide the knife from Tess*. She felt for it on the bed beside her, but it wasn't there. It must have fallen on the floor. And here she was, lying here in a pool of pee like a baby in a cot, unable to reach it. If it wasn't so stupid it would be funny.

*Ha ha ha. When the results come out you should get A-star for stupidity, Jo-girl.*

She heard the front door slam. A woman was giggling and a man was saying something Jo couldn't make out. Then there were footsteps on the stairs. "Hello!" called Jo, but then she thought maybe she hadn't said hello at all. There were more voices, a silence, then the man swore energetically. She didn't hear anything else.

There was something heavy on her leg. Maybe she'd fallen down a hole and got her leg stuck. And then she was moving, but she didn't know how, because she wasn't walking. It was all too confusing.

Then it came to her in a flash, like the answers to maths problems came to Pascale. She was in a *movie*, of course. A stunt had gone wrong. She was messing up in some way. That's obviously what it was. A movie with a 15 rating? Violence, clearly, or else why would her forehead be crushed against the vibrating window of a car, while something immovable pinned her to the seat? Oh, it was a *kidnapping* scene. She was bound by electrical cord. That's what kidnappers always used in movies. The camera was focused on her terrified face. She couldn't scream because she was gagged. And she was very, very thirsty, though the audience couldn't know that. Couldn't someone get her a drink of water?

Only a 15, though. Only moderate violence. No one had died.

# Chapter Fourteen

The pattern on the curtains round the bed looked like caterpillars having sex with slugs. Jo screamed in revulsion. A thin nurse in a pink tunic told her to calm down, and she screamed more. Then someone stuck a needle in her hand.

All around her were the sounds of people who'd had accidents or emergencies in the middle of the night. Jo stared at the tube embedded in the back of her hand, and at her bandaged leg. She was wearing a washed-out blue hospital gown. Was this still a movie? No, it couldn't be.

Tess was sitting on a plastic chair beside the bed. She didn't look much like she was in a movie. Her face was puffy and her eye make-up had made muddy tracks on her cheeks. She was clutching the arm of a man Jo had never seen before. "Oh my God, oh my God," she kept saying. "Oh my God."

The man was about thirty-five, not bad looking in a heavyset sort of way. His shirt, which had started out white, and his trousers, which had started out a sort of tan colour, were stained with a blotchy red and brown substance. He was in need of a shave, too. "I'm Mark," he said solemnly. His eyes were very pale blue. "You must be Jo."

"Hello," said Jo. She looked at her mother, who had put her head on the bed and was sobbing into the blanket. "Hello, Tess."

Tess's head came up. "Oh *darling!*" she wailed. "What have

you *done*?"

The pillow was soft behind Jo's head. And she didn't feel like screaming, or asking any more questions. She just felt sleepy.

Tess blew her nose noisily on a tissue. "Look at Mark, he looks like a butcher. If we hadn't come home just then..." She stared into nothing, seeing the scene all over again. "Anyway, he was a hero. He put his tie round your leg."

Mark looked at Jo, and she looked back. She was too tired to speak.

"Just sleep now," said the nurse. She had pointy cheekbones and pale, freckled skin. Jo wondered how old she was.

There was a silence. Mark blinked a few times. "Your daddy's coming all the way from Wales," he told Jo. "He should be here soon."

"If he hasn't been stopped on the motorway, since he's probably drunk," added Tess.

Jo's eyes filled with tears. "My daddy," she said. Then the urge to sleep overwhelmed her, and she didn't say any more.

\* \* \* \* \* \*

When she woke up, Trevor was standing beside her bed. "Hello, Jo-girl," he said.

Jo didn't say anything. Her throat hurt. Her bed was one of two in a side ward. The other bed was empty. A nurse was pushing a creaking trolley along the polished floor. The hospital smelled of hospitals.

"Tess went home to get some sleep," said Trevor.

There was a water jug and plastic beaker on the bedside locker. Jo looked at it, and Trevor poured her some water. Then he helped her drink it. She felt a fool.

"I feel a fool," she said croakily.

"Not half the fool I feel." A spasm of nervousness passed over Trevor's face. "You're not going back to that shop, are you?"

The thought of the shop, and Toby, and Gordon, made Jo's stomach hurt. "No," she whispered. Then, louder, "Do you know what happened, Trev?"

He nodded. "I think I get the general idea. I could wring their necks, the lot of them."

"Don't do that," said Jo. "I don't care any more. Is Holly here?"

"She was," said Trevor. "And Pascale. I saw them in the café. It's not visiting hours till two o'clock, but the nurse let me in because I've come all the way from Wales."

"And because you're my dad."

"And because I'm that."

They looked at each other. "Did Pascale say anything?" asked Jo. "About me?"

Trevor wasn't sure what she meant. A question came into his eyes. "Well, she was crying a lot," he said. "She's very upset."

Jo could imagine it. Deep inside her, way further in than her heart, she knew Pascale hadn't told Trevor or anyone else about the violence Jo had inflicted on her.

"Holly's pretty upset too," said Trevor with a small sigh. "She's been a pretty silly girl."

"I've been just as silly, Trev." Jo had to say it, though the confession was painful. "Or stupid, more like. Stupid about Toby. I thought – "

Her voice cracked. She was trying so hard not to cry that her throat felt as if someone's thumbs were pressing on both sides of it. This is what it feels like to be strangled, she thought.

"It's *Toby* that's been stupid, not you." Trevor had hold of

209

her hand again. He put his other arm around her shoulders and rested his cheek on her hair. "And a liar. If he was my son...well, I just hope his dad's got something to say to him, that's all." He paused before continuing in a softer tone, "but it's not just that. I wasn't here for you when I should have been Jo-girl."

Trevor's words had turned the key that had been stuck in her head for so long, and opened the door to the stuff she kept locked up. Hot, insistent tears flooded her cheeks and dripped off her chin. She wiped them away but they didn't stop. She held onto the front of his sweatshirt, sniffing frantically, hiccupping and snorting, but unable to stop either the tears or the words.

"His dad works overseas, and he's horrible to his mum, and she just cleans the house all the time. And Toby got expelled from school in Year Eleven. And Tess is so hopeless, and she's made everything so difficult for you, and I know you drink a lot but it's only because you're unhappy, and neither of you ever seemed to care what I felt like when you had fights all the time, and now she's got this boyfriend, and you'll get a girlfriend, and I'll just be a sort of...spare part." She let go of his sweatshirt. The tears were subsiding a little. "When you went off to Wales like that and left me with her, I thought 'he doesn't care about me'" – she shook her head as Trevor tried to protest – "of course I know you *do*. But it was just that I didn't have any *say* in anything, and I felt like I meant nothing. *Nothing*, Trevor! I felt like I needed to hurt myself just to make myself realise I was still *here*."

Jo's chest was still going up and down fast, but she'd stopped crying. Her voice was a whisper. "There just wasn't usually so much blood," she said. "I got good at it. I was really, really good at it. But then I wasn't."

Trevor was swaying a little, breathing unevenly. He took one of Jo's tissues and blew his nose, trying to compose himself, murmuring in Welsh. He only did this when he didn't know he was doing it.

When he started speaking English again it was to say, "Your dad's a bloody idiot, Jo-girl. But I'll sort it. I've told Mord to stuff his bed and breakfast. I want to be with my girl."

The possibility of Trevor changing his mind about Wales had never entered Jo's head. It had never even hovered *near* her head. "I'll move into a flat." He gave a collapsed sort of smile. "And with any luck we'll be able to keep the house. You're going to go on living there, with all your things, just like always."

Jo digested this. "So you're going to get a job here, in London?" Her voice still sounded as if she had tonsillitis, though the water had helped.

"Yep."

Compassion swept over her. "You sad old git," she said. "You never got it, did you?"

There was something in Trevor's face Jo had never seen before. He looked like Bruce Willis in *Die Hard*. He looked like a man who steps up. "No, but I get it now," he said seriously. "I don't think Tess will, though. She..." Trying to be kind to Tess, he failed to find the words.

"She always thinks everything's about *her*?" supplied Jo.

Trevor nodded ruefully.

"The more she went on about what would her friends think if I didn't go to university, the more I told her I wasn't going back to school."

He nodded again.

"Not productive." Something occurred to Jo. She didn't want to live with an unhappy, alcohol-dependent man who pretended he was still twenty-five. She had finished with that. But neither did she want to live with a woman who had no need

211

to pretend she was still twenty-five; she was far younger than that, and always would be. "If we do keep the house," she said, "do you think *she* might move out, instead of you?"

"Maybe, if this bloke she's got comes up with some dosh." Trevor rested his elbow on the bed and took Jo's hand. "It'd be bloody excellent, wouldn't it? I'll look after you." The Bruce Willis look was still in his eyes. "In case you're wondering, I'm going to get myself in a programme. You know, about the drinking. I don't need it, so I'm going to crack it."

He sounded so earnest, Jo smiled. "That's why you want me with you," she told him. "To keep you on the wagon."

"Rub – bish!" His accent had intensified. Jo saw his face flood with emotion. She watched him struggle for control. It was a few moments before he spoke. "I can do it on my own, but I don't want to," he said quietly. "I miss you, that's the truth. I want you to come home and live in our house, and go to school and me go to work, just like it was. Only this time, I won't act like such a tosser."

Something began to nag at the edges of Jo's mind. A memory, a note struck by Trevor's words. What was she thinking of? Older boys...*Ed can be such a tosser sometimes...so can older boys...who are you cheating on Ed with?*

Pascale had never told her about the nameless dark-haired boy who let Poins do card tricks with him. Had she told Ed? By now, Ed would surely know about what had happened at Holly's house, too. She thought about Ed for a moment. Then she raised herself off the pillows, leaning on her elbows, and looked at her father. "Look, I'll think about going back to school, OK?"

He tried not to look triumphant. Jo was touched. "Though of course, it depends on my results," she added.

"When are they out?"

Jo considered. Time had gone bonkers lately. Her fight with

212

Toby and Holly had taken place on Monday, the day Pascale had got home from Spain. The attack on Pascale and the unedifying scene in Toby's kitchen had both happened on the same evening, which must have been Tuesday. But was that last night, or longer ago?

"Is today Wednesday?" she asked.

Trevor nodded.

"Not tomorrow, but the Thursday after, then," she said. "The twenty-third. And I'm supposed to go and see Mr Treasure on the twenty-eighth."

She lay down again, watching Trevor, who rubbed his forehead, embarrassed at the memory. "I never did make that appointment with him, did I?"

"Nope." Jo had forgiven him long ago. "But it doesn't matter now."

Trevor looked at his watch. "Talking of appointments, the doc said she's coming to see you before visiting time. I'll make myself scarce, shall I?" He kissed her on both cheeks. "I'll just be downstairs."

"Thanks, Trev," said Jo, meaning it. "For...you know, coming back."

He nodded, and kissed her again. As he left the ward, he almost collided with the doctor, a young Asian woman. Under her harassed expression Jo could see the beauty she always envied, the gold-dark beauty of Asian women. They had brown hair like her own, but theirs always stayed up, and was thick enough to decorate gorgeously with combs and jewels. She wondered what Doctor Mandani would look like with her hair decorated.

"Blood pressure not great, but not terrible," said the doctor, looking at Jo's notes. "You lost quite a lot of blood, so we've got to keep an eye on it."

"Why did I lose so much?" Jo had been longing to ask this question ever since she'd realized that the substance which had ruined Mark's shirt and trousers was her own blood.

The doctor looked at Jo calmly. "You'd done it before, we could tell by the scars. And you've been lucky, because the top of your leg's a dodgy place to choose. Did you know there's a big artery there?"

Jo nodded, feeling childish. She *did* know that.

"Well, this time you got a bit too near it," said Doctor Mandani. "Any further and it could have been a lot worse."

Jo considered this while the doctor took her pulse. "People have bled to death from that artery, haven't they?" she asked her.

"They have. Now shush, I'm counting."

Jo thought a bit more while she waited. "When can I go home?" she asked when the doctor released her wrist.

"Tomorrow, maybe. I'll come and see you in the morning." The doctor wrote in Jo's folder, slotted it into the pocket at the bottom of the bed and put her pen back in her pocket. "It's visiting time now. But afterwards I want you to go to sleep." She smiled briefly. Her teeth were small and even. "See you tomorrow."

Jo closed her eyes, hoping no one would visit her. She couldn't stand the thought of Holly and Pascale trooping in with pinched faces, each thinking they were the one Jo had treated worse. The truth was, she'd treated them equally badly, reducing them to labels on the backs of DVDs, in an insane attempt to convince herself she was in control of them.

"Coo-ee!" It was Tess. She plonked a bouquet of roses on the bed and kissed Jo. "How's my darling girl?"

"I'm all right. I'm sorry about your boyfriend's clothes."

Tess smiled happily. Her hair was held back by a pink

headband that matched her skirt. Her lipstick was an exact match too. "Oh, I shouldn't worry about that. Mark can afford plenty of new ones." She widened her eyes at Jo. "Did you like him? He's sweet, isn't he?"

Unexpectedly, Jo felt a rush of affection. "Yes, he's sweet, Tess."

"And he was *so* competent, when we came home and found you...you know." Tess's eyes sparkled with pride. "I was in a state, as you can imagine, but he just took off his tie – a silk one, designer – and made a what's-it-called out of it – "

"A tourniquet," supplied Jo.

"That's right. And he's paid to have the bedroom carpet cleaned, too. He's just such a darling. You do like him, don't you?"

Trevor was right; Tess would never get it. "I absolutely adore him," she said.

"Oh, Jo!" Tess's eyes filled, but she blinked the tears away. "By the way, Holly and Pascale send their love."

"Are they here?" asked Jo. A small wave of panic lapped at her. "Trevor said he saw them downstairs in the café."

"I saw them too. I said they could come up to see you after two o'clock, but Holly said they thought it was better if it was just me and your dad, I can't think why. I mean, they're your best buds, aren't they?" She shifted discontentedly in the chair. "I don't know why they bothered to come to this vile place if they don't want to see you. Anyway, I've given you their love, like they asked."

Good old Holly, thought Jo. Always sensible. Always aware of how other people feel. The concern she and Pascale felt for Jo was clear to everyone except Tess. It wasn't that *they* didn't want to see *Jo*, it was that *Jo* didn't want to see *them*, and Holly knew it.

"I expect they'll pop in later," she said, to placate her mother. But she knew they wouldn't. The world the three of them had inhabited for so long had fallen over.

* * * * * *

The bit of sky Jo could see from the window had turned purply-blue, and she had switched on the light above her bed, when a nurse brought her a pink envelope which had been left for her at the nurses' station.

The envelope bore the words 'Miss Joanna Probert' in very familiar writing. Jo had witnessed that writing's creation, over the last 11 years. She had seen it through line-ignoring almost-letters, through a twelve-year-old's experiments with curls, loops and circles over the i's, to the teacher-pleasing clarity she now saw so often, and sometimes copied.

She tore open the envelope. Holly had written three words on the pink paper. One of them was the S-word Jo had never been able to extract from Toby. The others were 'Call you?' She must have gone home from the hospital that afternoon, sat down at her L-shaped desk, agonized over those three words, then come all the way back to deliver the note, and get the bus all the way home again. Alone, without telling anyone. Somehow, the trouble she had gone to was comforting.

Jo sank back against the pillow, the note in her hand. Poor Holly. Jo had labelled her 'Fairly adult', when all the time she was floundering in waters she shouldn't have stepped into, like a child who couldn't swim. She knew she would forgive Holly for not telling her about Toby straight away. She almost had already, really.

Thinking about Holly made Jo think about Toby. Accepting, denying, accepting and denying again, perhaps for years.

Universal viewing, suitable for all? Maybe not. His face appeared, his grey eyes dark, the pupils large. They bore into her, full of the desire to be forgiven. But how could she forgive him? He had admitted the truth to Holly, but he hadn't told *her*.

Things might be clear, but they were no less hurtful. Toby had tried to be Jo's boyfriend, but he hadn't given up his clubbing friends, or spent time with *her* friends. He'd stuck up for Jo about the mystery shopper, but now it was obvious why he'd been prepared to take such a risk with his job. He'd known Gordon wouldn't sack him.

She'd told him she loved him, but he knew she couldn't have really. That's why he'd changed the subject. And deep down she'd known she didn't. Especially after what he did in the taxi. In hindsight he'd tried to have sex with her in a place he knew she would refuse to do it, so that he didn't have to do it either. He'd acted aggressive and disappointed, when really he must have been relieved. And he'd told her that ridiculous story about being drugged and getting his phone stolen to cover the night he'd been with Mitch. Maybe she should have worked the whole thing out.

She started to think about Toby's mum and dad. His mum, a willing servant, didn't seem to know or care what Toby was doing, and his dad was never there. How had Toby felt, being left as the 'man of the house'? Jo had never considered the male perspective before. A man was expected to work, earn, support, protect, defend. Active verbs, as Mr Gerrard would say. Action, that's what men's lives were about. It was like sex. If the man couldn't do it, it didn't get done.

But supposing you didn't *want* to be the man of the house and the head of a family? Supposing you didn't *want* to have sex with a woman and produce children, and live with them forever-and-ever-amen? But if your mum and dad, and everyone else, expected you to, you would try to be what they wanted, wouldn't you? You might even go out with a girl who was too naïve to understand.

As Jo lay in the hospital bed with the pink tent of Holly's note on her chest, sleep began to enclose her. Her eyelids heavy, she reached out and retrieved her phone from the bedside cabinet. She wrote the three letters of 'Yes', and sent the text to Holly's number. Her leg throbbed; they'd give her some painkillers if she asked, but she decided not to. Sleep seemed like the better option. Sleep brought oblivion, and oblivion killed pain better than any pills.

* * * * * *

Jo was sitting in a garden chair among cushions with Blod on her lap, letting Tess show off in front of Mark by fussing over her and bringing her a drink with a little umbrella in it. Mark had an ironic way of looking at Tess which she hoped meant he wasn't overestimating her. Maybe he was content just to have his ego massaged, or regular sex, or both.

He pushed himself out of his chair when the doorbell rang. "I'll get it," he said. "And I'm going to stay indoors, Tess, OK? Got some work to do."

Tess nodded happily. Mark was some sort of broker. Not an insurance broker, something to do with financial institutions, Tess had told her proudly. It sounded to Jo like he might, indeed, come up with some dosh.

Holly emerged from the house. Jo watched her cross the lawn and sit down in the chair Mark had vacated. She looked like she usually looked, blonde tendrils in place around her face, smile ready, eyes full of that what-you-see-is-what-you-get expression. Jo knew now, though, that you didn't always get what you saw. "Hi, Hol," she said.

Tess stood up and gathered the empty glasses. "Well, I've got things to do," she said lightly. "And you two need to talk!"

*That's right, Tess, state the obvious.* Neither Jo nor Holly replied.

"Would you like a drink, Holly?" asked Tess. "It's so warm today."

Holly released the awaiting smile, though not widely enough to reveal her funny tooth to Tess. "No, thanks. But it *is* hot, isn't it?"

Didn't Holly ever give up trying to charm parents? Maybe, after so many years of practice, it came automatically.

"Anyway," said Tess, turning to Jo. "Call if you want anything, darling, I'll be in the kitchen." She turned back to Holly. "You won't tire her, now, will you? She's had a Very Bad Experience."

Holly's smile didn't falter. "Promise," she said.

Tess started towards the house, and Blod jumped off Jo's lap to follow her, hoping, as ever, for a snack.

When Holly looked at Jo her smile had become more tentative. "I'm so – " she began.

"Look, you don't need to apologize," interrupted Jo. "You've done that."

"I wasn't going to. I was going to say, I'm so glad you're out of hospital. They're full of bugs *and* they don't even have hot doctors like on TV. "

"The doctor I had was very nice-looking," said Jo, "but she was a woman."

Holly's smile tried to broaden, but the small talk wouldn't hold. Jo sensed what was coming and tried to head it off, "I don't care what happened, Hol."

"Well..." Jo could see that Holly was fighting dismay, but

what had she expected? That telling Jo what had happened would make it un-happen? "Look, I just *knew*. But I couldn't tell you, could I?"

"Why not?"

Holly's troubled look intensified. "After what you told me that day by the lockers I went into the shop when you weren't there and asked him about it. He sort of just gave in and told me about Gordon and pleaded with me to keep it secret." She glanced at Jo. "He stayed at Gordon's at weekends sometimes. You were suspicious, weren't you?"

"No," said Jo. "I just thought he had this group of friends he didn't want me to be part of. I thought he was ashamed of me, because I was only sixteen and couldn't get into clubs. We never even went to Press Gang because he said he didn't like it."

"Well, he had a reason," said Holly. "That guy behind the bar, the one with the tattoos, had been one of Toby's...er...lovers, and they fell out."

"Oh." Jo wished they *had* gone to Press Gang, and encountered the ex-lover. It would have saved a lot of trouble. "Well, go on, then. What did you say when he asked you not to tell me?"

"I refused. You know what I'm like, I can't stand lies – but he said he really wanted to make things right with you, and he was going to dump Gordon and stop going to Mitch's and all that, and be a proper boyfriend. He *promised*, Jo. And you seemed happy. You said you loved him! But..." Holly looked stricken at the memory. "This dumping Gordon, it didn't seem to happen. On Monday night, when you turned up at his house, I'd gone round there to moan about it. But he fobbed me off, saying that Tuesday would be the last time ever, promise, promise. And you know how persuasive he can be, and how...I don't know, how *all right* things sound when he says them. But then, on Tuesday, I couldn't stand it any more. I went round to his house to tell him I wasn't going to cover for him any more, and he'd have to deal with the consequences. I said I wouldn't leave unless Gordon came with me, but they went upstairs anyway. I sat in the house not knowing what do and then you knocked on the door. You were so worked up, but I was worked up too. I just didn't know *what* to do."

The two girls, one each side of the table, their faces shaded by the umbrella, looked at each other silently for a long moment. This really *is* the final scene of a movie, thought Jo. The symmetrical, meticulously-set-up shot of the two characters, the slanting sunlight, the deep shadows, the lush, mid-August foliage. The slow pull back, to reveal the garden, the street, the city. And then the credits.

Jo pictured Holly, her loyal defender, pleading that day by the river. She'd always known, without ever really thinking about it, that Holly loved her. Holly's attempt at lying had gone so deeply against her natural morality that she had suffered intolerably. When she'd let Jo in the back door of Toby's house, it was because she'd collapsed under the unendurable strain.

"You've been as big a fool as I have," Jo told her.

Holly had gone pink. She looked insanely pretty. What was it with Tom Clarke, that he hadn't made his move, properly, on her? Perhaps it was best not to wonder, thought Jo ruefully.

"Anyway," went on Holly, "then I found out he'd been expelled from St Bede's." Her eyes met the question in Jo's eyes. "There was a long list of trouble," she said, still very pink. "But possession of cocaine was the final straw apparently."

Jo nodded, sighing inwardly. "Well, that's not as bad as dealing, I suppose." *Or seducing younger boys.* "Go on."

"OK, I tried to get Toby to...er...end the relationship, but he didn't. So I told you about him getting expelled, and tried to make you see what a loser he is, so that you'd dump him."

Jo almost smiled. If it wasn't so brutally embarrassing, it might be hilarious. It would, she thought vaguely, make a neat idea for a movie. Or had the gay-guy-straight-girl craze run its course?

"And all the time, he kept promising to tell you the truth. But he never did, and when you threatened to smash the door down on Tuesday night, I was so relieved!"

Jo said nothing. Holly still didn't know, and with the smallest bit of discretion on Ed's part she never *would* know, that Jo had thought Toby was cheating on her with Pascale.

"And all the time it was going on," went on Holly, "I kept telling myself it was Toby that was in the wrong. But it was *me*, wasn't it? *I* made you cut yourself, and nearly die, didn't I, little Jo?" Her voice wobbled, and tears rushed to her eyes. She blinked, and they splashed onto the table. "I know you'll forgive me, because you're you. But I don't deserve it."

Jo watched her cry for a few moments. She replayed Holly's words in her head and as she did so, the truth became inescapable. She slowly leaned forward and laid her left arm on the table, underside up. The scars left by the scratch-patch and the compass were displayed in all their glory.

"It's not you, Hol" said Jo. "And it's not Toby, or Trevor, or Tess, or anyone. It's *me*."

# Chapter Fifteen

Jo studied the file. She didn't know what to do with the labels, because things had become clear. And when something was already obvious, you didn't need to label it, did you?

She held her breath, ready to delete the names and labels, but she let her breath out and stared at them, wondering. Supposing she re-classified them? A movie X-rated thirty years ago might be a 15 now. Times changed. People changed.

She hovered the mouse arrow over Pascale's label. Pascale had proved to be a true friend; Jo didn't deserve to be forgiven, and yet Pascale had forgiven her. She considered the space beside Pascale's name carefully. Then, before she could change her mind, she deleted 'Explicit sexual content' and her fingers clattered out 'Strong scenes of violence'. *On your part, Jo, that is.*

And Ed. What you see is what you get. He was always, always honest. Jealously, she'd tarred him with the same brush as Pascale. But the 'Strong sex references' label had nothing to do with what Ed was really like, on the inside.

In its place, she wrote 'Fit for viewing by persons generally', and was satisfied. When she'd got rid of Toby's 'Suitable for all' label, she typed 'Suitable for persons of 18 years and over'. *There.* She'd liberated him, setting him loose in the adult world, where he wouldn't have to pretend that he was something he wasn't. He might even one day break into fashion buying.

Immediately, without having to think about it, she exchanged 'Fairly adult' for 'Mild peril' beside Holly's name. Holly was like the fish in *Finding Nemo* – all at sea, venturing into an unknown world, suffering the real, but not mortal, peril caused by a force stronger than herself.

After a moment of indecision she added her own name to the list. She stared at the chunky little two-letter word, chewing her lip. Then she typed, 'Contains adult material' beside it.

If Trevor could step up, so could she.

It was Results Day tomorrow. With a small sigh she opened her Facebook page. There was a message from Holly asking everyone to meet at 10 o'clock at school. 'I'll be there', she typed in the Comment box. Then she added, as an afterthought, 'xxx', and pressed 'Enter'.

\* \* \* \* \* \*

"But no-one gets *six* A-stars!" gasped Holly.

Jo was standing in the corridor staring at the slip of paper in her hand, with her friends hanging on to each of her arms, staring too.

"And three ordinary As, and a C for Maths. Oh, *Jo*!" Pascale, almost in tears, hugged and hugged her. So did Holly. By the time they'd finished looking at each other's results, all three of them were crying.

"You've got A-star for Maths, Pascale!" exclaimed Jo. "You must be a genius!"

"I wonder what Ed got for Maths," pondered Pascale. She blew her nose. "If he didn't get A-star he's going to be mad jealous."

Pascale had two other A-stars too, and Holly a total of four. "I got A for French!" she said for the third time. "For *French*!

How clever am I?"

"Clever, clever, clever! But six..." said Pascale, grinning at Jo, "six is ridiculous. Especially when you don't even know if you're staying on."

"Oh, Jo, you *must* stay on!" cried Holly, her eyes still shiny with tears.

Jo put the results slips in her bag. "I might, I think."

Holly and Pascale both stared at her. Holly recovered first. "*Brilliant.*" Her eyes were alight with relief. "When did you decide?"

"I haven't decided. But maybe, now that Trevor wants to..." began Jo. Then she stopped. She didn't know what to say.

"Wants to what?" demanded Holly.

Jo wiped her cheeks, keeping the tissue ready in case more tears came. "Oh...to be, you know..."

"A dad?" supplied Pascale unexpectedly. Her tone was tentative, her dark eyes serious.

Jo gave her a grateful look. "I suppose so. Instead of a liability."

"Well, thank God for that," said Pascale in her what-a-load-of-bollocks voice.

Jo put her arms around Pascale and held her tightly. It wasn't the usual girl-hug that everyone in their class had given each other when they opened their envelopes. It wasn't even the friend-hug Jo, Pascale and Holly always did when they met or parted. It was a love-hug. There was no doubt in Jo's mind: she loved Pascale, for her faults, her innocence, and, though it sounded a bit po-faced, for her nobility.

"Thanks, Pascale," she said into Pascale's hair. "I care much more about you than you know."

Pascale's body shuddered. She was making big efforts to keep control. "Oh, *bollocks!*" she said.

The tension was broken. They both laughed, embarrassed and relieved. Jo had made her apology, revealing the depths of her shame without needing to re-visit the event, and Pascale had understood.

"I could murder a cup of coffee," said Holly, her watchful gaze flipping between Jo and Pascale. "Come on, or those greedy bastards will have drunk it all."

They set off in an untidy saunter, with people shrieking and embracing all around them, along the corridor to the dining room, where coffee and cake was being dispensed by last year's Lower Sixth. Teachers gathered at the door, commiserating with and congratulating people. "Well done, Jo Probert," said Mr Treasure. "See you on Tuesday."

Jo smiled. "Thank you, sir."

The three girls went out of the French windows and sat at the picnic tables under the trees by the field. Most of their year seemed to be there. Everyone was excited; it was as noisy as a primary school playground. Jo liked it. It was such a familiar sound, and such a familiar place. The insipid coffee, the feel of the bench on the back of her legs, the marks on the dining-room windows left by the Christmas stickers Year Seven always made. Jo looked round, wondering whether she actually *would* stay on. Or did she – just a little bit – still want to hold up that placard saying 'Look at me! Aren't I special?'

Their table had filled up suddenly. Almost before Jo had time to notice him, Ed had sat astride the picnic bench beside her and spread his results slips on the table. "What do you think of *that*, then?"

He had three A-stars. "One for Maths, thank God," he said, with a sideways glance at Pascale. Pascale didn't look at him, but got up and started speaking to someone at another table, her coffee cup in her hand.

"That's great!" Jo told him warmly. "I got the results I wanted, too."

"So are you staying on, then?" He said this with such artless expectation Jo's heart began to murmur.

"I'm thinking about it," she said.

His expression seemed to ignite. "Yeah? That's...um, really good." He regained control of his face. "Did Pascale tell you?" he asked in a low voice.

"Nope. What about?"

"About her and me."

Jo smiled. "If you dumped *her*, she'll never tell me. If she dumped *you*, I'll hear about it eleven hundred times."

"Nobody dumped anyone. We came to a mutual agreement."

"Really?" Jo was surprised. "How come she tolerated that?"

Ed began to chuckle. Jo liked the sound of him chuckling. It was more masculine than a giggle, but more musical than the drunken cackle she'd heard so often from Trevor. "Because she's in *lurve*. Her new bloke's called Tarquin!" His voice was almost a squeak. "I mean, who's called *Tarquin*?"

"Um...well, not many people are called Pascale," Jo pointed out. "Or Poins." For a moment, she was jealous that Pascale hadn't told *her* about Tarquin, but then she remembered that before this morning, she hadn't seen Pascale since the Very Bad Experience. And Holly hadn't seemed to know either. "So how did she meet this Tarquin?" she asked.

"At some party she went to at her dad's firm," said Ed, "where they had to dress up as eighties stockbrokers. I tell you, if she'd asked *me* I'd have refused. I'm never going to go to a fancy dress party again my life."

"I think you'd look OK in a striped shirt and red braces," said Jo, beginning to smile a lot.

Ed was grinning too. "It gets better. This Tarquin's got a twin brother called Torquil. What are these people thinking of?"

Jo giggled. "Poor Tarquin! Because he wears Rose and Reed jeans and has got dark hair, he caused all this trouble and he doesn't even know it!"

Ed started drumming his heel on the ground. His knee bounced up and down. He only did that when he was nervous. "Toby OK these days?"

"I haven't seen him."

He stopped drumming his heel and stuck his hands in his pockets. "Finding out your boyfriend's gay must be so *weird*," he said quietly. "I'd be furious if that happened to me." He smiled bashfully. "If my girlfriend went off with another girl, I mean."

Jo took a few seconds to work out what she wanted to say. Ed waited patiently, watching her face. She was aware of him watching her, but the anxiety she'd always felt about what he was seeing – was her hair stranding, or her nose shiny? – wasn't there. "To be honest," she said at last, "I was more furious about things that happened *before* that night." She looked at him earnestly. "I never felt like Toby was...you know, a proper boyfriend, but I didn't know why. I thought there was something wrong with me."

He gave her something approximating to The Look. "There's nothing wrong with you, Jo."

"Um..." She knew her neck was going pink. "Well, anyway, it was all a bit difficult."

Ed put his elbow on the table, leaned his head on his hand and went on looking at her. "And you and Holly are still friends, are you?"

Jo nodded. "Amazingly enough, yes."

He seemed to be awaiting an explanation.

"We worked it out," she said.

He grinned knowingly. "And Pascale's come out of this with her reputation intact, hasn't she?"

Jo wished she could tell him the truth. Her attack on Pascale, though scary for both perpetrator and victim, was the straw that had broken the back of the whole Toby thing, and ended up sorting it out. "She's a brilliant person, you know, Ed, even if she can be a bit mean about boys."

"That's an understatement." There was admiration on his face. "She really likes you, you know, Jo. She was hysterical that day when you were in hospital. She kept saying it was her fault, and Holly kept saying it was *her* fault." Another grin. "Me, I think it was Tarquin's fault."

Jo smiled, and the smile turned into a laugh. Ed slid a little further along the bench, so that his thigh was pressed against hers. "This party at Tom Clarke's on Saturday," he said softly. "Will you come with *me*?"

Jo didn't know what her face was doing. She hoped she was smiling, but she could hardly speak because her heart had turned into a battering ram. She could feel Ed's hipbone sticking into her and his breath going in and out. "That would be nice," she said. Then she thought of something. "But *you* can't go, surely?"

He frowned. "Why not?"

"Tom says it's fancy dress."

"So?"

"You said you're never going to a fancy dress party again."

"Did I? When?"

"Just now, when you were telling me about Tarquin."

He took hold of her hand under the table, right there in front of everyone. No-nonsense Ed. Do what you feel like doing. "The trouble with you, Jo," he said, "is you're too clever."

Jo fished her results slips out of her bag and waggled them

at him. "Six A-stars!"

\* \* \* \* \* \*

It was the sort of late summer day when the sky is cloudy but it's too hot to wear a jacket. None of Jo's clothes seemed suitable. And what *was* suitable for an appointment with your headteacher in the holidays anyway? In the end she put on jeans and a loose blouse, and a necklace. She tied back her hair in a pony tail, but on the bus she caught sight of herself in the window looking about twelve, and shook her hair out over her shoulders.

The sliding glass panel revealed that the secretary's office was empty, but the door to Mr Treasure's office was open. When Jo tapped on the glass he called out, "That Jo? Come in!"

He looked different without his usual dark suit. His short-sleeved shirt and casual trousers made him look lightweight, with less authority than he actually had. She noticed that he'd recently had a haircut, ready for the start of term. While Jo had been on the bus the sun had come out, and the Venetian blinds made stripes of light across Mr Treasure's desk.

"Thanks for coming," he said.

"You said it would be doing you a favour."

He nodded. He hadn't smiled yet. He put his forearms on the desk and linked his fingers. "Did you do me the other favour I asked for?"

"Well, I told my dad to make another appointment, and that you don't like being messed around." As she said this, Jo thought how little she, too, liked being messed around. "I kept reminding him, but he didn't do it."

"No, he didn't." Mr Treasure leaned back in his chair with his arms folded. This was the position he always adopted when he was in prosecuting-lawyer mode. Jo's spirits wilted a little under the certainty of more and more questions. "However, things have moved along a little since last term, haven't they?"

Jo swallowed. Mr Treasure knew. Jo didn't mind him knowing, just like she didn't mind Ed knowing, because neither of them would tell anyone else. "Yes, I suppose so," she said cautiously.

Mr Treasure gave a small nod. "And has your opinion about your future moved along at all since last term?"

"Yes, sir."

She looked at him. Blinking, she realized that although he wasn't exactly smiling, he didn't look stern, or smug, or anxious, or any of the things teachers usually looked like when they were trying to be a psychiatrist. He was just sitting there, as impassive as his spectacles, listening to her being her *own* psychiatrist.

"I think I've realised what it's been like for my parents," she told him. "They must have loved each other once, and to lose that...well, Trevor being a drunk must have been as bad for Tess as it was for me, and her being so...difficult, must have been as bad for Trevor as it was for me, but I only saw how bad it was for *me*, and blamed them. And neither of them could make sense of what I was doing."

One of those silences that aren't really silent at all fell between them. Mr Treasure went on looking at Jo, and Jo went on looking at him. She knew what he was thinking, and he knew what she was thinking. She could hear a wasp butting against the open window behind the blinds, and the sound of the mower cutting the grass on the school field. She felt calm and safe in familiar surroundings, like when she went to sleep with her face in her pink rabbit's belly.

In the end, Mr Treasure spoke. "You've made sense of it, though, haven't you?"

She nodded. She thought about the gouges on her arm and the cuts on her leg, but she kept her face expressionless unless Mr Treasure's super-sensitive antennae picked up her brainwaves. "I worked so hard for my GCSEs while threatening all the time to leave school, because the only way I could make Trevor and Tess notice me was to do something that hurt them. Though it hurt me more," she said softly. Then she thought of something, and smiled. "I'm a case-study in a psychology textbook, aren't I?"

Unfolding his arms, Mr Treasure leaned forward with his elbows on the desk. "No, you're not. This is a big thing in your life. This is about *you*, and *your* parents."

Jo knew he was right. Newspaper articles about divorce, alcoholism, scarred girls, hospitalized girls – articles that made you shake your head sorrowfully when you read them – were about things that happened to other people, and you forgot them immediately. But to those who were experiencing them, they were the biggest thing in the world, and would never go away.

"Will we see you back on the first day of term, then?" asked Mr Treasure.

Jo didn't know whether she felt embarrassed, or stupid, or relieved, or something else altogether. "Um...yes, sir," she said.

Mr Treasure didn't say anything.

"My dad's looking for a new job, and he's in AA," she blurted unexpectedly. "I'll make sure he sticks at it."

Mr Treasure nodded. "And what does your mother think about this?"

"Oh..." Jo had to consider before she spoke. "Well, she's got a new boyfriend and doesn't really notice my dad. But that's OK. The only way to deal with her is not to have very high expectations. Anyway, they're not going to sell the house, and one of them'll live there with me." She paused, smiling a little. "My mum's boyfriend's there at the moment, and Trevor's staying with his friend Ken. But Mark, that's my mum's boyfriend, has got a big house of his own, in Hertfordshire or somewhere, big enough for Tess. And all her shoes. So I expect it'll be me and my dad again."

Mr Treasure didn't smile. "I'll write to your father," he said crisply. For a moment he looked like the usual Mr Treasure who stood on the stage in Assembly and walked quickly down corridors with his shoes clicking. "And your mother, too."

"All right, sir."

He stood up. The interview was over. "First day of term, nine o'clock, Sixth Form Assembly," he said.

"Yes, sir," said Jo.

He didn't say anything else, and Jo turned and left the office. She went down the corridor and out into the deserted school grounds, where bits of newly-mown grass swirled in the air and an aeroplane drilled its way across the sky.

At the gate, Ed was waiting.

"I thought you'd be longer," he said, taking her hand.

"We didn't have much to say to each other. He asked if I was staying on and I said yes."

"You didn't burst into tears or anything?" He was grinning.

"Nope." She looked at him grinning, and thought how stupid it was that they'd spent the whole summer messing around with Pascale and Toby. "I've done enough of that bursting into tears stuff to last me for a while, I think."

They began to walk towards the bus stop. "Does he know about...you know, the VBE?" asked Ed. They'd taken to calling it that. Even though it was Tess's invention, it was a useful code to use when there might be other people listening. Ed liked it so much he used it even when there weren't.

She nodded. "He was pretty nice about it."

He didn't look at her, but drew her more closely against his body. "So he bloody should be. He's got clever Jo Probert in his precious Sixth Form, hasn't he? He should be arranging a red carpet and a photo-shoot, let alone being *nice*."

She put her arms around him. His body felt smooth and tubular under his T-shirt, and his breath smelled minty; he'd cleaned his teeth especially for her. The bus came round the corner, and they hurried and caught it. Then they went upstairs and sat in the back seat, and kissed contentedly all the way home, just like they did in the movies.

Anyone affected by any of the issues covered in this book can seek help and advice from the following organisations:

## Selfharm.co.uk

Selfharm.co.uk is a safe, pro-recovery project dedicated to supporting young people impacted by self-harm. We also offer advice, training and resources for parents and professionals and work to de-stigmatise society's view of self-harm through the media.

Visit www.selfharm.co.uk or email info@selfharm.co.uk for more information.

## ChildLine

For advice and information about self harm visit childline.org.uk/selfharm. Or you can talk to ChildLine for free, 24 hours a day, whatever your worry - 0800 1111. Find out more at childline.org.uk.

# About the Author

Veronica Bennett taught English for many years before leaving the profession to become a full-time writer. She is married with two children.

Veronica is the author of eight young adult novels in her own name, and also writes the successful *Poppy Love* series under the pen name Natasha May. More information can be found about the author on her www.veronica-bennett.com.